W9-BWL-126

CHILD'S
PLAY

LONDON PUBLIC LIBRARY
WITHDRAWN

BOOKS BY ANGELA MARSONS

DETECTIVE KIM STONE SERIES
Silent Scream
Evil Games
Lost Girls
Play Dead
Blood Lines
Dead Souls
Broken Bones
Dying Truth
Fatal Promise

OTHER BOOKS
Dear Mother (previously published as *The Middle Child*)
The Forgotten Woman (previously published as *My Name Is*)

Angela
MARSONS
CHILD'S
PLAY

bookouture

LONDON PUBLIC LIBRARY

Published by Bookouture in 2019

An imprint of StoryFire Ltd.

Carmelite House
50 Victoria Embankment
London EC4Y 0DZ

www.bookouture.com

Copyright © Angela Marsons, 2019

Angela Marsons has asserted her right to be identified
as the author of this work.

All rights reserved. No part of this publication may be reproduced,
stored in any retrieval system, or transmitted, in any form or by
any means, electronic, mechanical, photocopying, recording or
otherwise, without the prior written permission of the publishers.

ISBN: 978-1-78681-569-9
eBook ISBN: 978-1-78681-493-7

This book is a work of fiction. Names, characters, businesses,
organizations, places and events other than those clearly in the
public domain, are either the product of the author's imagination
or are used fictitiously. Any resemblance to actual persons, living or
dead, events or locales is entirely coincidental.

This book is dedicated to Jez Edwards.
Simply, Thank You.

PROLOGUE

WINTER 2010

'*Come on, what do you want?*' *she snaps, rubbing her hands together, reminding me of when I was a child.*

But I'm no longer a child. I'm a grown-up and I'm angry. But she doesn't need to know that. Yet.

'*And what are we doing here, anyway?*' *she asks, looking around the deserted park. It is mid-January and one degree above freezing, twenty minutes before the sun falls completely.*

My promise of having something for her had lured her here as I'd hoped.

I pat the seat of the roundabout beside me. '*Sit with me and I can give you your present.*'

She looks unsure but curiosity gets the better of her.

I've been dreaming of this minute for eight years.

'*Come on, what's this all?…*'

'*Remember bringing me here to play when I was little?*' *I ask.*

She hesitates. '*Err… I…*'

'*Do you remember pushing me on the swings, sitting with me on the see-saw, playing with a ball on the field?*'

'*Come on now, it's late. I want to get home,*' *she says, and I hear a note of fear in her voice.*

She knows that something is wrong.

She moves away from me.

I grab her arm.

'You don't remember? No? Oh, that's because you never did, you fucking bitch,' I say, turning her around.

'What the?…'

I've rehearsed this in my mind so many times. I know exactly how it is going to work.

I raise my right arm and punch her in the temple, knocking her clean out.

A genuine smile lights up my face. That felt almost as good as I have imagined.

I work quickly as the day begins to fade, unsure how long she'll be out.

She starts to groan as I finish the last tie to her ankle.

'Hey, what you?…'

'Comfy?' I ask, standing back to admire my handiwork.

Her legs are spread-eagled and tied to the metal frame of the spider's web roundabout, facing down. Her body is bent at the waist so her upper half is hanging down towards the floor, the top of her head touching the concrete base of the ride. Her hands are tied behind her back.

'Look, I'm gonna puke…'

'Least of your problems,' I say, enjoying the fear in her voice as she tries to move.

'Aargh,' she cries out as the barbed wire bites into the flesh of her wrists. A nightmare to apply but worth it to see the bright red results of her struggles.

'You should have brought me here just once,' I spit as I begin to push the spider's web around.

She screams as her head is dragged across the surface.

I smile and keep pushing, safe in the knowledge she won't be heard. The houses the park had been built to serve were condemned and emptied years ago, after two fell into an old mining pit.

The only kids that use it now come from miles away but not on a night like this.

'P... please... st...'

'Shush. It's my turn now,' I say, pushing the frame harder. Clumps of hair are being left behind with each revolution. 'You're going to wish you'd played with me,' I say, speeding up the pushes.

Her breath is coming in short, sharp bursts in between pain-filled screams as her flesh is dragged across the gravel.

The screams have turned to yelps now, and I guess she's fading in and out of consciousness.

I stop the web from turning and push back the other way. The barbed wire cuts deeper into her flesh as the momentum builds again.

And finally we're playing a game. A game that I have chosen.

A trail of blood is forming in a circle around the gravel.

I push harder, causing the roundabout to whiz past me at speed.

'You should have listened to me,' I cry, pushing as hard as I can.

The sounds coming from her are no more than a whimper.

The blood on the ground is pooling, clumps of flesh are sticking to the concrete base.

The crying stops completely after I hear the sound of the fracture of her skull.

I give one last good push of the spider's web and stand back.

'You really should have played with me,' I tell her again, although I know she can no longer hear.

I walk away as the slumped, lifeless body continues to turn.

CHAPTER ONE

Kim Stone arrived at the cordon tape at 11.29 p.m. The sun had been down for almost three hours but late August warmth still lingered in the air.

She had instructed Despatch to place a call to her colleague, DS Bryant, but his Astra Estate wasn't yet visible amongst the squad cars, ambulance and coroner's van. She looked at those two vehicles side by side. Surely only one or the other was needed.

As she removed her helmet she wondered from what activity her colleague had been disturbed when he'd received the call. Knowing Bryant, he'd been about to fall asleep with the crime channel playing on the TV in the background.

She'd been preparing to take Barney for his late-night walk. She'd left him after a quick visit out to the back garden and the promise of a run at the park when she got home. Whatever the time. She'd neglected to mention it was Haden Hill Park to which she'd been called, feeling he wouldn't forgive her absence quite so readily if he knew she was visiting a park they frequented often for an early morning walk.

Haden Hill House was a Victorian residence built on parkland in 1878 by George Alfred Haden Haden-Best. He had originally intended to demolish the grand Haden Hall and extend his home but his elderly aunt, widow of the squire, lived in the Old Hall, and by the time she died in 1903 he had lost the will to enlarge Haden Hill House, so the two buildings remained side by side. Upon his death in 1921, the house, the Old Hall, gardens and 55 acres of land were bought by public subscription for use as a park. In the years since, the Old Hall and House had been used as a refuge for evacuees and a bombing raid shelter. The Old Hall had lain in ruins for years following a fire until lottery funding had helped restore it to its former glory.

Kim had been directed to the entrance off Haden Park Road that led onto the kids play area at the top of the grounds, a short walk away from the refurbished buildings. A dozen or so onlookers were already craning their necks to see beyond the police officers and vehicles and more doors were opening as locals gave up the pretence of looking through downstairs and upstairs windows.

She showed her ID and ducked under the cordon tape, heading towards the collection of fluorescent jackets and multiple torch beams shining in the absence of street lighting.

Officers moved aside as she headed to the centre of the crowd, passing paramedics who had obviously been dismissed but remained in discussion beside the giraffe-emblazoned play slide.

'Hey, Keats,' she said, spotting the diminutive pathologist, who reached for something from his equipment bag which had been perched on some kind of cartoon character on a spring.

He shook his head, sorrowfully, causing Kim to wonder exactly what she'd been called out to. And then the reason for his dismay clicked in her mind and it had nothing to do with the crime scene.

'He'll be along shortly,' she said, acknowledging the fact that the man liked her colleague far more than he liked her and made no attempt to hide it. It didn't bother her. Most people felt that way.

A slow smile began to turn up the man's dour mouth.

Clearly, Bryant had arrived.

'Evening, Keats,' her colleague said, with a smile and an outstretched hand.

She offered him a look that he ignored.

Keats smirked. 'Now, that's how you greet—'

'Sorry, but did someone say there was a body here, somewhere?' Kim asked, pointedly looking around.

'There is indeed, Inspector, and the poor soul has not been touched except to check for life signs.'

'Okay, well, point me in the right—'

'Guys,' Keats said, nodding to the group of uniformed officers.

Suddenly, by collective torchlight, like a solo performance on a darkened stage, the area to the left of her lit up as though a switch had been flicked.

It took a few seconds for her eyes to adjust as Bryant came to stand beside her.

His sharp intake of breath mirrored her own.

'What the bloody hell is this all about?' he asked, taking the words right out of her mouth.

CHAPTER TWO

At first glance Kim saw a late-middle-aged female sitting on the far-right swing. Her handbag was positioned neatly beside the metal frame. It wasn't open, it wasn't strewn, it was placed with the shoulder strap coiled to the left.

Kim began her second detailed perusal of the strangely macabre sight before her.

The woman's hair was thick and grey but well styled. Even by torchlight Kim could see the glisten of lipstick on an attractive face that showed signs of wear but had not yet given itself up to deep wrinkles.

Small pearl studs decorated each earlobe and matched a single strand around a neck that had not escaped the ageing process as well as the face.

The string of pearls disappeared into a white collared blouse covered by a thin summer cardigan with three-quarter sleeves.

The skirt was flared, patterned blue with small yellow flowers; it fell just below the knee but was probably longer if she were standing. Nylon covered her legs down into blue court shoes with two-inch heels.

So, just a middle-aged lady pausing for a go on the swings as she took a walk through the park. Reliving a childhood memory or unable to resist an impetuous urge. Harmless.

Except for two things: the bright red stain colouring the front of her blouse and the barbed wire that was tied around her wrists.

Her body was trying to slump forward but was held in place by the vicious wire entwined into the hanging chain of the swing. Her legs were slightly bent, the tips of her shoes dragging against the ground.

'Some kind of sexual game gone wrong?' Bryant asked.

'Dunno yet,' Kim said, struggling to pull her eyes away.

Take away the barbed wire, and in the daylight the picture of this woman laughing and moving to and fro on the swing beside her grandchild expelling whoops of delight would elicit smiles and laughter. Late at night even without the blood and barbed wire the scene offered a more sinister and compelling sight.

'Who found her?' Kim asked, to no one in particular.

'Chappie over by the climbing frame, and avoid that puddle by the gravel. That belongs to him too,' said one of the uniforms.

Bryant turned and nodded towards him. 'Want me to go over and?…'

'No,' she said. 'You take a look in her handbag. Keats is less likely to have a paddy at you.'

The pathologist didn't much like things being touched until the techies had been through them, but the bromance between the two of them offered Bryant a bit more leeway. Antagonising Keats at the beginning of a case rarely worked out well for her.

She knew much of Keats's affection for her colleague grew out of sympathy at Bryant's plight of being stuck with her every day. Keats felt the man had enough crosses to bear. And she didn't necessarily disagree with him, she thought, as she stepped around the pool of vomit to approach the fair-haired male sitting on the ground.

His back was against the climbing frame, his knees bent with his arms resting on them to support his head as he stared down at the ground.

She guessed him to be mid-twenties, wearing dark jeans and a sweatshirt.

'Hey,' she said, showing her ID.

He pushed himself to stand.

'It's okay, you can stay on the—'

'I just want to go home, officer. I was told that once I'd spoken to a detective I could…'

'Okay, okay,' she said, looking to the female police officer standing beside him.

'Eric,' she offered. 'Eric Hanson of—'

'Thank you,' Kim said, assuming the young man had not lost the ability to speak.

His gaze had automatically lifted and been drawn back towards the swings. He started to shake his head.

Kim stepped in front of him and blocked the view. She nodded towards the plastic water bottle in his hand. 'Take a sip, mate.'

'I'm fine, thanks,' he said, shaking his head.

'So, Eric, what happened?' she asked.

'She was just… I looked and…'

His eyes were staring straight through her, locked on to the picture he'd stumbled across. She didn't need him replaying the horror over and over. What she needed were facts.

'Okay, back up for me, Eric,' Kim said, bringing him to the present. 'What time did you come into the park?'

'Half ten-ish,' he said, lifting his attention to her face. 'I just wanted to walk off that last pint of lager I downed at the club. Just fancied stretching my legs.'

'So, you came from that direction?' she asked, nodding towards the path from the club.

Although not a part of the park there was a path that led from Old Hill Cricket Club along to the entrance where she'd just parked.

'Yeah, had a few pints with my mates and…'

'And no one passed you as you were walking along?'

Another shake of the head.

'Did you hear anything as you approached?'

'Nothing. It was dead…'

His words trailed away as that one single word returned his mind once again to what he'd seen.

'So, you saw and heard nothing and called the police straight away?' she asked.

He nodded.

'Then what did you do?'

Guilt flashed across his face. 'What do you mean?'

'Did you touch her at all?'

He hesitated before shaking his head.

'Are you sure, Eric?' she pushed. They had to know.

'I'm sorry, but I didn't check. I mean I just couldn't…'

Kim understood the source of his guilt and evasion. He felt bad because he hadn't had the courage to approach her and see if she was still alive.

'It's okay. I don't think there's much you could have done to help her.'

He offered her a grateful smile as Bryant approached.

'Okay, Eric, we'll be in touch if we need anything further, and if you remember anything more give us a call.'

He nodded his understanding as she met the gaze of the officer still standing to the side of him. 'Get someone to take him home.'

'Will do, Marm.'

'Anything?' she asked, turning to her colleague.

'Mitch is here and is discussing with Keats the best way to remove her from the swing.'

'Do we have her name?'

'Belinda Evans, sixty-one years of age, lives in Wombourne and drives a BMW 5 Series. Less than two years old.'

She raised an eyebrow. His last few minutes had been much more productive than hers.

'Car keys in her handbag, along with her purse, untouched, her driving licence, a small make-up bag, a pen, glasses and a pack of breath mints. No mobile phone.'

'And her car is?'

'Parked correctly about fifty yards from the park gates. Locked and with no evidence of foul play.'

'Good work, Bryant,' she said, heading towards the entrance to the park. 'Most of that information is utterly useless, but you've identified one piece of information that is incredibly helpful and relevant.'

'Which is?'

'That Belinda Evans came to the park of her own accord.'

CHAPTER THREE

Kim entered the squad room and immediately realised that something was not right. It had nothing to do with the fact that when she'd left the room at 7.30 a.m. to brief Woody on the events of the previous evening, the office had been empty and was now full. No, it wasn't that. She'd expected that to be the case. The change was more subtle than that.

Ah, she got it.

'Bryant, why is Betty on your desk?'

Not once had he been awarded the prized plant for his work efforts.

Stacey sniggered. 'Told you.'

'Just looking after it, guv, with Penn being away for most of the week.' He paused. 'And I kinda wanted to see how it looked.'

'Then earn it,' she said, placing it back on the windowsill.

She turned back to the room. 'And what the hell are those on your feet, Penn?' she asked, folding her arms.

'Trainers, boss.'

Unlike the man who had occupied the place in her team before him, Penn was not a man easily given to smartness. His normal attire of plain black trousers and white shirt were presentable and met her standards, just. But put the man in a suit and somehow the suit managed to look just as pissed off as he did.

Not that she knew much about men's current fashion in suits but with its thick grey pinstripe, his court outfit looked as though it had crawled out of the Nineties. His unruly curly blonde hair did little to help, but she was pleased to see the bandana was missing and the curls had been tamed by some kind of man hair products.

But the trainers.

'Look, Penn, I don't know what Travis put up with but when you're going to court, even for one of your old cases, you are part of this team now and as such you're representing both—'

'They're under the desk, guv,' Bryant said, behind her.

'Huh?'

'His shoes... they're under the desk. I couldn't let you do it. You were falling for it way too easily.'

Penn smirked before reaching down to untie his laces.

'Jesus, you're dead funny, you lot,' she said, shaking her head.

'I'll be back after though, boss, eh?' he asked, hopefully. 'Court finishes around four-ish.'

Both Bryant and Stacey waited expectantly for her response too.

She was sorely tempted to agree.

'No, Penn. Go straight home. Woody ain't budging.'

A collective groan sounded around her.

'Not my rules, guys,' she said, holding up her hands in defence.

She'd seen the memo sent out a month ago to all supervisory staff across the West Midlands Police Force. And initially she had quite happily ignored it. Until she'd been called up to Woody's office and presented with a printed copy by her boss.

The force was in crisis. Recruitment figures were down, violent crime was up and staff burnout rates were at an all-time high.

'You work them too hard,' Woody had said, waving the memo in front of her face.

'This is my fault?' she asked. She had a team of three which, even if she burned them all out, wouldn't touch the overall figure.

'You know what I mean,' he growled.

'I keep an eye on them,' she defended.

'They're like dogs, Stone.'

'Excuse me, sir?'

'They hide their illnesses,' he clarified. 'Police officers hate to admit when there's something wrong. They battle on, soldier through it. You won't know until it's too late.'

'So what am I supposed to do?'

'Rest them, Stone. You have to manage them and ensure they get enough downtime. Try to stick to shift patterns and look for tell-tale signs like emotional changes.'

She raised an eyebrow.

'Okay, maybe in your case you should look for behavioural changes and physical signs like being withdrawn, irritable, aggressive. It's all here,' he said, waving the memo at her again.

'Noted, sir, and I have only one question,' she said, glancing at the piece of paper in his hands.

'Go on.'

'Did the criminals get the memo too?'

If her memory served correctly that was the point at which he'd thrust the memo at her and told her to leave.

Penn's court case could not have come at a worse time. Any time over the last few weeks would have been fine by her, while they'd been working routine cases since their last major investigation into the sicko who had been recreating the most traumatic events in her life.

Unfortunately, the CPS didn't consult her diary when programming murder trials, and as it had been Penn's last major investigation with West Mercia, she'd had no choice but to free him for the trial. Especially as he'd been the arresting officer.

'Okay, let's get cracking,' she said, perching on the edge of the desk facing the wipe board. 'Belinda Evans, sixty-one years of age found tied to a swing, late at night at Haden Hill Park. Smartly dressed, presentable, arrived there under her own steam but no mobile phone on her person. Lives in a nice area of Wombourne and hasn't come to our attention before. Stace, find out everything you can about our victim. Bryant and I will be heading over to her house before meeting with Keats for the post-mortem at ten.'

'Got it, boss,' she said, turning to her computer.

'Woody has delegated statement taking to Inspector Plant and his team seeing as Penn is taking a holiday this week.'

Follow-ups normally fell to Penn. He shook his head. 'Who the hell would want to hurt a little old?—'

'Hey, sixty-one ain't old, matey,' Bryant said, being the closest person in the room to that age. 'And my money is on Eleanor.'

'Eleanor who?' Kim asked, frowning.

'Don't know her last name but she's rumoured to glide around the park looking for her lost love, a monk who was walled up in a passage alive and...'

'Or it could be Annie Eliza,' Stacey said, widening her eyes. 'She lived there allllll alone, never married or had children and...'

'Or it could have been Yvette?' Bryant added.

'Another bloody ghost?' Kim asked, moving towards the Bowl.

'Nah, she's real. Does *Most Haunted* programme and they've been to investigate—'

'Enough, guys,' she said, grabbing her jacket.

Kim glanced back at the white board that contained just the barest of details. Right now, Belinda Evans was a bullet-point list, a collection of facts gained solely from the crime scene and already Kim had the feeling that the woman was going to become much more than that.

CHAPTER FOUR

Wombourne was a village in South Staffordshire with Anglo-Saxon origins that managed to hold on to its sense of community despite the numerous housing developments that had sprung up as an overspill housing solution for the nearby city of Wolverhampton.

Bryant pulled up behind a squad car on Trident Road, a few streets back from the village green.

As she got out of the car Kim noted that the double-fronted detached bungalow had been recently painted. A waist-high slatted fence enclosed the front garden and disappeared around the back. A hanging basket was placed either side of the door, both bearing identical flowers coloured pink and white. The property was tidy and pleasant and appeared to have been designed for low maintenance.

'Wish my missus would go for something like this,' Bryant moaned, holding his ID up for the constable on the gate. 'Damn flowers back home have me sneezing all over the…'

'Hang on,' Kim said, stepping back to the officer on the gate. 'Any interest?' she asked, looking around the street.

'Plenty, Marm,' he said. 'Lady at number seventeen watched from her bedroom window for over an hour before leaving twenty minutes ago. The person at number twenty-one doesn't realise we know they've been behind that net curtain for forty-five minutes and Mr Blenkinsop from number fourteen along the road makes a very nice cup of tea.'

Kim smiled. In her experience, there were four types of neighbour. The first, and her favourite on a personal level, were the ones that really couldn't give a shit what was going on beyond their own front door. The second were the ones who wanted to know what was going on but didn't want to show it. The third group were the openly curious but easily bored, and then there were her professional favourites: The Blenkinsops; the ones that were openly curious and made the effort to engage with police and find out what was going on.

'Cheers,' she said, catching up with Bryant who was already in the hallway.

'Observant guy,' she noted, glancing back to the officer.

'Give the man a plant,' Brant said, turning left.

His failure to earn the plant had become a standing joke in the squad room. One which Bryant played for all it was worth.

'Basic layout by the looks of it,' he noted. 'Living area on the left and bedrooms on the right. Decent size.'

The hallway was decorated with an embossed wallpaper that had been painted with bland magnolia matt emulsion. The rooms offered a similar colour palette which gave the impression of fresh, clean but coolly detached somehow.

'How much?' Kim asked, looking around the lounge. Bungalows were pretty expensive around the area.

'I'd guess around three hundred grand,' Bryant said, frowning.

'I'd have expected a bigger property,' Kim said, honestly, purely based on the car model and registration of the car that the victim drove.

'My thoughts exactly,' he said touching the top of a sideboard. 'It's a nice place but…' His words trailed away as he pulled open the top drawer of the cupboard.

'Empty,' he said, looking her way.

Kim shrugged, and continued walking around the room. The television was flat screen but not much bigger than a computer monitor. An old-fashioned stacker system music centre sat on a two-drawer unit in the opposite corner. She could see no speakers attached and it appeared to be just for show.

She opened the drawers. 'These are empty too.'

They moved along to the kitchen. The heart of the home. In this property it appeared to have suffered a cardiac arrest. The space was a functional area of boxes, hard edges and sharp corners. Nothing softened the space or brought it to life. No chopping board, place mats, canisters for tea bags, bread bin, teapot. All the things that people have and don't really use.

Again, Bryant began opening doors and drawers.

'A few bits and pieces but little more than we found in the lounge. Not sure we're gonna find any evidence to help solve her death when we can barely find anything to prove her life.'

Kim turned to her colleague.

'Bloody hell, Bryant, you been reading books again?'

'Actually, Carl Jung says—'

Bryant's words were cut off by a cough that came from behind.

Kim turned and her breath met a brick wall in her chest.

'Jesus,' Bryant whispered, as they both stared at the person before them.

She had the feeling they were looking at a ghost.

CHAPTER FIVE

'Marm, I'm sorry... she just...'

Kim waved away the constable's apologies. Judging by the look on the woman's face the entire day shift kitted out in riot gear would have struggled to stop her.

She took a moment to process the sight before her. From the floral skirt to the plain blouse to the pearl earrings and matching necklace. The face was a little more worn but the resemblance to Belinda Evans was uncanny.

'May I ask what you're doing in my sister's house?' she asked in a clipped, stern voice that held no Black Country twang.

Kim stepped forward. 'Mrs?...'

'It's Miss Evans, like my sister and my name is Veronica,' she stated, as Kim's phone began to ring.

'You can ignore that call and explain what you're doing in my sister's home,' the woman said with steel in both her voice and expression.

'Yeah, I'm probably not going to do that,' Kim said, turning away. Even Woody didn't speak to her like that, but right now she had to force herself to remember that this person was about to find out they'd lost a family member.

'Stace,' she answered.

'Next of kin, boss, is sixty-five-year-old Veronica Evans, lives at—'

'Thanks, Stace, I'll get back to you,' she said, ending the call and wishing it had been just two minutes earlier.

'Miss Evans, I think you should take a seat,' Kim said, pointing back towards the lounge.

The woman ignored her advice.

'Is she dead?'

'Miss Evans,' Bryant said, stepping in to take over the sensitivity portion of their job description.

'If you could just step into…'

'I'll take that as a yes, then?' she said, looking from Kim to her colleague.

Okay, so it appeared that Bryant could put his kid gloves away for the time being.

'Yes, Miss Evans, I'm afraid—'

'Veronica, please, or we'll all get confused. How did it happen? In that fast car of hers, I suppose. Ridiculous how she drove it. I've been telling her for months that she needed to act her age, but—'

Bryant stepped forward. 'Miss… Veronica, I really think you should come into the lounge and…'

The woman speared Bryant with a look. 'Officer, will my sitting down make my sister any less dead?'

'Absolutely not,' Kim answered for her colleague who was nonplussed by the woman's manner.

Kim had seen it before. Sometimes relatives remained stoic for days, weeks, months and then broke down because of something trivial or a certain memory. Whatever the reason Kim was going to make the most of it.

'No, Veronica, your sister will be no less dead but the situation is more complicated than you suspect and would be better discussed sitting down.'

'Complicated, how?'

Kim took matters into her own hands and walked past the woman into the lounge. She stood in front of the sofa thereby directing the woman to the single seat.

After all his efforts to make Veronica sit, Bryant remained standing in the doorway.

'Veronica, I'm sorry to tell you that your sister was murdered.'

Kim waited for an emotion to cross her face. Any emotion would do but she wasn't expecting the one she saw.

Annoyance.

Kim couldn't work out if it was annoyance that her sister had died or because her demise was not in the manner that Veronica had prophesised.

'No, I'm sorry but you must be mistaken. It's either an error of her identity or the way she died but there's no way Belinda—'

'There's no mistake,' Kim said. 'Your sister was murdered at Haden Hill Park by a single stab wound to the heart.'

Veronica's hand went to her throat as though she'd just been told there was a fly in her soup.

The lack of emotion caused Kim to wonder how close the sisters had been. It appeared that Veronica lived close by due to the time in the morning she'd just happened along for a visit. They had uncannily similar interests in clothes and jewellery and both still went by their maiden names.

'Veronica, I'm sorry, this must be an awful shock but do you have any idea why your sister was at the park last night?'

Kim had checked and there had been no events, at either the park or house.

'I have absolutely no idea.'

'Was it a favourite place of hers?' Kim pushed. 'Maybe something from your childhood?'

As people got older they liked to wander down memory lane, relive particularly happy memories.

'Belinda was found sitting on a swing,' Kim offered, leaving out the detail of the barbed wire that had been securing her.

'Murdered while sitting on a swing late at night?' she asked, trying to stare Kim down. 'Is this some kind of ridiculous joke?'

'I'm afraid not. Your parents never took you to Haden Hill Park?' she repeated the question that had not been answered.

'No. Our parents were not park people and Belinda had no interest in swings,' she said, with exasperation, as though Kim had lost her mind.

'Had she spent a lot of time at the park or Haden Hill in general?'

'Not that I know of.'

'The cricket club, did she perhaps socialise there now and again?'

'Belinda didn't drink. At all,' she emphasised. 'And I can think of no reason for her to be there unless taken by force.'

'Belinda's car was parked and secure with no evidence of any kind of struggle.'

'I'm sorry but the place means nothing to me,' she said, dismissively.

'Any husband or?…'

'Never married. Either of us,' Veronica said. 'Although she did have a friend from the college that she sometimes kept company with.'

Kim heard Bryant's notebook open behind her.

'Name?'

'Charles, Charles Blunt. He's in the physical education department at Halesowen College, where my sister worked until seven months ago when she retired.'

'As?'

'Professor of child psychology.'

Kim wondered if they'd learn more of the woman from her colleagues than they were learning from her sister.

'And did Belinda have a phone?'

'Of course she had a phone.'

'It wasn't in her handbag or car,' Bryant offered.

Veronica shrugged. 'Probably stolen. It was a big cumbersome thing with lots of those appy things on it. She liked the bigger screen so she didn't have to use her glasses to make a call. Prone to vanity, at times, I'm afraid.'

'May we take the number?' Kim asked. 'We'll contact the service provider…'

'It's Vodafone you want,' Veronica said, taking an old Nokia from her bag. 'She swapped after I told her I was getting a better deal.'

Kim detected a note of triumph as Veronica read the number out to Bryant.

'Okay, Miss Evans, thank you for your help. If I can just ask about something that's puzzling us?'

'Of course,' she answered, smoothing her hands over her skirt.

Kim glanced around. 'There doesn't seem to be much evidence of your sister here. Just a lot of empty drawers and cupboards.'

'Oh, I'm sorry, officer. I assumed you already knew. My sister also owns the house next door. If you want to know more about her, you really should go there.'

CHAPTER SIX

Penn arrived at the entrance to Birmingham Crown Court at three minutes to nine. He would have made the run from the train station quicker if the boss had let him keep the trainers on.

'Bloody hell, Penn,' Lynne said, smiling. 'Talk about cutting it fine.'

'Bloody trains,' he said, unsure how to greet her.

A hug seemed inappropriate but no contact felt cold. He held out his hand.

Lynne gave him a strange look but shook his hand anyway.

'Hey, mate,' Doug said, dropping his cigarette and thrusting out his hand.

Penn shook it and quickly appraised them both.

In the four months since he'd left West Mercia, Lynne appeared to have lost a few pounds and Doug appeared to have found them. He'd swear that the sergeant had done something different with her light brown hair, maybe grown it a couple of inches. Her normal inch-high boots had been replaced with expensive-looking high heels that disappeared beneath her navy trouser suit. He was pretty sure she was wearing make-up, too. Her court outfit had taken way more money, time and consideration than his.

Detective Constable Doug Johnson was wearing the exact same thing he wore for work every day. A slab of black suit and a light blue shirt. The whole team had ribbed him about having a wardrobe full of black suits and blue shirts. He had retorted that this way no one ever knew when he was wearing dirty clothes.

'Good to see you both,' Penn said, as they headed up the steps. And he meant it. He'd worked alongside these officers for more than four years and he'd wondered how he would feel seeing them again. A comfortable familiarity washed over him as he followed them into the building.

He was struck by the cold functionality of the Elizabeth II Law Courts that housed Birmingham Crown Court. He always found himself wishing he was at the other place. When the new Crown Court opened in 1987 it had taken major cases away from the Victoria Law Courts on Corporation Street. The older court house, now a Magistrate's Court, was a Grade I redbrick and terracotta building drenched in history ever since Queen Victoria laid the foundation stone in 1887.

Now *that* place felt like a law court, Penn thought, with its great hall and chandeliers made to resemble Queen Victoria's coronation crown. The place demanded reverence and respect.

The newer building resembled a collection of square, efficient boxes. Here they used recording machines instead of a stenographer and laptops had replaced case files.

He underwent the normal security measures as he remembered his reason for being here. It was to see Gregor Nuryef finally face the justice he deserved.

Gregor Nuryef had brutally stabbed a man to death for refusing to hand over the night's takings from the family petrol station business.

Penn had been forced to admit he'd been wrong in his first assessment of the crime.

Initially he'd suspected a local gang headed by two brothers, Alan and Alec Reed, of being behind the crime. Having moved into the area in the mid-Eighties after a few close shaves with the Met, the brothers had eventually taken over organised crime in the city of Worcester and surrounding areas.

Their empire had been founded on identifying small businesses with limited or no CCTV and carrying out violent armed robberies, but despite diversifying into prostitution, drugs, racketeering and snack vans, armed robbery remained a mainstay of their business model.

The challenge to identify vulnerable businesses had become harder for the brothers over the years as small businesses had learned the benefits of a security system, but there were still struggling traders who thought a dummy camera would suffice and others who had broken systems they never bothered to get repaired.

Two years earlier West Mercia had introduced an initiative of visiting vulnerable premises and offering advice on basic safety measures proprietors could implement inexpensively. Sometimes they'd listened and sometimes not.

Mr Kapoor senior had largely listened but due to finances had not acted and had lost his twenty-three-year-old son as a consequence.

Penn shuddered at the memory of what he'd found when he'd attended the scene.

Of course, DI Travis had been the officer in charge of the case, but as the first responder Penn had always felt it was his case. Not least because young Devlin Kapoor had occupied his dreams for weeks.

He hoped the trial would finally allow him to put this case to bed. It was one that still kept him up at night as he waited for his mind to release it completely, for his brain to accept that it was over, the way a funeral offered closure to the relatives. This case was like a sentence written and erased but the indent of the letters remained.

He followed his colleagues into one of the sixteen courtrooms as an uneasy sensation stole over him.

And for the life of him he couldn't think why.

CHAPTER SEVEN

Kim waited as Veronica took the spare key from her bag and opened the door to the run-down property next door.

When she'd asked the woman why Belinda had owned the second property she had offered a secret smile, almost childlike and said, 'You'll see.'

The woman pushed open the door but didn't attempt to step inside.

'Welcome to my sister's real home,' she said, waiting for a reaction.

Kim's eyes widened as she looked into the space before her. What had once been a hallway that mirrored the clear one next door was now a narrow walkway with columns of books and newspapers on either side. The walkway was a good few inches above floor height with more of the same trampled down.

She turned to Veronica. 'She got in and out of here?'

Veronica nodded and stepped inside. Kim followed, tracing the woman's footsteps and holding out her arms for balance. Two strides in and Kim was hit with the smell of the place that reminded her of Barney after he'd run through a muddy puddle.

'Any pets?' Kim asked.

'None,' Veronica answered without turning.

Kim dreaded to think where that smell was coming from or what might be found beneath the piles of rubbish.

As she travelled forward Kim could see that every room was the same. A raised walkway which was filled from floor to ceiling with all kinds of objects including empty boxes, bike parts, tapestries led into each room. A single wing-backed chair remained untouched in the middle of the lounge.

Kim was unsure if the walls matched the magnolia colour next door as no wall space was available to view.

Kim couldn't compute the woman they'd seen last night, so tidy, so well turned out, living like this.

'I don't get it,' Kim said, entering the kitchen. There was not an inch of work surface to be seen. An electric kettle was just visible on the drainer unit of the sink. Bryant sneezed twice behind her, and Kim could feel the dust settling on her lips the way it had attached itself to the cobwebs straddling the corners of the ceilings and the light fittings.

'It started when our parents died, thirty-four years ago,' Veronica explained. 'This bungalow was theirs. She moved in and wouldn't throw a thing away that belonged to them and then began collecting things she felt were of value. Every time I came round it seemed that another part of the house had become unusable, another corner filled with junk. She insists that she needs every item here.'

Still talking as though her sister was alive, Kim noted.

'And the house next door?' Bryant asked.

'Came up for sale around the time I was threatening to have her committed if she didn't do something about it. She bought the bungalow next door dirt cheap and promised she'd sort all this stuff out while living next door and then we'd sell it and split the proceeds.'

'But?...'

'I think she snuck back in and slept here every night,' Veronica admitted.

'But how did she hold down a responsible job until just a few months ago?' Bryant asked.

'Why wouldn't she?' Veronica snapped. 'She wasn't crazy or stupid. She was just trying to hang on to something that didn't exist. She functioned perfectly fine and I find your comment a little bit insulting.'

Jeez, Kim thought. Bryant had pissed someone off more than she had. Now that might earn him the plant, after all.

Unusually it was time for her to don the United Nations Peacekeeper cap. 'I think we're just surprised given the way she looked and the cleanliness of the car that…'

'She was good at keeping up appearances, officer. We both are.'

Kim had already sensed a strange dynamic between the sisters but now she wanted to know more.

'You were older than Belinda?' she asked.

'Oh yes, officer, I certainly was. I suspect that had Belinda come first my parents wouldn't have bothered to have any more.'

Kim waited for further explanation of such a strange observation but Veronica met her gaze silently, waiting for any further questions.

'So, you looked out for her?'

Belinda raised one eyebrow. 'Whatever gave you that idea?'

'You live close by. You seem to have the same taste in clothes and jewellery. You check on her. You obviously took care—'

'Officer, I'm sorry to disillusion you but my sister and I really couldn't stand the sight of each other.'

CHAPTER EIGHT

'You know Keats is gonna be pissed off, don't you?' Bryant asked, as he neared Russells Hall Hospital.

'Yeah, cos that'd make a change,' she offered drily. 'And I'm not sure what you're worried about. It's not like he's going to take it out on you, his favourite detective.'

'Can't help the fact that folks like me,' he said, smugly.

'Except Veronica Evans. You're not her flavour of the month, and thank the Lord I was there to smooth over that little faux pas about Belinda holding down a job.'

'You were thinking the exact same thing.'

'Immaterial, my dear Watson. But if you're going to start pissing people off we really are in some shit. Woody might decide to split us up.'

'Really, it's that easy?' he asked.

'So, what do you make of our sisters?' she asked, hoping he would say something to dispel the uneasy feeling in her stomach.

'Damned weird if you want the truth.'

Or not, she thought.

'The likeness between them was eerily freakish. Her total lack of emotion at her sister's death. Didn't really ask us any questions about the circumstances. Didn't ask if we had any suspects. No pleas for us to find whoever did this,' he continued.

'Her admission that they didn't get on even though she lives close by and visits seemingly often,' Kim added.

'Yeah, and the fact that neither of them married and that's before we even get on to the hoarding.'

They looked at each other.

'Damned weird,' they said together as Bryant parked the car.

'Couple of references to their childhood that she chose not to elaborate on,' Kim said, across the roof of the car.

They fell into step together and headed for the main entrance.

'That thing about keeping up appearances,' Bryant said.

'And that comment about her parents not having any more kids if Belinda had come first. Do you think Belinda was a problem child?'

Bryant shrugged as they headed along the corridor to the morgue. 'Don't know, but I do know one thing: that information is not going to help us establish what Belinda Evans was doing tied to a swing at Haden Hill Park last night.'

'You may be right, Bryant, but I'd still like to know.'

'Hey, Keats,' she said, stepping into the morgue.

'You're late,' he said, peering over the rim of his glasses.

'Yeah, Bryant wanted to stop off for a full English even though he knew you'd be pissed, so how do you like him now?'

'Still better than you as you've now added liar to the list of your less favourable attributes.'

Kim shrugged. Looked like she wasn't breaking this bromance up any time soon.

'May I?' she asked, stepping closer to the table.

Keats nodded as he continued to make notes on his clipboard.

Kim gently drew back the white sheet to reveal Belinda's face. She looked past the complexion that always reminded her of raw pork and focussed on the features.

In this position, on her back with her head pointing towards the ceiling and her hair falling away from the face, the resemblance to the woman they'd just left was less striking.

There was a softness here, a gentleness to the features. Belinda carried a few more pounds than her older sister which appeared to soften the high cheekbones and sharp nose. There was a fullness to the lips instead of a sharp determined line. The most striking resemblance had come from the hair, clothes and jewellery, the similarity of which was still at the front of her mind.

'Belinda's sister will be along later to formally identify the body,' Kim said re-covering her face.

'I'm not completely finished,' Keats admitted, checking something on his clipboard before leaning against the stainless-steel counter top.

'But I will share what I've found so far. This lady was in excellent health and would have been for someone ten years younger. She's never smoked or drank excessively and all her major organs were functioning well and still intact. There is evidence of arthritis in her elbow and knee joints but nothing that would have incapacitated her or even slowed her down at this point. May have required surgery in approximately ten years.'

Kim offered him her 'not at all helpful' look, which he ignored.

'I find no evidence of broken bones or major injury which, strangely…'

'Why strangely?' Kim asked. She was ready for anything out of the ordinary that might explain why this academic, educated lady had taken a knife to the chest.

'Strange, because I've rarely had a customer, especially of this age, without some kind of broken bone or injury. I myself have a broken bone in my wrist from not holding the cricket bat correctly when I was a child.'

Bryant stepped forward. 'I got a broken toe from kicking a football when I was six.'

'Oh yeah,' Keats responded. 'Well I broke my thumb falling out of a tree.'

'Cracked jaw on the rugby field,' Bryant countered.

'Fractured femur when I fell from a two-storey building trying to catch a murderer,' Kim piped up.

They both turned her way.

'Fair enough,' said Bryant.

'Exactly my point, Inspector. All three of us have suffered major injuries.'

'Perhaps she never played cricket, football, rugby or chased murderers around rooftops,' she suggested.

'I didn't say it was a smoking gun, only that it was curious,' Keats said.

'So, general health was good and the cause of death was the single stab wound to the chest, which was a direct hit on the heart. The murder weapon is clearly a knife blade of seven to eight inches with a smooth sharp edge. The thrust was confident and decisive. There was no hesitation and it was accurately placed. Death would have been near instant.'

So, the aim had not been to cause as much pain and suffering as he or she could.

'And the barbed wire?' Kim asked.

'Was wound around her wrists only moments before death,' Keats answered. 'Judging from the blood loss from the wrist wounds.'

'Okay, Keats, as ever you've been—'

'Your impatience is equalled only by your rudeness, Inspector,' he said, moving towards the tray. 'You should know by now that I like to leave a little something until the end. A finale if you like.'

'Like something that might help?'

He ignored her. 'Bryant, can you stand the other side, please?'

Her colleague did as he was asked and they faced each other across Belinda's upper body.

Keats rolled the sheet down to her breastbone and placed his right hand on her shoulder to prevent the sheet slipping further.

'Pull her gently towards you,' he instructed Bryant across the body.

Bryant did as he was asked, and she watched as Belinda was rolled on to her side.

'Lift up her hair at the back,' Keats instructed.

Kim did so and took a sharp intake of breath at what she saw.

An X had been carved into the skin.

CHAPTER NINE

Penn glanced around the courtroom as both the prosecution and defence readied themselves to begin.

His eyes wandered over the modern light wood and cream paint that made the space more like a conference room than a court of law.

His gaze rested on Mr Kapoor, sitting straight, staring ahead in the public gallery, surrounded by people nudging and whispering, without a clue that he was the only person in the room whose life would never be the same.

As the man stared into space Penn couldn't help wondering if Mr Kapoor was remembering Devlin's first word, first step, first day at school. Maybe he was reliving a sporting achievement during his school years or a party for his eighteenth birthday. He hoped it was any one of those things instead of the sight of his young son lying on the floor of the family business saturated in blood.

Mrs Kapoor had not been able to force herself to attend the trial, just as she had not been able to step foot in the service station since the death of her son. Truth be known Mr Kapoor wanted shot of the place, but with two teenage daughters to feed and clothe he didn't have many options. His older brother had stepped in and between them they were keeping the place afloat.

Memories of Mr Kapoor had stayed with Penn. He had taken the news of his son's death with dignified silence. Not because he didn't feel the loss. Penn had seen the sudden emptiness that had crept into his gaze. And as Penn had listened to Mrs Kapoor's hysterical outpourings of grief he had also seen the resolution that had kept the man's own emotions at bay.

He had stepped forward to hold his trembling wife, offering himself as a rock onto which she could cling.

Throughout the investigation the man had quietly and respect-fully enquired about progress in finding his son's killer. He had not shouted, screamed or accused and that had prompted Penn to want to find the bastard who had done it even more.

'Looks lost, doesn't he?' Lynne whispered beside him.

Penn nodded his agreement as his gaze continued along the public gallery. Doug sat on the other side of Lynne staring straight ahead.

Penn's eyes rested on another solitary figure staring straight ahead. Irina Nuryef, Gregor's wife.

He tried to read her expression now as he had twice before. The first time was when she'd been giving her husband an alibi, and the second time was when she'd admitted she'd lied and taken his alibi away.

And that one admission had thrown the case wide open.

He stared at her hard, trying to pinpoint exactly what had changed since the last time he'd seen her.

On that second visit her hair had been unwashed and lank, hanging around her shoulders like a blanket. Her face had been pale and drawn. Understandable, given that she was admitting her husband was a murderer.

But right now, a phrase he didn't use often entered his head. She looked put together. Her hair was stylishly cut and her skin looked smooth and healthy.

As though sensing his attention her cool gaze turned his way. There was no register of either recognition or emotion as her scrutiny held for a second and then moved along the row.

Penn couldn't explain the shudder that ran through him as the court clerk announced the beginning of the session and instructed them all to rise.

CHAPTER TEN

'So, what do you make of the X on the back of the neck and why are we heading straight back to Wombourne?' Bryant asked.

'I'm still thinking about the X, but we're heading back cos I want another look around those houses without the overbearing sister and Mitch is on his way there now.'

'Oh, he's not gonna thank you for sending him in to that mess,' Bryant observed. 'You read the memo about that guy working a case in York?'

Kim shook her head.

'Techie guy died falling through a warehouse floor at the scene of an attempted murder. Wife and two kids left behind.'

'What's that got to do with Mitch?' she asked.

'Guy's boss is being blamed for failing to risk assess the area properly. You know how this works. Mitch is gonna be extra careful, which'll take a lot of extra time. Shit rolls downhill as they say but in my experience it goes to the sides as well. A bit like us all having to suffer with this stress and burnout stuff because a few city coppers had a bit of a paddy.'

'Bryant, I think the figures reflect a bit more than—'

'I'm just saying that Mitch is going to be extra careful right now.'

'Too bad,' she answered, unsure what choice they had. The woman had been murdered and they had to look for clues.

Kim still hadn't been able to let go of the image of the woman tied to the swing by barbed wire. The juxtaposition of those two items, the innocence of a child's swing and the barbed wire, sharp, pointed and biting into the flesh.

The carved wound into the back of the neck had been inflicted after death, Keats had advised. It hadn't been to cause pain or additional injury. In her experience, symbols were not meant for the victim. They were used either to purge something from the killer or to send a message. Make a statement. It was personal.

'Uh, oh,' Bryant said, as he turned into the quiet road.

Mitch was suited, booted and leaning against the bonnet of his van.

'You are kidding?' he asked, as she got out of the car.

Clearly, he'd taken a look in the hallway and got no further than that.

'Gotta be done, Mitch,' she said, leading him up the garden path. 'The woman's dead and much as I wish she'd tidied up first—'

'Come on,' Mitch interrupted. 'This is more than a messy house. This is hoarding at its worst. It's not safe for my guys to enter. I need to risk assess…'

'Bloody hell, Mitch. I've seen you work at height, underground and in confined spaces. You've entered rooms that smell like Keats's defrosted fridge, so man up and make a trail across a few nick-nacks for your guys. Jesus.'

'A few nick nacks?'

'Exactly. Glad you're seeing it my way.'

He shook his head and sighed. 'Given that this is a fair few miles from the crime scene, what exactly are you hoping we'll find?'

'The floor would be a start,' Bryant quipped behind her.

'I wouldn't presume to tell you your job, Mitch, but this woman was in her early sixties, brutally murdered in a kids' park and we need to find the bastard that did it. Like now.'

He raised one eyebrow.

'And you know I'd never ask you to do anything I'm not prepared to do myself.'

He groaned, rolled his eyes and called over the rest of the team. 'You owe me.'

'Cheers, Mitch,' she said, as his guys filed in behind him.

'We going in, guv?' Bryant asked.

'Not a chance,' she said, heading straight back down the path. 'We've got somewhere way more interesting to be.'

CHAPTER ELEVEN

For once Stacey was pleased to have the office to herself, although the noise she'd hoped would go away was still blaring loudly in her head.

In one way she was pleased to have the distraction of another major case, God forgive her for the thought. The last few weeks of plodding through the mundane had given her too much time to think. Too much space for the doubts, for the negative thoughts running around her mind. She'd been asked a question and right now she didn't have the answer. Was she prepared for her whole life to change, to leave the safety of the familiar, move out of her comfort zone. Quite honestly, she didn't know.

She pushed the thoughts away and tried to focus on the mobile phone records of Belinda Evans, while ignoring that her own phone had just dinged an incoming message. The phone hadn't yet made it out of her satchel. She didn't want it staring at her accusingly from the desk, taunting her into a response. She could ignore it so much easier if it was out of sight. And right now, that was exactly what she needed to do.

Having Belinda's phone number and the provider had made her job considerably easier. Susie at Vodafone had already confirmed that all activity had ceased on the number at 11 p.m. the night before.

Stacey was guessing the phone had been destroyed which told her the device was important, that there was some kind of link to the killer on that phone. Otherwise it would have remained on her person.

Helpful Susie at Vodafone was still working on the tracking information and was pulling data from the masts, but in the meantime Stacey had the phone activity to focus on.

She laid out the four pages emailed by Susie which covered the previous twenty-eight days.

As she began to scour the data she heard her own phone ding again.

She shook her head at her satchel as though it could understand her.

And then she got back to work.

CHAPTER TWELVE

'Guv, do you want to explain what you hope to find here?' Bryant asked, as they entered the second property belonging to Belinda Evans. 'We already know she spent all her time next door, so surely any clue will be there.'

Kim turned to him. 'Even in death did Belinda Evans appear unkempt, unclean?'

Bryant shook his head.

'Could you even have guessed at the squalor she lived in next door?'

'No.'

'Did the inside of her car in any way reflect it?'

'A simple answer to my question instead of twenty of your own would have been nice,' he grumbled.

'There was conflict, Bryant. A part of her needed that chaos next door. I'm not sure why yet but she also craved order and simplicity, organisation.'

'I still don't?...'

'I'm getting there,' she said, moving along the bare hallway and into the lounge. She looked in drawers and under cushions as she went.

'Where did you keep stuff when you were a kid?' she asked.

'Everywhere. Clothes on the bed, in corners, trainers strewn around the room, school books in a pile on the bedside cabinet, just everywhere, really.'

'What about important stuff? Things you wanted quick access to or to know where they were at all times, love letters, your favourite miniature Corgi car, pictures of half-naked…'

'Top drawer of the bedside cabinet,' he said, as her logic finally dawned on him. 'You're thinking Belinda used this house like a drawer. It's where she kept important stuff, away from the chaos of next door?'

She nodded as she opened the bottom drawer of the sideboard.

'Aha,' she said, lifting out a pile of paperwork.

'And what exactly are we looking for?' Bryant asked.

'I have no idea,' she said, handing him the pile. 'But I'll leave you to look through that lot while I take a look around.'

She did a cursory inspection of the kitchen but moved quickly on. There was little evidence of the woman enjoying any kind of cooking, which was something she could relate to.

And yet she was finding out little else about their victim. Normally she got a feel for the person by roaming their home. In this case she had two homes and was none the wiser about the person tied to a swing.

Usually she would find evidence of their life, their interests. She'd glance at books, magazines, style of furniture, ornaments and nick-nacks left lying around, but right now Belinda Evans was a 61-year-old academic, a former college professor of child psychology. Where was Belinda the woman? What were her passions, her fears, aspirations? Kim wanted the meat on the bones, the flesh that made her individual, unique. How had she grown up with Veronica as a sister and what story was hiding there.

She hadn't been expecting to find framed photo albums and sentimental trinkets. The woman had never married. There had been no children's or grandchildren's images to fill the mantelpiece but still Kim didn't get it. Her own home held one single photograph of herself and Mikey when they were six years old, and although her space was sparsely decorated she saw evidence of herself everywhere. Dog bowls, bike parts, magazines, psychological studies of serial killers, a dead plant on the windowsill. An oil stain on the carpet that just wouldn't come out.

But here there was nothing, which, for a woman who was clearly complex, made absolutely no sense.

She bypassed the spare bedroom that held not one stick of furniture and headed for the bedroom at the back.

This one held a double bed, a bedside cabinet with lamp, a dresser, a wardrobe and a full-length mirror.

Kim headed straight for the bedside cabinet. Top two drawers were empty but the bottom one held a copy of *Fifty Shades of Grey* and a pair of glasses.

Kim felt her lips turn up. Finally, a glimpse behind the curtain.

She strode to the first of the two wardrobes and found a small selection of pressed clothes similar to what she'd been wearing the night before, with a couple of added pairs of slacks. A shelf held underwear and flesh-coloured tights.

Her eyes passed quickly over the clothing to the item on the right.

She removed the overnight bag and placed it on the bed as Bryant entered the room.

'Anything in the paperwork?'

He shook his head. 'A few recent bills, a couple of solicitors' letters from the completion of the house purchase and a few bank statements. You?'

Kim pulled back the zip and started to remove the contents of the case. Two skirts, one pair of trousers. Two shirts, a pack of white lace lingerie, unopened, one pair of shoes, basic underwear, a small pill container already filled and one other small item nestled in the side pocket.

'So, where was Belinda Evans going?' Bryant asked.

Kim held up the packet of three condoms. 'And, more importantly, who was she going with?'

CHAPTER THIRTEEN

Penn pushed away the second half of his sandwich.

'You not eating that?' Doug asked, screwing up the packet of his second bag of cheese and onion crisps.

Penn shook his head as Lynne smiled tolerantly.

'Doug, I swear you've got a hollow leg or something.'

'Hate waste,' he said, reaching across the table.

Penn didn't mind. It was a bland egg mayo on brown bread. Had he been at home making lunch with his brother he'd have gone heavier on the mayo, added a sprinkling of salt and then spread the mixture between two chunks of thick white bread. But even that wouldn't appeal to him now.

He hated court days. He understood the need to give evidence to finish the job and close the case. And he'd done his bit. As the arresting officer, he'd been first to stand up and read his statement. A few questions had followed from the defence which he'd braced himself for, but they'd been pretty harmless.

'That barrister went so soft on you I thought he was going to offer to rub your feet while you were up there,' Lynne observed, wiping her mouth with a napkin.

Yeah, that's what Penn was worried about. In his experience, the defence team either went after the police or the witnesses. If they were going after police they questioned everything about the procedure. They recited passages word for word from the PACE book, analysing every action taken, search warrants, arrest procedure, questioning and covering everything from police brutality to whether the suspect had been served lunch.

Penn knew that every procedure had been followed to the letter but he had expected some kind of battle from the barrister.

So, if it wasn't the police they were going after, what did they know about the witnesses?

'Yeah, the guy was almost plaiting your hair,' Doug agreed.

'Hey, don't knock it,' Lynne said, nudging Doug. 'We're up next and I'm not in the mood for a mauling.'

He winked. 'I'll maul you any day of…'

'Doug,' Penn warned.

'Try it, buddy,' she responded with steel in her voice.

Penn knew Lynne didn't need him to fight her battles. Half the team had been frightened to death of her, but sometimes Doug stepped a bit too close to the line.

Doug rolled his eyes at what he felt was an overreaction on Penn's part, and took out his phone.

'Frustrating, isn't it?' Lynne asked. 'Having to hang around?'

Penn nodded. He'd given his evidence and now had to sit through the rest of the trial when his own team was working a murder investigation.

'Good to have you back, though,' she said, nudging him.

'Yeah,' he agreed, glancing around the room. People were starting to look at their watches as they sensed the end of lunch break approaching.

'Off outside for a smoke,' Doug said, pushing his chair back.

'Mate, you've got less than—'

'Stop fussing,' he responded with amusement. 'Just tell 'em to start without me,' he said, slapping Penn on the shoulder.

'Count to ten,' Lynne advised.

'It's not enough.'

'And don't think I didn't notice your lukewarm response to my comment about having the old team together again.'

'Course it's good to be back,' he said, glancing at the clock.

'Okey-dokey and now you're done insulting my intelligence or forgetting just how well I know you. We'll park that one right there.'

Had they not been in court Penn would have laughed at the knowing expression on her face.

As he'd been getting ready that morning a part of him had been looking forward to seeing his old colleagues again, being around people with whom he was so familiar, people he'd built friendships with along the way.

And yet he'd forgotten that he'd often had to play nursemaid to an officer who was almost fifteen years his senior.

But there was something else he'd realised. His old team lacked balance. The team was bigger and was an assortment of constables and sergeants but despite their individual skill sets it was a bit of a free for all when it came to task apportionment. And in some ways he could understand how that strengthened the team long-term. By making them all interchangeable no one's absence brought down the team.

But there was no clear team cohesion, no sense of place or belonging.

In his new place their roles were defined clearly due to the size of the team. The boss and Bryant would be forging ahead, not in the office long enough to warm their seats. Stacey would get right on to data mining and online investigation. And he would do either depending on the nature of the crime. Sometimes he was data mining along with Stacey and other times he was out doing follow-up interviews, door-to-door enquiries, checking alibis or following his own instinct. Which is probably what he'd have been doing right now.

'Hey, how's Jasper?' Lynne asked, interrupting his thoughts.

'Doing good,' he said, smiling. 'Still talks about beating you on the go-karts.'

Lynne threw back her head and laughed.

The two of them had met when Travis had arranged a team-building day at the go-karting course for all of them following a particularly harrowing child murder case, and he had taken Jasper along. The final race had been between his brother and Lynne who had recently completed her advanced police driver training course.

He knew she had let him win and he had appreciated the gesture. He met her gaze, realising how much he missed her. It was Lynne he'd been looking forward to seeing again.

'Yeah, well, thanks for letting him take the…'

'I did no such thing. The kid beat me fair and square.'

Penn's smile and response froze on his lips as Philip Maynard hurried towards them wearing a pensive expression beneath his CPS wig.

'One of the witnesses has gone missing,' said Philip, urgently.

'Ours or theirs?' he asked.

'Theirs,' he answered although it didn't really matter. Any missing person had the power to disrupt and derail the trial, preventing a guilty man getting the justice he deserved.

'Who?' Penn asked. Last time he'd checked everyone had been present and correct.

The recall bell sounded behind them.

'Dexter McCann. He slipped out twenty minutes ago and hasn't been seen since.'

Gregor's neighbour, who insisted the man was at home on the night that Devlin Kapoor was murdered.

The man was no threat to the prosecution and the alibi he was providing for Gregor Nuryef was as thin as 1-ply toilet paper, but the bad feeling in his gut was not going away.

In fact, it was starting to get worse.

CHAPTER FOURTEEN

'Guv, I am willing to bet my car that the distance between those lobelia plants is spot on,' Bryant said, as they traversed Mr Blenkinsop's paved pathway, along which was a one-foot-wide border on either side holding purple, and only purple, lobelia blooms.

'Even if you offered something decent I wouldn't bet against you,' she said, taking in the symmetrically planted hanging baskets on either side of the door.

Vertical hanging blinds adorned both the upper and lower windows. A way of maintaining privacy but allowing the occupant to see out. Perfect for the nosey neighbour.

'Mr Blenkinsop?' Kim said as the door was opened by a man in his late fifties.

The smell of lemon hit her nostrils and she wasn't sure if it came from the house or him.

His jeans had a crease pressed into the front of each leg and his short-sleeved white tee shirt was spotless.

A pair of glasses hung on a cord around his neck.

He nodded.

'May we come in?'

He didn't step aside but nodded again, as he looked down. 'Of course, if you'll just remove your shoes.'

Kim looked at Bryant and then back at the man.

'I'm sure our footwear is reasonably clean, Mr—'

'Please remove them,' he insisted.

In all her years as a police officer she had never once been asked to remove her shoes before entering a property.

'Never mind, sir, we were hoping you could assist with the events along the road but we'll continue on our way to the next property.'

'Okay, okay,' he said, opening the door. His obvious need to be involved trumped his need for carpet control.

'If you wouldn't mind talking in the kitchen,' he said, pointing along the hallway.

Damage limitation. They were not being allowed into the reception rooms with their shoes still on.

She headed past him towards what appeared to be the epicentre of the zesty smell.

The kitchen was surprisingly modern, light and airy, with flagstone tiles. A bistro table was set before a patio window looking out to the garden. A small fish pond was surrounded by colourful blooms.

'So, Mr Blenkinsop, what can you tell us about Belinda Evans?'

'Well, I didn't know her all that well. I mean, we waved and said the odd hello, exchanged Christmas cards and such but…'

'I understand,' Kim said. It was way more than she did with any of her neighbours except Charlie, Barney's best friend. 'So, what can you tell us about her habits? Did you happen to notice anything?'

'Well, it's all a bit strange, if you ask me. Unmarried, no children, no partner, buying the house next door for goodness knows what reason.'

So, the man had never been in her home, and looking around his own pristine surroundings it could very well have been the death of him.

'Did you ever notice any visitors, strangers coming to the house or hanging around outside?'

He shook his head. 'She seemed to go out a lot, late at night. Sometimes came back early hours of the morning, occasionally gone overnight.'

'Any idea where?' Kim asked, thinking about the overnight bag. He shook his head.

'Or with whom? Maybe her sister?' Bryant asked.

'No, I don't think so,' he said, frowning. 'Very strange. Hard to tell the two of them apart. Same hair, same clothes, similar car. A bit like they were trying to be twins.'

Except that by all accounts they couldn't stand each other.

'Two to three times a day the other sister turned up, sometimes just for a few minutes or half an hour but it was like they couldn't bear to be apart for more than a few hours at a time. Most strange for two women in their...'

His words trailed away as Kim's phone began to ring. She had to agree that these observations were not matching Veronica's description of their relationship.

'Excuse me,' she said, heading back into the hallway.

'Go ahead, Stace,' she said, out of earshot.

'Boss, I know you said the sisters weren't close but it might be worth finding out why they spoke to each other on the phone at the very least ten times a day.'

CHAPTER FIFTEEN

Penn watched as Ricky Drake took the stand and placed his hand on the Bible.

Although not a religious man, Penn wanted to rip the thing from beneath his palm.

Even now he couldn't account for the instant dislike he'd felt for the man, which he'd buried well during the investigation, due to him being their star witness.

It wasn't the first time he'd met someone like Ricky Drake, low-level scum always on the take and busted for house robberies two years earlier. It was unfortunate that you couldn't choose your witnesses, but the man saw what the man saw.

Penn was pleasantly surprised that he'd taken the time to make an effort. The dirty grey jogging bottoms had been replaced with a pair of black trousers and the navy fleece had become a long-sleeved white shirt that covered most of the tattoos that decorated his body.

He couldn't help but wonder if jury members still fell for the illusions and games played on both sides of the courtroom. Clean someone up to make them look more respectable, shave off facial hair to make them look younger. Surely every courtroom drama on the TV meant that jurors no longer fell for that crap.

And yet when Ricky Drake had entered the courtroom not one face in the jury had registered any kind of emotion. He knew full well the distaste that would have travelled across their faces had he not been cleaned up. But his benign appearance had caused no offence and therefore the jury was prepared to listen to him without prejudice, without judgement.

Yeah, the prosecution team did good in turning him into a credible witness, and he could see Doug nodding approvingly in the direction of where he stood.

All three of them had been surprised when Ricky Drake had offered them information on an armed robbery in exchange for leniency on a petty shoplifting charge, because Penn had thought he was seasoned enough to know that kind of stuff really did only exist in films. And after a sandwich and a cuppa from the station canteen he'd given up his info anyway.

He'd told them how he'd left The Crying Dog pub at around ten twenty to beat the rush into the chippy. He'd walked on the other side of the road, glanced into the brightly lit shop and seen the male in what he'd assumed to be a normal transaction. He'd stopped to light a cigarette, taken another look and realised he knew the guy vaguely and then carried on along to get his supper.

Both himself and Doug had been surprised – they'd been barking up the tree of the Reed family, having felt the incident had all the markings of one of their jobs – but they couldn't ignore a witness who had walked by the location during the actual incident. This man's statement had changed the direction of the whole investigation and eventually led to the apprehension of the murderer.

Ricky Drake had been instrumental in giving them enough detail about the man to track down Gregor Nuryef and question him. Initially his wife had provided an alibi and a search warrant had been out of the question.

However, guilt had driven Irina Nuryef to retract her statement and admit she'd lied about her husband being at home on the night of the murder.

This admission had enabled them to obtain the search warrant for the Nuryef home.

Doug had found nothing in the house, but Penn had struck gold in the garden shed where he'd found a bloodstained tee shirt rolled up in a carrier bag. Testing had matched the blood to that of Devlin Kapoor.

And despite the fact that Ricky Drake had handed them the crowbar to crack this case wide open there was still something in the man that almost brought bile to the back of his throat.

He tuned back in as the prosecutor drew the witness to the business end of his statement.

'So, you glanced towards the lit shop once as you walked along the road?'

'Yeah, that's right,' Ricky answered, seeming to be enjoying himself. Looking towards the jury as though they were his very own audience, all present to witness his solo performance. He was caught up in the moment, distracted as he played to his fans.

'But then you paused to light a cigarette...'

'Nah, chippy's only up the road and yer cor tek yer fag in...'

Penn's breath caught in his chest as every head on the side of the defence table shot up, and he could understand why.

Ricky had maintained from day one that he'd got a good enough look at the killer because he'd stopped to light a smoke.

The prosecutor was desperately trying to get Ricky to backtrack and remember the events accurately. The way they'd been recorded on the statement in front of him.

The defence team were furiously scribbling notes.

And Penn was trying to swallow down the bile that was now well and truly in his throat.   •

CHAPTER SIXTEEN

Veronica's house was not what Kim had been expecting and yet somehow it suited her completely.

The property was a four-storey town house including the garage that was at ground level and could not have been more different to the single-storey dwellings of her sister. And yet the height, the imposing structure of the dwelling, mirrored the woman perfectly.

'Bloody hate these places,' Bryant moaned as they approached the front door. 'Had an aunt that lived in something similar, too many stairs and weird layouts normally.'

Kim ignored him and knocked the door.

'I mean who wants a bedroom beneath the kitchen or a—'

'Good evening, officers,' Veronica said, opening the door. There was no surprise in her tone at seeing them there.

She'd changed into smart jeans and a V-neck tee shirt with a rose embroidered over a chest pocket. Her hair had been let down and her feet were encased in flat deck shoes.

Unlike either of Belinda's homes, a warm aroma, musky but not cloying, reached out and welcomed them in.

'Please, go up,' she said, pointing to the staircase that ran alongside the double garage. 'My office is on the first floor.'

Only Kim heard Bryant's tut as they took to the stairs.

The first landing opened up into what Kim guessed was more than a study.

The space immediately beckoned you in with its warm mix of period furniture. A vintage mahogany desk that caught the light from the south-facing window. A comfortable chair before the fireplace, mismatched cushions that looked worn but homely. An entire wall given to leather-bound books. Another wall with old framed movie prints. Glass jars spaced around the room containing liquid and wooden sticks. Her own attempts at keeping the air fresh in her own home was a few squirts of Neutradol and an apple-scented plug-in. But this was a room that wasn't trying to be anything except a comfortable space in which to spend time.

'My favourite room in the house,' the woman said, stepping in behind them. 'I spend most of my time here,' she said, crossing the room to open a door that led into a bright modern kitchen that was completely at odds with the space in which they stood.

'May I get you anything to?...'

'We're fine, thank you,' Kim said.

Veronica closed the door and pointed to the comfy chairs in front of the fireplace.

She took the left giving only one of them the opportunity to sit down. Taking the only remaining chair behind the desk would have been too familiar, intrusive.

Bryant moved towards the book wall as Kim found herself wondering if the two sisters had spent time together sat here bathed in the firelight as they sipped a glass of wine.

'How may I help, officer?' Veronica asked, crossing her legs at the ankles and folding her hands neatly into her lap.

Kim suspected the sisters had not sat side by side enjoying the space, given what Veronica had already told them about the relationship, which brought Kim to her first question.

'Miss Evans...'

'Veronica,' she corrected quickly.

'My apologies. You told us earlier that the relationship between—'

'Please be careful with those, officer. Many are First Editions,' Veronica said, without turning her head towards the sergeant.

Bryant stepped away from the book wall like a scolded child. Kim again marvelled that they appeared to have found someone that related to her more than they did to her colleague.

'You told us that the two of you weren't very close.'

Veronica's mouth lifted in something short of a smile. 'That's not exactly what I said but it's near enough.'

Yes, Veronica had said that the two of them couldn't stand the sight of each other.

'And yet you spoke to each other countless times every day, judging by her phone records.'

'Absolutely we did,' Veronica answered. 'We are sisters.'

'But you didn't like each other?'

'Correct again, officer, but I fail to see your point.'

Which was unbelievable for a smart, educated woman.

'My point, Veronica, is that siblings who don't get along tend to go their separate ways and choose to have as little contact as possible,' she said. They don't dress similarly, drive the same car, live within a few minutes' walk of each other and speak twenty times a day on the phone, is what she wanted to say.

'Each other was all we had left after our parents died.'

'Did that bring you closer?' Kim asked, trying to understand.

'Not at all. Our childhood dictated that we would never be close.'

'Could you explain why?'

'Absolutely not, as it has no bearing on the case and will not assist you in the slightest.'

'How can you be so sure of that; would you not want to do everything possible to help us catch the person that did this to your sister?' Kim asked.

'If I thought events from half a century ago were connected to her murder, I would share them but they are not.'

The mild curiosity in Kim's stomach was now developing into a raging need to know what had existed between these women, and she would be the judge of what would help move the case forward.

'Veronica, I really—'

'Officer, your only interest in me should be where I was at the time of Belinda's death, which is what I assumed to be the purpose of your visit and why I invited you into my home. I was here at my desk on a Skype call to the editor of the *Daily Telegraph*, which can easily be verified in a single phone call. Once you have established that our business is concluded.'

'May I ask what the Skype call?...'

'Thirteen across and eleven down.'

'Excuse me?'

'The crossword, officer. That's my job. I devise cryptic cross-words for newspapers. My editor felt that two clues in particular were far too difficult, which I argued against, but he insisted I change them.' She stood. 'Now, if there's nothing else?'

'Actually, there is,' Kim said, staying exactly where she was. 'Your sister had an overnight case in her wardrobe. Do you have any idea where she was planning to go?'

Kim caught the surprise in her expression. 'Damn it, we agreed...'

'You agreed what, Veronica?'

'Nothing, it doesn't matter. I'm sorry, officer, but I have no idea where my sister was planning to go.'

Kim hated barefaced lying and that's exactly what this woman had just done.

'Or why she was taking a healthy supply of condoms along?' Kim pushed.

'I'm sorry, Inspector, but I will not answer any more of your questions and I'd really like you to leave. Right this minute.'

Damn this woman's obstinacy but right now she had no cause to push her any harder than she already had. Knowing that she was lying was not a good enough reason in the eyes of the law.

Kim stood, bid her a terse goodbye and headed down the stairs. Veronica didn't follow them down and Bryant closed the door behind them.

'Blimey, that cooled down very quickly, but we didn't learn a fat lot,' he observed as they headed to the car.

On the contrary, Kim thought, remembering what the woman had said about the crossword puzzle, and her own cleverness.

She had the distinct feeling that they'd found the sister that liked to show off.

CHAPTER SEVENTEEN

Penn sat at the table and sighed heavily, trying to expel the fatigue that had settled in his bones and had nothing to do with hard work.

Sitting in a courtroom listening all day knackered him far more than a full-on twelve-hour shift. The inertia drained him as restless energy coursed around his body with no place to go.

He'd called in to the boss who had told him to go straight home. He'd considered arguing with her, wanting to insist there was something he could do to help, but the boss had told him to save his energy. He'd wanted to tell her that he'd been saving his energy all day but she'd ended the call. So, when Lynne had suggested a quick cuppa he'd been happy to accept. As had Doug, although Penn wasn't sure the invitation had been an open one.

'What do you think, then?' Doug asked, loosening his tie and taking out his mobile phone.

'Of what?'

Doug nodded towards Lynne who was loading three flat whites onto a tray.

'Her new car. Leather interior, satnav as standard, alloy wheels and…'

'It's hardly new, Doug,' Penn said, with a smile. 'Just not as old as her last one.'

'Yeah, well, you DSs like to flash your cash about, buying drinks, new cars.'

Penn was tempted to tell him to go for promotion himself and remembered just in time that he had and had failed the exam. It wasn't something the man liked to be reminded of. Not that the increase in pay was a lot to shout about.

'You seen the piece of shit I drive?' he said, taking the cups from the tray as Lynne laid it down.

'You moaning about my car again, Douglas?' she asked, using the full name she knew he hated.

'Fuck off,' he bristled.

'Love you more,' Lynne joked, sitting beside him and nudging him in the ribs.

Doug's face relaxed as he put his phone on the table.

'Any news on Dexter McCann?' Penn asked of the missing witness. He was no longer in the West Mercia email loop.

Doug shook his head.

'Not gonna lose too much sleep over it,' he said, adding two sweeteners to his drink. 'Their witness not ours. Gotta be lying anyway. We know we got our guy.'

'But why lie?' Penn asked. 'He's only a neighbour, so what's he got to gain?'

Doug narrowed his eyes dramatically. 'You switching sides, dude?'

Penn had to admit that one of the things he didn't miss was just how annoying Doug could be when the mood took him.

Penn shook his head, ignoring the 'dude'.

Doug turned to Lynne. 'You think Dexter McCann is lying?'

Lynne thought for a minute and then shook her head.

'I think he's confused. He knows the guy calls his dog to come into the house at ten thirty every night. How can he remember every single night exactly?'

Which was precisely what they'd all said at the time.

She sipped her drink and continued. 'I reckon we've got enough bother with our own witnesses without worrying about the ones for the other side.'

'Yeah and wasn't that a bloody slip-up?' Penn asked. He turned to Lynne. 'That's what he said, wasn't it? I mean from the very first statement?'

Lynne gave him a look of irritation mixed with something else he couldn't quite read.

'Nah, I made it up cos like I really don't know how to take a statement,' she snapped, slamming her cup back into the saucer.

'Come on, Penn,' Doug said, looking at Lynne and then at him. 'It's what the tosspot has said throughout. He made a mistake.'

'A mistake?' Penn asked. The guy had forgotten what he'd been doing when he'd actually seen the guy on the premises.

'You saw him up there,' Doug continued. 'Overconfident, drunk with being on the right side of the law. He got cocky and slipped up.'

Penn couldn't help wondering how being an arrogant prick affected your memory of events but he wasn't going to argue with his colleague and friend. Judging by Lynne's pensive expression, he'd done enough of that already.

'Anyway, no permanent harm done,' Doug said, reaching for his phone. 'Jury didn't take much notice and seemed to believe him.'

Penn remained silent and took a sip of his coffee.

Yeah, the jury seemed to believe Ricky Drake, all right, but Penn wasn't sure he did.

CHAPTER EIGHTEEN

Stacey switched off her computer at 5.45 p.m. and sat back in her chair. The boss had told her to go home and she'd learned to read the signs.

She glanced around the empty room as a memory came back to her.

She'd been new to the rank of detective constable and freshly assigned to the team. On the first day, the boss had called in and told her to go home.

As she'd gathered her things together her new colleague, Kevin Dawson, had looked up at her aghast.

'What're you doing?'

'Going home,' she said, pointing to the phone. 'The boss just said—'

'Forget what the boss just said. We've got a dead body and three active lines of enquiry. You really think the boss wants you to go home?'

Stacey was confused. 'But why would she tell me to go, then?'

'Cos it's the end of your shift. You ain't getting paid for any more hours.'

Stacey stood, coat and bag in hand, feeling ridiculous, unsure what to do.

Dawson studied her for a second or two before speaking.

'This is where you get to decide what kind of copper you want to be. Commit or don't commit but make your choice and stick to it.'

Stacey smiled at the bittersweet memory. She remembered thinking what an arrogant knob he was and how that opinion had changed as they'd become friends.

And he'd been right of course. Two hours later when the boss and Bryant had returned to the squad room there'd been a silent nod of acknowledgment in her direction.

Dawson's advice of commit or don't had served her well, and she'd learned to read the signs. If the boss was going home, they were all going home.

Except, she didn't want to go home, she realised, as she headed down the stairs, right into the mêlée of uniform shift changeover.

She dodged around and walked in between mates and colleagues on shift handover, either catching up or relaying a particular incident that had happened throughout the day. An arrest, an Asbo, a hands-on scuffle.

She finally found herself at the front reception and the automatic doors as two more squad cars pulled up.

She reached the end of the car park and hesitated.

If she turned left and stayed on this side of the road, the bus would take her to her small flat in Dudley, a half mile from her mum's house.

If she turned right and crossed the road, the bus would take her to Devon's flat, where she'd been spending most of her time.

She thought about the text message still unanswered on her phone.

Commit or don't commit but choose now, she heard again.

She took a step forward and turned left.

CHAPTER NINETEEN

Kim pressed the play button on her iPod and 'Der Ring des Nibelungen' filled the garage. The sound of Wagner's tuba wafted around her combining the tonal elements of the French horn and the trombone.

Since returning home she'd washed, ironed, fed the dog and vacuumed. Given her own way she'd have still been at work delving deeper into the life of Belinda Evans, but she'd had the memo.

So, here she was, home before dark, relaxing.

The silent argument in her head raged as Barney took his place by the door to the kitchen.

There's a body in the morgue.

There's always a body in the morgue.

You have a duty of care.

My team are all adults.

But they may try to hide it.

'Oh, for fuck's sake,' she cried, throwing a spanner across the floor. How the hell was she supposed to know what to do? Damn it, she'd never wanted kids and wasn't afraid to admit it. She'd never wanted the responsibility of another life in her hands and she possessed enough self-awareness to know the kid wouldn't fare so well either. She wasn't so sure Charlie down the road would have come and walked it daily the way he did with Barney. And she worried enough about him. No, having a child was definitely not for her and somehow she'd ended up with three of them. Big ones.

Barney raised his head and looked at her.

'I'm relaxing, honest,' she said, crawling on her knees to retrieve the tossed spanner.

He stood and walked past her. His tail wagged two seconds before a knock sounded on the garage door.

'You in there?'

'Bugger off, I'm relaxing,' she called back to her colleague.

'Yeah, I heard.'

'Come round,' she called back getting to her feet, eager to be out of the garage.

Normally she loved her time in her favourite room of the house. She loved nothing more than to focus on the jigsaw of bike parts that would eventually make a whole, but only when she felt she'd earned it and deserved it.

She reached for the percolator jug as Bryant came in the front door.

Barney blocked further access with a resolute stance and a whooshing tail.

'Here you go,' Bryant said, paying the entry fee of one apple. The definite way to her dog's heart.

'Couldn't sleep,' he said, launching himself on to the bar stool on the other side of the breakfast bar.

'Bryant, it's not even nine o'clock,' she said, smiling.

'Ah, that'll be why then.'

'You gotta relax,' she offered.

'Tried it,' he said, shrugging. 'Got bored.'

'How?' she asked turning. 'How exactly did you try and relax and why isn't Jenny keeping you busy?'

Normally wives appreciated a bit of help from their husbands.

'Started weeding the front garden. How desperate is that for something to do?'

Knowing how much he hated gardening that was pretty much rock bottom.

'And?'

'Apparently we pay a kid who's putting himself through college to do that.'

She smiled. Yep that sounded like Jenny.

'I put the washer on. Apparently it's not the right day for that cos now she's got washing hanging around until ironing day. I mean who knew washing machines and irons only worked on certain days of the week?'

'Bryant, you're giving these things way too much thought.'

'Yeah, that's what Jen said right before she sent me round here.'

Kim laughed out loud. If she was honest, she loved Jenny almost as much as Bryant did.

Never once had she been threatened by the friendship that had grown between them over the years. The long hours, the late nights, the focus that excluded all else when a heavy case came up. Jenny got it and was totally secure in her husband's love.

'She's having trouble adjusting,' he said, turning a drinks coaster onto its edge and trying to twirl it.

'She is?' Kim asked, pointedly.

He put it down and began tapping it.

'You know, I've often heard folks talk about all the things they've done in that time between shifts. Visited parents, out with friends. Date night, whatever the hell that is, cleaning, cooking, playing with kids and I've thought how nice to be able to fit all that in. You know, actually have a life.'

'Yeah, well now you've got the chance to…'

'I don't want it, guv… sorry, Kim,' he said, remembering her 'first name at home rule'.

'And it's not good for my marriage, either.'

Kim pushed his coffee towards him. 'You're joking?'

He shook his head. 'We've never been that kind of couple. We don't need to be with each other every minute. Jenny has her work mates, book club, a few old school friends and I have rugby and… well, work.'

'Jesus, Bryant, seeing as you're not doing much of the rugby thing right now that leaves you in a bit of a sorry state.'

'Ain't that the truth?'

'You never did tell me why you've cooled the rugby thing. I mean I know you were getting beaten black and blue most games but that's been going on for years.'

'No particular reason,' he said as a shadow crossed his face. If she recalled correctly it had happened during their last major case where the killer had been copycatting the traumatic events of her life.

She shuddered as she pushed the memories away.

'Anyway the point is that some couples can have too much time together. It can be detrimental to their psychological and physical—'

'Jenny hit you?' she asked, stifling a smile.

'Threw the remote at me when I switched off *Emmerdale* and asked if she wanted to go out for a walk.'

Kim laughed out loud. 'Methinks you're gonna have to find yourself some man friends.'

'Or I could just do my job the way I've always…'

'Sorry, but I'm under orders. You know Woody's really getting his knickers in a twist over this burnout report.' She hesitated. 'I mean we both know you don't do anything quick enough to even worry a friction burn but…'

'Cheers, Kim,' he said, running his hand through his hair.

'Hands are tied.'

'Woody doesn't have to know. We could work out of here once the shift ends and…'

'Not happening.'

She'd had the team working there for 24 hours during the last case and she wasn't likely to invite that situation in again.

'Thing is, I can't get Belinda Evans out of my head. All I can see is her sitting on that swing with the barbed wire around her wrists, her foot turned at the ankle, slouched against the chain like a rag doll.'

'Yeah, I know what you mean,' she answered, taking a good sip of her drink.

The vision had been with her since she'd walked back in the door.

'And her sister. I mean there is some weird shit going on between the two of them.'

'And yet Veronica won't even talk to us about their childhood. I wonder if Stace…' Her words trailed away as she raised an eyebrow at her colleague. 'Very clever, Bryant, but we're not talking about this any more. Pretty sure that counts as work and we're off the clock.'

'Bloody hell,' he said at the end of a long sigh. 'You know, at my age I have to make the most of my active brain cells cos there'll come a day when…'

'Either talk to me about the weather or piss off,' Kim advised.

'Jeez, Kim. You're really following the rules?'

Yeah, even she was surprised. Her response to rule following was selective at best but not when it came to the welfare of her team.

'So, that shower we had earlier…'

'Not a chance,' Bryant said, edging off the stool. 'Not sitting here discussing weather. I am gone.'

Kim smiled at his retreating back.

'Good, go home and get relaxed.'

'I am fucking relaxed,' he shouted at the top of his voice before he slammed the front door.

She had the sudden feeling it was going to be a very long week.

CHAPTER TWENTY

'Okay, guys, look lively eh?' Kim said, glancing around the room at her team.

Penn was looking at something on his mobile phone, Stacey was staring over his head at something out the window and Bryant was wearing the same scowl that had been on his face the night before.

Oh yeah, her team was looking totally energised from their extra downtime.

And from her point of view she almost felt as though she hadn't seen them for days.

She had followed the rules herself, to set an example, and hadn't entered the building until 7.45 ready for the mandated 8 a.m. briefing. She wouldn't mention the half hour she'd spent sitting in the car.

'Penn, anything to offer before you get off to court?'

He put his phone aside. 'Just checking if I need to go, boss. Not sure what's happening.'

'Thought the case was pretty straight forward?'

She'd been hoping to have him wrapped up and returned to her by the end of the week. Having to trust Inspector Plant and his team with the follow up interviews did not sit well with her.

'Defence witness went AWOL yesterday. Uniforms went out looking but no update yet.'

'Everything else, okay?'

He hesitated. 'Fine boss, but I could easily have come back for a few hours last night.'

'You read the memo,' she reminded him.

'We really still sticking to that?' he asked, causing another two heads to raise in hope.

Jeez, Kim thought, it was like trying to force a kid to eat their greens. You knew it was good for them but they fought you at every mouthful.

'Yeah, we're sticking to it,' she said, as Penn's phone sounded receipt of a text message.

He read it. 'Still no neighbour but the defence is calling their only other witness, which is his wife, so that should be fun seeing as she's a hostile witness.'

Kim nodded as he pushed his chair away from the desk. This was what happened sometimes. Witnesses were rearranged to provide continuity and keep disruption for the jury to a minimum. Once a case had started no one wanted it interrupted, schedules had been cleared, meetings postponed, experts booked, family members primed for a result one way or the other. Every effort would be made to keep the trial going.

'And then there were three,' Kim mused as Penn disappeared out the door.

She headed over to the board.

'Okey-dokey, good work on the phone calls between Belinda and her sister yesterday, Stace. Still got no explanation about the weird relationship between the two of them and I want you to keep digging on that. I want to know everything you can find out about these two ladies: their parents, childhood friends, neighbours, boyfriends, everything.'

In her peripheral vision she could see Bryant's expression questioning the instruction.

'Go on, spit it out,' she said, without turning.

'Veronica has an alibi and you can't seriously think…'

'And check out that alibi while you're at it, Stace,' Kim instructed. 'Skyping with the editor at the *Telegraph* shouldn't be too hard to prove, and then we can rule her out completely.'

'Got it, boss,' Stacey said, making notes. Kim was relieved to see the tension slipping from her face.

She turned towards her colleague. 'And why should we rule her out without checking her alibi, grumpy boy?'

'She hardly—'

'Don't you even dare say she doesn't look the murdering kind. Tell me the last time we arrested someone that did. And you never hear of sororicide?'

'Err... no,' Bryant answered. 'And if you've got it, is it contagious?'

'The killing of one's sister,' Kim elaborated. 'Primarily when sibling rivalry gets out of hand. Ronald DeFeo Jr. shot both his sisters in 1974. The murders became the inspiration for *The Amityville Horror* books and films. Karla Homolka and Paul Bernardo raped then killed Karla's sister Tammy in 1990, and Yuki Muto murdered his sister in—'

'Someone appears to have spent their downtime doing some research last night,' Bryant observed, tapping his fingers on the desk.

'Yeah, just fell on this article that happened to be open on the laptop,' she lied.

Twenty minutes after he'd left she'd been unable to resist just taking a look.

'Aah, I get it,' Stacey said. 'If we happen to open our computers and there's something there to...'

'I've told you. It was an accident.'

'Yeah, she tripped and fell into Wikipedia,' Bryant said around her as she walked between them.

'Boss, there's still some phone numbers on the call register to work through so?...'

God damn it, right now she could have done without Penn in court. Stacey's workload was going to get pretty heavy.

'Finish that off first and then start on the other stuff.'

Stacey nodded her understanding.

The detective constable was going to have a busy day and yet Kim had the feeling that she wouldn't mind.

'Bryant and I will be focussing on her last place of work, the man she was seeing and trying to find out where she was going.'

'She had condoms in the case?' Stacey asked with wide eyes.

'She was being responsible,' Kim replied.

'But I mean…'

Bryant folded his arms. 'Stace, if you're talking about her age, folks still have normal desires beyond retirement, you know. And being in your sixties doesn't prevent you catching sexually transmitted diseases.'

'Yeah, I get it, but it's just…'

'Stacey Wood,' he blustered. 'How can you write someone off just because they've reached…'

'Ignore him, Stace. He's just getting worked up cos he's approaching that stage of life himself.'

Stacey chuckled as Bryant opened his mouth to respond.

Kim held up her hand to stop him as her mobile began to ring.

'Keats,' she answered.

'I need you here.'

'And good morning to you too.'

'I have something to show you. I found the answer.'

The line went dead in her hand.

She didn't even know there had been a question.

CHAPTER TWENTY-ONE

Penn arrived at court with a few more minutes to spare than the day before.

He entered the building and clocked Lynne and Doug holding up the coffee bar at the far left of the space. He hesitated when he spotted Mr Kapoor dead ahead at the end of the line waiting for access to the public gallery.

He headed towards Mr Kapoor. The man was not a witness, so communication between them was not an issue.

'How are you holding up?' Penn asked, offering his hand.

'Truthfully, sir, I want it to be over. I want to remember my son for other things.'

Penn understood. The man had lived twenty-three years of Christmases, birthdays, school, college, graduation and all Mr Kapoor could think about were the events of the last few minutes of his son's life. And until the bastard that had done it was punished that would be all he could think about. Penn wanted nothing more than this man to have some kind of peace.

'How is Mrs Kapoor?'

He looked down at his feet. 'She still blames me and I understand. I was stupid. I should have listened to you,' he said, raising his head and nodding towards the others at the café. 'I should have installed CCTV. We were an easy mark for anyone but I couldn't afford it. We were losing money week after week but I should have found it.'

Penn felt for the man. The opening of a mini market along the road had hit him hard. His few bits and pieces of grocery couldn't compete with the light, bright and shiny premises along the street, and if the rumours he'd heard about a Tesco superstore a mile and a half away were true the man would barely be able to give his petrol away either.

Penn could feel the man's regret: had he known what he was going to lose he would have begged, borrowed or stolen to get more security, but he hadn't, his son was dead. Penn wanted the murderer to pay so this man could begin to rebuild his life.

'Is all okay with the case, sir?'

Despite his urging the man refused to call him anything else.

'I noticed some sort of upset yesterday. Is all well?'

Penn realised he must mean the discovery that one of the witnesses had gone missing.

'Nothing on our side, Mr Kapoor,' he reassured the man, touching him on the arm. 'If there's anything you need to know, I'll find you,' he said, before turning away.

'Any more news?' he asked Lynne and Doug as he approached.

Lynne shook her head, and Doug shrugged in a 'Who Cares' expression.

'The defence is calling Gregor's wife, to give the uniforms more time to track McCann down,' Lynne said.

'Well, this should be fun,' Doug said, rubbing his hands together, as they began to file into the courtroom.

Penn was sure they were expecting a hostile witness but they had yet to meet Irina Nuryef.

He'd met the woman twice and neither occasion would he have described as fun.

CHAPTER TWENTY-TWO

Kim knew what Bryant was going to say before he said it. She was only surprised he managed to keep it in until they were walking towards the morgue.

'You saw Stacey, right? You know she's miserable being sent home at five each night?'

Of course she'd seen her colleague. 'It's an adjustment period. She'll get used to it. With all this extra time you'll make new friends, too, take up cake decorating; now get off my back. There's nothing I can do.'

'And what time do you call this?' Keats asked, as they entered the cold, sterile area.

'Don't even start,' she advised.

'Working half days, now?'

And of course, asking him to stop doing something only encouraged him more.

'So, what you got?' she asked, placing her hands onto the metal dish.

'Hands off,' he said, wrapping her knuckles with the ruler in his hand.

'Oww,' she said, rubbing at her hand.

'I've just cleaned it,' he said, reaching for his clipboard.

She looked to Bryant and silently asked him if that gave her permission to haul him over the dish by his lapels.

Bryant's brief shake of the head said no.

As the ruler was still in his hands she placed her own into her pocket, not least to protect them from the ruler but also from tightening around the pathologist's throat.

'So, Belinda and I have been chatting some more and she seemed to have a little more to say. I can confirm that she was sexually active and—'

'Blimey, Keats, how the devil do you deduce such a thing?' Kim asked, wondering about the physicality of such a discovery.

'Because of these,' he said, placing a photo on the metal dish between them.

She looked down to see raised bobbles of pink skin.

'Genital warts, Inspector,' Keats explained. 'HPV: human papillomavirus. These little terrors are sore, painful and very easily transferred by sexual contact.'

Kim took a moment to digest the information, trying to compute the image of the professional, educated middle-aged lady, well dressed, well presented, appearing to be highly sexed.

'And that's not all,' he said, placing two more photographs on the table.

She reached out, placed them side by side and then shuffled them, unsure exactly what she was looking at.

'Hands,' Keats said, again cracking her fingers with the ruler.

'Keats, I swear if you do that one more time, I'll…'

'What you're seeing here,' he said, pointing to the first photo with the ruler, 'is a magnified image of the corners of Belinda's mouth. Here,' he said pointing to his own mouth where the lower lip met the upper lip. 'There are minute tears to the skin on both sides. And this', he said, turning the second photo around to face her, 'is the imprint of a circle close to her ears on both sides, cleverly concealed with make-up.'

Kim shook her head.

'A ball gag, Inspector. Commonly associated with sado-masochism. The ball is placed in the mouth and a leather strap is buckled around the back of the head.'

'I still have no idea...'

'Bryant, google it for her, will you?'

Her colleague took out his phone, pressed a few buttons and turned the screen her way.

'Oh, okay,' she said, wondering how the hell such an object could enhance sexual pleasure.

'Keats, how on earth do you?...'

'It's my job to know these things, Inspector.'

'So, it looks as though our victim not only liked sex but also liked sexual games.'

'I think we need to find out who she was playing those sexual games with,' Bryant said. 'And we might just find our—'

'It's not sexual,' Kim said, walking around the table, her hands firmly back in her pockets.

'Come on, guv,' Bryant said, incredulously. 'The woman took condoms wherever she went, she had a sexually transmitted disease and she liked to play games.'

'Precisely. She was sexual but the murder was not.'

'Could have been a sex game gone wrong,' he pushed.

She shook her head, stubbornly. 'It has none of the signs of a sexually motivated murder. There was no sexual contact—'

'There doesn't have to be sex for it to be a sexually motivated murder, guv,' Bryant argued.

'Agreed but no clothing was removed; there was no mutilation of sexual organs. Nothing had been removed or tampered with and the marking on her neck was done in an area where her garments didn't need to be touched.'

'But if she'd passed on the disease to someone who was less than pleased with the gift?'

'Still wouldn't be sexual though, would it?' Kim observed. 'That would be revenge.'

Bryant turned to Keats. 'Help me out?'

Keats tapped his chin with the ruler. 'Sorry, but, much as it surprises me on this occasion, I have to agree with your boss, may the lord forgive me,' he said, looking heavenward. He continued. 'In my experience, sexually motivated murders are unmistakeable: clothing has been removed, destroyed, genitals are on display and often mutilated, interfered with or totally removed. It's a statement. It's the first thing the killer wants you to notice whether it be a fetish or whatever the reason. It's normally on display for the symbolism to be clear. It's their message.'

Bryant still appeared unconvinced, and Kim had a good idea why.

'You're allowing her age to colour your view,' Kim said facing him across the table.

'Don't be…'

'If we were looking at a twenty-something victim, you'd take the information about her sex life as part of her story, but because she's older you're assuming this is her only story. If she's in her sixties and having kinky sex then that has to be the reason for her death.'

'Keats, are you hearing this rubbish?' Bryant implored.

Keats shook his head. 'Remaining silent right now as even I can't stomach agreeing with the inspector twice in one day. And much as I'd love to stand and watch you argue this one to the death, I do have other customers to deal with, so…'

'Thanks, Keats,' Kim said, heading towards the door, her mind whirring with what they'd learned.

'Not so fast, Inspector. I do want you gone, admittedly, but you still don't have the answer I called you here for.'

'And the question was?'

'The cause of the forty-seven nicks in the bones of the left hand.'

'And?' she asked.

'I'd have thought that was now perfectly obvious,' he answered, with a coy smile.

Her brain clicked.

'The ruler?' she said, rubbing at her left hand.

Keats nodded. 'At some stage our victim's knuckles were being constantly rapped forcefully with a sharp, metal ruler.'

CHAPTER TWENTY-THREE

Penn held his breath as Irina Nuryef strode to the witness stand, offering a filthy sideways look to everyone in her path.

Again, he couldn't help but notice the difference in her appearance from the other two times he'd seen her.

With a face set in a permanent scowl she looked like a feral animal ready to strike at any second. The hair may be better styled, the make-up more expertly applied and the jewellery finer but the hostile expression he'd know anywhere.

He studied her as she took her oath and realised that she hadn't looked at her husband once.

The defence barrister stood and smiled in the direction of the witness, who glowered in response.

'Mrs Nuryef, the court understands that you are in fact a hostile witness to the defence team of your husband who is currently on trial for murder.'

Still she didn't glance in his direction and managed to remain silent, clearly coached to stay shtum unless asked a direct question. Knowing her as he did Penn could only wonder at how long that would last.

'It is your testimony that your husband was not at home on the night of the twenty-sixth of October last year.'

'Yes'

'And that you have no idea where your husband was that evening?'

'Correct. I already—'

A shake of the head from the prosecution cut her off, but the real Irina Nuryef was just dying to break free.

'And to the best of your memory this information is accurate and true?'

Penn began to relax. This questioning was not doing them any harm at all. Every time she repeated her answer the jury heard her say it again.

'I've already said—'

'Just answer the question, Mrs Nuryef,' the barrister said curtly causing the anger to flash in her eyes.

'You say he left at approximately 9 p.m. and returned around 11 p.m.?'

'That's what I said, didn't I?'

'Eventually, yes,' said the barrister. 'But I'll come to that.'

Penn suddenly knew exactly where the barrister was going but had no idea how much this was going to hurt them. He had a feeling it would come down to the credibility of the witness and that was the cause of his concern. And that of his colleagues judging by the tension on their faces.

'And you recalled that he didn't come straight into the house. He went into the garden first?'

'Yeah, bastard was—'

Shit, the genie was out the bottle.

'You don't actually know what your husband was doing in the garden, do you?'

'He was hiding the fucking—'

'Did you see your husband hiding anything in the garden, Mrs Nuryef,' the barrister asked curtly.

Penn could see the prosecution breathe a sigh of relief every time the barrister cut her off or interrupted her. They were relieved she was being shut up, but what they didn't realise was that the barrister was doing it deliberately, taunting her, cutting her off, which was firing her up more. He was opening the gate long enough for her to poke her head out and then slamming it in her face. When he was ready, when she was straining at the leash and dying to have her say, he would open the gate completely. He could see it and he couldn't stop it.

'So, you told the police that he was out hiding something in the garden and then went straight upstairs to clean himself up? Is that correct?'

'Yes, the bastard went and washed the blood—'

'And you saw that? The blood, I mean?'

'Well… no… but…'

'So, he may have just run upstairs because he was desperate for the toilet?'

'No way. He was—'

'But he could have done.'

'No, it was—'

'And you're sure this was 11 p.m.?'

'I looked at the—'

'It couldn't have been 10.45?'

'I fucking told—'

'Or 10.40?'

'I know what—'

'How do you know it wasn't 10.35?'

'I can tell the fucking—'

'And you remember all this clearly?'

'Objection, your honour,' called the prosecution. About forty seconds too late in Penn's opinion.

He understood the team was giving her a moment to collect herself, rein in her temper. Think before saying something she'd later regret.

'Sustained,' said the judge offering the defence barrister a warning look, which he acknowledged.

'So, you are sure of your memory of all those events on the night concerned?'

'Yes,' she growled.

'And there is no doubt in your mind?'

'No,' she spat.

'Then please explain to the court why your original statement, the one closest to the actual event, states that your husband was home with you all night?'

'I was confused,' she said, colouring.

Most jury members were frowning yet riveted.

'Confused about the date, time, your husband's whereabouts, which is it, Mrs Nuryef?'

'Yes, no, I mean…'

'Four days after the murder of Devlin Kapoor you stated that your husband was with you at the time, yes?'

'I had the wrong date. I couldn't recall…'

'Aah, you couldn't remember exactly but you gave your husband an alibi for the murder?'

'I assumed he was at home.'

The colour in the woman's face had spread down her neck towards her breastbone.

'Aah, you assumed. So, your memory is not to be trusted?'

'No, I remember it clearly now. He was—'

'You remember events more clearly now, months after the event, than four days later?'

'Yes, I do,' she snapped as the hostile defensiveness wiped out the nervous red stain on her skin.

'So, you would have no ulterior motive in changing your story?'

'Why would?…'

'Nothing happened in the time between you changing your statement?'

She shook her head as though not trusting herself to speak.

'Please answer the question.'

'Nothing happened.'

'No arguments?'

'Nothing.'

'No physical fights?'

'I already said.'

'I'm sorry, Mrs Nuryef, but I put it to you that your memory has failed you once again, or that for some reason known only to yourself you are perjuring yourself on the stand.'

'I am telling the truth. He did it. I know he did.'

'I put it to you, Mrs Nuryef, that you are telling barefaced lies to the court for some reason.'

'He's the fucking liar not me,' she screamed, pointing at her husband and looking in his direction for the first time. 'He's the one who has been lying for fucking years.'

Her eyes were filled with hatred and her tongue dripped venom as her gaze locked on her husband.

'I fucking hate you; now rot in hell you lying, cheating bastard.'

Penn let out the breath he'd been holding throughout that exchange.

It was over and the courtroom was silent.

Penn didn't need to look at the prosecution, the defence or the jury to gauge how much that had hurt them.

It had kicked them in the nuts.

CHAPTER TWENTY-FOUR

Halesowen College began its life in 1966 as one large building. In the early Eighties four more blocks were added and in the years since a further eight blocks had been added to incorporate Sports Studies, Media, Music and Performing Arts, ICT, Science and Animal Care. In addition, the college had a Science and Technology centre at Coombswood and a Hair and Beauty facility right by the Shenstone traffic island.

'You feeling like we've done something wrong?' Bryant asked as yet another member of staff passed them and glanced their way.

Sitting outside the principal's office was not something she'd ever done well, and she was glad that the college had not yet commenced its autumn term giving them thousands of students as a further gawping audience.

They were five minutes early for the pre-arranged 10 a.m. meeting with Felicity Astor, the head of the college. The woman was taking it to the exact minute by the looks of it. And it wasn't as if they had a murderer to catch.

Kim stood up and began to pace in front of the glass window that looked into the admin office. Not every desk was filled as term hadn't started, but the five women inside shared little conversation as they stared at the screen and typed busily.

All except one.

'Wonder who she's talking to that can be more important than us,' Bryant observed. The receptionist had called through to let her know they'd arrived.

Kim took another pass of the window and tried not to stare.

A couple of heads raised and looked in her direction but her attention was on one single lady right at the back. She stood out from the others for a few reasons. First she was a good twenty years older than everyone else in the office. Secondly, her plum ruffled blouse and full face of make-up contrasted heavily with the jeans and tee shirts worn by the rest of the staff, and thirdly she was the only one wearing headphones.

Old school, Kim realised. The practice of audiotyping was dying due to voice recognition software, and the skill of shorthand was almost extinct.

But that wasn't the main reason the lady had caught Kim's attention. It was because despite staring at the screen and having her fingers poised above the keyboard, her foot hadn't touched the foot pedal controls once.

'Guv, what the?…'

'Shush, I'm in stalker mode.'

'In front of a clear glass window?'

Kim approached the clear glass window and knocked on it. The woman nearest almost jumped out of her skin and then offered Kim a terse expression.

Kim ignored her and pointed to the woman at the back of the room.

Eventually the older woman looked her way and Kim motioned for her to come forward. She removed her headphones and walked towards the glass. Kim pointed towards the door.

'Guv, what the hell are you doing?' Bryant asked as the woman negotiated the last couple of desks to get out of the door.

Kim held up her ID as she looked at her questioningly. She introduced herself and her colleague.

'Ida Lincoln,' she said, moving from one foot to the other.

'Ms Lincoln, we're investigating the murder of Belinda Evans. Did you know her well?' Kim asked.

She had been the only person in the office who seemed unable to concentrate on her work.

Tears gathered in her eyes. 'We were all called in last night and told the news. It still hasn't sunk in yet. I know she didn't work here any more but knowing that she's gone, I mean, really gone, is just…'

Her words trailed away as she reached into her sleeve and retrieved a handkerchief. Kim gave her a few seconds.

'Were the two of you close?'

'I wouldn't say close but we had a lot in common,' she said, glancing behind her. 'Both started to feel like old farts amongst all this youth.'

Kim hadn't expected that word to come out of this lady's mouth.

'There were times in the staff room when the conversations just went over our heads. I'm not into all the new technology and she wasn't either. We didn't get all that social media stuff they chat about in there. If I wanted to see cute kittens I'd buy one. We talked about books a lot. I don't know if you're aware but she was a very intelligent woman. You wouldn't have wanted to get into an argument with her.'

'Why's that?' Kim asked, wondering if the woman had been known to show aggression or temper.

'Because she always had a fact to prove a point at her fingertips. Very clever.'

'Did the two of you mix out of work?' Kim asked, noting the absence of wedding rings on Ida's fingers. These two women could have been good company for each other.

'We met up for an evening drink, non-alcoholic of course as Belinda didn't drink. We started chatting about a recent documentary on African burial rites but it was cut short.'

'Why's that?' Kim asked.

'Her sister must have called a dozen times during the short time we were there. Belinda was clearly annoyed at the intrusion but wouldn't switch the phone off. Eventually I left realising I'd get a more focussed conversation from my cat. I don't actually have a cat but you know what I mean. Strangest thing, though,' she said, looking up and to the left.

'Strange?' Kim asked. She liked strange. Strange lived in the same house as unusual and anything out of the ordinary could produce a lead.

'Could have swore I saw her sister on the car park outside but that wouldn't make any sense, would it?'

'Did you mention that to Belinda?' Kim asked.

'No, not at all. By the morning I was sure I'd been mistaken.' Right now Kim wasn't so sure.

'And that was the extent of the friendship?' Kim asked.

Ida shook her head. 'A week or so later Belinda asked if I'd like to grab a coffee after work, but conveniently her sister had some type of fall right before we were due to finish. I mean I can't be sure but—'

'Officers, I'm ready to see you now,' said a voice from behind.

Kim hadn't heard the door to the principal's office open.

'Yes, we'll be with you in a minute,' Kim said, without turning. 'Please continue, Ida. What were you going to say?'

'Oh nothing much, really. I was just going to say that I got the impression that her sister didn't much like her spending time with anyone.'

CHAPTER TWENTY-FIVE

Kim knocked and entered the door that had just closed behind her.

A plump woman with a severely cut shock of blonde hair offered her hand. Bryant stepped forward and shook it while introducing the two of them.

Kim watched the woman make her way back to the other side of the desk and got the impression the three-inch heels were not adding as much height as she would like them to.

'We're sorry for the loss of one of your colleagues,' Bryant said, taking one of the seats with blue cushions on the door side of the desk.

A laptop sat open on the generic desk, and Kim noted that while spacious and pleasant the office was by no means opulent. The furniture was mismatched and appeared to have hailed from whatever department had been budgeted a refit.

'We are very shocked as you can imagine. Belinda only left us a few months ago, although we begged her to stay.'

'You did?' Bryant asked.

Kim was happy to allow him to lead while she fought down the irritation at being kept waiting. Ida had more than adequately filled the time, revealing little about Belinda except that she tried to keep her life completely compartmentalised. Ida clearly knew nothing of her friend's sexual appetites and probably wouldn't have believed them had they been honest with her. More interesting was what they'd learned about the sister that wasn't dead. If they disliked each other so much, why the involvement in each other's lives?

'Of course we asked her to stay,' Felicity Astor said, turning her full attention towards Bryant. 'She was one of our most popular professors. Standing room only in her classes.'

'Any particular reason?' Bryant asked.

'Child Psychology is always a popular class. The qualification is an asset in so many professions: counselling, teaching, social work and your own police force but Belinda's class was particularly popular.'

Bryant said nothing but nodded for her to continue.

'She didn't teach the subject, she lived it. I make a point of sitting in once a year on all my professors, and her lessons were just electric. Her knowledge of the child's psyche was encyclopaedic especially in the area of mistreatment.'

'Go on,' Kim said, sitting forward.

Felicity turned her way. 'Belinda was particularly expert on the long-term repercussions of early mental cruelty.'

Felicity looked heavenward and offered a sad smile.

'In one of her lessons I was captivated by one of her studies. She talked of a little boy she met when he was nine years old. The poor thing had been locked in a small boxroom for most of his life. He was fed once a day and left in the dark. There was no interaction and no love. He wasn't chained and the door was not locked. He had been trained, conditioned to never leave. The boy had been born to two addicts.'

'Drugs?' Bryant asked.

'Alcohol?' Kim asked.

Felicity shook her head at both of them.

'Computer games. They spent every hour glued to the Xbox playing each other and other folks online. The woman hadn't even known she was pregnant until the little boy popped out. They didn't know what to do, so they put him in the spare room and watched YouTube videos on feeding.'

'Is this for real?' Bryant asked, although Kim remembered reading about something similar in the newspaper.

'Oh, it's real. Life went on as normal for the couple. Fed the child once a day, kept him in nappies and only got found out when the council insisted on inspecting the property's boiler following a recent fatality in a similar home.'

'What happened?' Bryant asked.

'Neighbours were horrified, parents were imprisoned, authorities began pointing fingers and the little boy was put into care.'

'And?'

'And now you can see why Belinda's classes were electric, officers. She made the students care. She told stories of real children, real situations, people she'd met and interacted with.'

'And the boy?' Bryant insisted.

'Is unlikely to see the outside of an institution for the rest of his life. Belinda explained that the conditioning of those nine years had destroyed his ability to love, trust and communicate. He couldn't bear to be touched. Even someone brushing against him would prompt hysterical reactions. He hadn't learned anything and consequently was locked into a world that no one else could understand.'

'How awful,' Bryant whispered.

And Kim agreed but was no stranger to the harm that parents could do. Then something else occurred to her.

'But Belinda was a teacher, a professor not a medical health practitioner, so how did she know of these children?'

'She studied them, Inspector. Any chance to interact with a troubled or damaged child was a gift to her. She never wanted to stop learning of the lasting effects of early childhood experiences.'

There was something here that was feeling unpalatable right now: the idea that the woman had met with damaged and broken children to study and analyse them and their suffering, but without the clinical training or knowledge to help them.

'We suspect Belinda was planning to take a trip. Would you have any idea where?' Bryant asked.

Felicity shrugged. 'To my knowledge she rarely took holidays or mini breaks, so if she was going somewhere it was probably to further her knowledge.'

'Okay, thanks,' Kim said, standing. 'And would you mind pointing us in the direction of Charles Blunt?'

'Of course, but why?'

'We believe he was Belinda's last known lover.'

'Are you sure?' she asked, making no attempt to hide her shock.

'We believe so,' Kim repeated, realising that Belinda had managed to keep her relationship secret from everyone. Her friend hadn't known and her boss hadn't known, yet the sister she didn't like *had* known. Their relationship was growing stranger by the minute.

'I think you're mistaken but I'll take you to Mr Blunt myself.'

Kim fell into step behind the woman, already wondering what they were going to find.

CHAPTER TWENTY-SIX

'What the fuck was that about?' Lynne hissed as they exited the courtroom.

The judge had asked for the jury to be excused and was speaking to both barristers privately.

Penn had no clue what was going to happen next.

'Come on, Lynne, we were expecting the defence to rough her up a bit,' Doug said, taking out his phone. 'The woman did a complete about turn in her statement, and although we felt she was telling the truth the second time, you can understand why the jury might—'

'Not that you gonk,' Lynne said, exasperated. 'Of course, I expected that, but what was this cheating bollocks she was screaming about and does it have anything to do with her change in testimony?'

'Doesn't matter,' Doug said, smiling. 'The jury won't forget the bloodstained tee shirt in a hurry. Her statement got us the warrant, and that's when we found the tee shirt in the shed. Dev Kapoor's blood on his clothes is kind of indisputable, don't you think?'

The man had a point. Forensic examination had linked the accused to the crime, but Penn had seen juries rule out forensic evidence if they felt that witness testimony was weak or fabricated. It destroyed their trust in the police, the case and the process. And it took both a strong stomach and a watertight case to convict for murder. Jurors hung on to the 'beyond a reasonable doubt' so they were not party to the irrevocable change of a person's life.

Which went double for anyone who had watched the Netflix show *Making a Murderer*.

Unfortunately, the response boxes on the jury service notification didn't include an option marked 'I don't feel I could ever convict'.

'It'll be okay, though,' Lynne said, wringing her hands. 'We'll get the conviction and we can all get back to work.'

Doug shrugged. 'Don't mind being paid to sit in court all day. Easy money.'

'Jesus, Doug,' Lynne blustered but there was a smile in her voice. Doug would always be Doug.

'Sir, do you have a?…'

'Mr Kapoor, of course,' Penn said, stepping away.

'Are things going wrong?' he asked, quietly.

Penn shook his head. 'No, everything is fine. The judge has decided that both barristers need telling off. Prosecution should have prepared the witness better and the defence was guilty of needling her but they'll be finished in a minute and the trial will resume,' he said, as he saw Lynne put her mobile phone to her ear.

'I'll come find you afterwards and we can have a better chat, okay?'

Mr Kapoor nodded as Penn moved back to his old colleagues.

'Everything okay?'

Lynne looked troubled and shrugged in response.

'No idea but the boss, Travis to you, wants us back at the station. Now. And he said that includes you.'

CHAPTER TWENTY-SEVEN

Stacey sat back from Belinda's phone records, which now resembled a rainbow. Using different coloured highlighting pens she'd ruled out most of the phone numbers on the sheets, which were overwhelmingly yellow for her sister's mobile phone. Stacey shook her head. She'd never spoken to one person so many times in a day. Ever. Never mind every day.

Blue was for ruled out harmless calls. Mainly incoming from PPI scavengers and other marketing calls.

Pink represented service calls she'd made and received: hair, nails and a recent podiatrist appointment, taxis and a twelve-minute call to her internet provider.

Only three numbers remained. Two outgoing and one incoming.

She tried the first which was to a mobile number that went straight to voicemail. Bog standard message with no indication of who should be at the other end. She put a little pencil mark by it and moved on to the next. It was a landline that just rang out until it eventually cut off. No message option. Stacey put a small pencil mark by that to indicate she hadn't yet ruled it out.

Then she dialled the last number, a landline that had called Belinda early on the day she was killed.

Stacey waited patiently for the call to be answered and was surprised by the greeting when it was.

CHAPTER TWENTY-EIGHT

Kim instantly understood Felicity's doubt about the relationship between Charles Blunt and Belinda Evans the second the woman pointed him out.

After berating Bryant for being judgemental she'd fallen into the exact same trap herself and the man was not what she'd been expecting.

Felicity strode across the empty sports hall towards an athletic-looking man in his early to mid-forties. His short black hair was showing strands of silver at the temples. His face was pleasant and open and he exuded health and fitness in khaki tracksuit bottoms and a plain white tee shirt that showed off the dark hairs that ran down his arm to a sports watch fixed at the wrist.

'This is Charles Blunt who runs our Sports and Exercise Science HND class, and many other things too,' she said, touching his arm.

He smiled in their direction as Felicity continued.

'These police officers would like to speak to you about Belinda.'

He nodded and then looked at the college head, who appeared to be waiting for the conversation to start.

Clearly Felicity Astor liked to know everything that went on in the college.

'Thank you, Ms Astor, we can take it from here,' Kim said, pleasantly, and waited for the woman to walk away.

She caught the amused expression on the man's face as he watched her leave.

'Nice lady,' she observed.

'How may I help?' he asked, offering no response to her statement.

Kim regarded him for a few seconds.

'I'm trying to think of subtle ways around this but sod it. Were you sleeping with Belinda Evans?'

He smiled at her candour. 'Not recently but in the past, yes,' he answered, making no effort to hide the fact.

'I'm really sorry to ask but…'

'You want to know why?' he asked, ending her discomfort.

She nodded. 'I really don't mean to be rude but age differences happen more commonly the other way around, and I don't mean to imply that there was anything wrong—'

'Please stop, Inspector,' he said, holding up his hands. 'I do understand your point and I'm not offended by the question.'

'Was it a secret?' Kim asked. Had he been ashamed of the relationship?

'Only from her,' he said, nodding towards the door through which Felicity had left. 'She likes to get in everyone's business. Makes and changes rules to suit herself.' He tipped his head. 'Officer, I'm not ashamed of our time together, and I'm truly sorry that she's dead,' he said, regretfully.

He moved towards three piles of mats in the corner of the room and took a seat.

'How did it start?' Bryant asked as they both took seats on the mats opposite. 'If you don't mind us asking?'

'I'm not sure you mind asking?' he said, aiming the ghost of a smile her way. 'Christmas party last year. Both hunting the buffet for wheat-free options. Got talking and couldn't stop. Met for coffee during the college break and the same happened again.'

'And what attracted you?'

'Her intelligence, Inspector. Not every relationship begins with a physical attraction and it never has for me. I've always enjoyed the company of older women but you have to understand that Belinda was not like other women. She was the most intelligent woman I've ever met. Her brilliance was both alluring and attractive. She was confident and assured and yet childlike sometimes.

'She was an exceptional pianist and would play for hours but not difficult pieces, easy, jolly songs and then clap her hands in delight afterwards.'

'Sounds a little strange,' Bryant observed gently, echoing her own thoughts.

He shook his head. 'Not for me. I enjoyed every minute we spent together.'

'Who ended it?' Kim asked, hearing both fondness and regret in his voice.

'I did, but not for any reason you might think.'

'Go on,' Kim said.

'It wasn't about the sex, the relationship, I mean. Not for me. It was a part of it but I just enjoyed being with her. The sex became more important for her,' he said, colouring.

Kim appreciated his total honesty so far but could see this conversation was growing increasingly uncomfortable for him. And she hadn't even started on the hard questions yet.

'I'm sorry we have to ask but…'

'No, I understand. Belinda became more demanding sexually. She wanted to try new things, toys, dangerous places, games, rough games, which isn't something I find appealing. She was insistent, so I had no choice but to end it.'

Kim realised that Belinda had struck lucky with this guy. On the face of it he was a decent, caring man who had been attracted to her for the right reasons.

And yet it hadn't been enough.

'It seemed to be some kind of escape for her, a compulsion beyond making love and I didn't feel the same way.'

'But you loved her?'

'Oh yes, officer. I loved her.'

'Which makes my next question almost impossible to ask,' she said, recalling the photos shown to them by Keats.

'Given what I've already revealed to you about our private life, that surprises me, but please ask anything you need to.'

'Did Belinda pass on an STI to you or you to her?'

The sudden shock on his face gave her the answer.

'Definitely not,' he answered. 'Are you saying?...'

Kim nodded. 'I'm afraid so and it appears she was determined to play those games with someone.'

He shook his head and looked to the ground.

Kim felt as though they'd trampled over their relationship enough but she still had other questions.

'Did you meet her sister?' Kim asked.

'Only a few times but that was enough.'

'Why's that?' Bryant asked, shifting on the mat.

'She was strange, they were strange together. Belinda changed into a different person around her sister.'

'Can you explain?' Kim asked, remembering the things Ida had told them.

'It was as though they couldn't stand each other. They bickered about all sorts of things, disagreed on everything but had to be in contact with each other all the time.

'I remember one time they started arguing over the recipe for their mother's cheesecake. It ended with Belinda physically throwing her sister out of the house. Two minutes later she was pacing the room and fretting over whether she was okay. Belinda called her and they continued the argument until Veronica was back at her own home, and once Belinda knew she was okay, she ended the call. The dynamic between them was off, but they thought it was perfectly normal.'

'Did Veronica ever try to get in the way of your relationship?' Kim asked.

He thought for a minute. 'Not intentionally, I don't think. I could always kind of feel her presence due to the level of contact they had but she never openly tried to come between us.'

Was it that somehow Veronica had been more threatened by a platonic relationship with a female like Ida than she was by a sexual liaison with Charles?

'Did Belinda ever talk about her childhood?' Bryant asked.

Charles shook his head. 'Never.'

Whatever had formed them had started there.

'And lastly, can you tell me where you were on Monday night? We have to ask.'

'Of course. I was at The Cock Robin pub in Romsley in a pub quiz with my old football team. Left at 10.45 and I'm happy to give you all of their names.'

Bryant took out his notebook as Charles scrolled through his phone offering names and numbers.

Kim stood and offered her hand.

'Thank you,' she said, as he shook it. His palm was cool and dry. 'We'll be in touch if…'

Her words trailed away as her phone rang.

She stepped away and listened to the findings of her detective constable.

She ended the call and walked back.

'My apologies, Mr Blunt, but it looks as though we're not quite done with you yet.'

CHAPTER TWENTY-NINE

'Why here?' Penn asked, as they turned the corner into Curzon Street. Before they'd even reached the car the instruction had changed via a text message to Doug's phone.

'Not a clue. The boss just... Jesus Christ, what's this all about?'

A cordon had been placed across the road between two lamp-posts. Beyond it were three squad cars, an ambulance and Detective Inspector Travis on the phone. The street was residential formed of mid-priced semi-detached and detached properties three miles north of Kidderminster.

Without words Lynne parked the car and they all jumped out.

Doug pushed forcefully through the crowds as Lynne followed with shouts of 'excuse me', while Penn nodded apologies to people being barged out of the way.

He understood it was a West Mercia crime scene. What he didn't understand was the reason he'd been summoned to attend. And what the hell could trump a trial for murder?

'Guv?' they all said together and it really did feel like old times.

Travis ended the call and looked none too happy.

'Trial has been suspended for now,' he said, holding up the phone, confirming that's what he'd just been told.

'Guv?' Lynne repeated.

He looked across the confusion shared by all three of them.

'Follow me,' he said, heading along a pathway that separated two detached houses.

At the end of the path was a steep bank with a path trodden between the overgrown weeds.

They scrambled up the bank in single file and stood together when they reached the top.

Penn spotted an arm first, severed just beneath the elbow, approximately twenty feet along the railway track. The stump of the limb was flesh-coloured mulch, deep red with dried blood. Loose flesh looked as though it was trying to crawl away. Sinews hung from the pulped muscle.

Beyond the limb was a crumpled, bloody mess surrounded by white suits. Another clutch of white suits was bunched further up the line, telling him this poor soul had been deposited in bits over a seventy to eighty feet stretch.

'Bloody hell,' Doug said.

'Indeed, Doug. Seven different bits of him strewn across the track.'

As horrific as the scene was Penn still didn't understand why he was there. If the trial of Gregor Nuryef had been suspended, it was time for him to get back to his own team.

'Look closer,' Travis said.

Penn looked back at the solitary arm. The shirt, the suit.

A wave of sickness rose within him.

'Oh shit, is that?...'

'Yes, Penn. We're looking at bits of Mr Dexter McCann, witness for the defence in our murder trial.'

He turned back to them, rage mottling his features.

'So, tell me, guys, how the hell did you fuck this one up?'

CHAPTER THIRTY

Charles Blunt showed them back into the general office. Ida looked up and Kim smiled in her direction.

'Lou can tell you much more than I can,' he said, folding his arms.

Kim noted that all the female employees had looked up at the sound of his voice. She also quickly realised that not one of them except Ida had a chance. Amongst the rest there wasn't one of them above the age of thirty-five.

'May I ask what's going on here?' Felicity Astor asked from the entrance of a doorway on the other side of the office.

'And if there's nothing else I can help you with, I'll get back to work,' Charles said, backing away.

Kim thanked him as Bryant stepped towards the head of the college who, although wearing a polite smile, didn't seem thrilled they were still there.

'A phone call was made from this location to Belinda's phone on the day she died and we need to know who made that call,' Kim explained.

Felicity stared towards the other door. 'Given what you've told me I'd say that was perfectly obvious.'

'I don't think so,' Kim said. Charles had already confirmed that he'd had no contact with Belinda for over a month and following his honesty on everything else she had no cause to doubt him. His alibi would be checked along with everyone else's whereabouts. 'But feel free to give us the data that proves us wrong.'

Only the main number of the college had registered on Belinda's phone records, but Kim was guessing there were hundreds of extensions that all had access to an outside line.

'All calls in and out are routed via the computerised switchboard,' Felicity said, tapping the screen on an empty desk. 'Any call from these premises will register the main number but there are almost three hundred extensions.'

'Please tell me you record all calls,' Kim said, hopefully.

She shook her head. 'Just a little too invasive, officer. We have call monitoring on the sales extensions and the help lines.'

'So, is there any way of finding out who made that call?'

'I didn't say we don't monitor at all, Inspector. We do like to know that our staff aren't spending all day on the phone.'

'So?...'

'So, there is a database that logs all information of every phone call out of the premises, time made, duration et cetera.'

'And the database is searchable?' Kim asked, hopefully.

'I think you'll find that Louise is waiting right now for the number called.'

'It's Belinda's—'

'We don't keep staff details in there, data protection.'

Bryant took out his notebook and read the number off to her.

She typed it in and waited for a few seconds while the screen loaded.

'Here we are,' Louise said. 'The number was called from the college on Monday morning at 9.55.'

'That's the one,' Kim said.

'Call lasted two minutes thirty-three seconds and was made from extension number 27, which is... Oh.'

Louise picked up her phone and pressed the two and seven. She waited a few seconds and then shook her head.

'It's an active line but...'

'But what, Louise?' Felicity asked, frowning.

This was a woman who did not like surprises.

'It doesn't exist. There's no extension 27 on the list.'

'Don't be silly,' Felicity said, coming around to the other side of the desk. 'There has to be.'

Louise shrugged. 'It's not on the list,' she said, tightly.

Felicity looked over her shoulder. 'So extension 26 is the Biology office and extension 28 is the Physics lab.'

'But they were all swapped over and kept when—'

'Excuse me,' Kim said to remind them she was there.

'Follow me. The Science block is one of the oldest parts of the complex,' Felicity explained, as she headed towards the door through which she'd come. Both she and Bryant followed.

'Hence the lower extension numbers. Right now, we're in the process of moving the entire lab to the new block but it's only part complete.'

Kim followed the woman whose heels were in no way detrimental to her speed. They travelled corridor after corridor, down stairs, upstairs and crossed from one block to another.

'We're keeping the extension numbers the same to avoid any confusion, but extension 27 appears to have slipped through the net.'

Felicity pushed open a heavy set of double doors as Kim's phone signalled the receipt of a text message. She hung back and read it quickly.

She frowned at the text and the sender.

A cryptic text from DI Tom Travis was unlikely to add anything positive to her day. What the hell could he possibly want?

She put the phone away and joined the two of them in the corridor.

Felicity was pointing. 'That's the old Biology office and right next door is the Physics lab. There's no phone in between.'

Kim looked to the door on the opposite side of the corridor. 'What's in?...'

'That's just a cleaner's cupboard,' Felicity said, as Kim opened the door.

She was right, Kim realised, noting the industrial mopping machine, buckets, brushes, shelving, as well as the phone on the wall.

'Oh my... I had no...'

Kim turned to Bryant. 'Unlikely we'll get anything but give Mitch a call to see if there are prints.'

Bryant nodded and turned away.

'We need this door locked, Ms Astor. No one is to enter this room until scene of crime officers have been in.'

Kim had no idea how many times the phone had been used since, or even if the call had any link to Belinda's murder, but it was the best lead they had so far.

'Who has access to this area of the building?' Kim asked. The list of people couldn't be endless which would give them somewhere to start.

'Students, teachers, maintenance, cleaners. Pretty much everyone.'

'I'll need a list.'

'We're talking thousands,' Felicity said.

'Absolutely, but if it's everyone who has access our killer will be on there somewhere. It's not like we're searching the whole world.'

Felicity began to pale before her eyes.

'Did you say the call was made on Monday morning?'

Kim nodded with the sudden feeling this was going to be a bad thing.

'Sorry, Inspector, but you may be searching the world after all.'

'I'm not sure what?...'

'Monday was our open day. We had literally thousands of people come through the doors.'

Kim closed her eyes in frustration.

Because it could have been any one of them.

CHAPTER THIRTY-ONE

'And he didn't say what he wanted?' Bryant asked, taking their drinks from the tray.

Kim shook her head. His text had said:

> *'NEED TO MEET*
> *NAME THE PLACE.'*

She had texted back 'Barnett Hill', a Wyevale garden centre, shopping village and café that wasn't far from the border of the two constabularies. But in truth was much more their neck of the woods than his.

Clearly, he wanted something from her and he could do the mileage to get it.

'Said he'd buy us lunch,' she said, smiling.

'You don't normally eat lunch.'

'It's an event if Travis is putting his hand in his pocket.'

Bryant laughed and then sobered. 'Hard to remember that a couple of years ago the two of you couldn't be in the same county without squaring up and now he's offering to buy you lunch.'

Oh yeah, the two of them had history. The five years they'd worked together had counted for nothing when she'd privately challenged him one day about his rough treatment of a suspect. Right before he'd punched her in the mouth. She had chosen not to report him and had only found out the real reason for his transfer to West Mercia when they'd been forced to work a hate crimes case together eighteen months earlier.

'Bit of a bust at the college, though,' Bryant said. 'Really thought we had something, but with that many folks coming in and out we're stuffed.'

Kim nodded her agreement.

'Mitch is gonna be lucky to get anything helpful from the phone, but Felicity is going to send over some CCTV covering the event. You never know. We might get lucky.'

'Except we have no idea who or what we're looking for, so our killer could walk right up to the camera, give us the thumbs up and we still wouldn't know it was them. We already know the CCTV around the Science block has been disconnected.'

'Yeah, but how does our killer know all that, eh?'

'Good question,' Bryant said, as a squad car pulled up outside the front entrance.

'He's here and it looks like he's in a hurry,' Kim observed as he entered the double doors. Kim raised her hand, surprised to see him in a high-vis jacket.

His tight expression as he weaved through the tables towards them told her he didn't want to borrow a cup of sugar or tap her up for a bit of intel.

His jacket rustled as he took a seat beside Bryant.

'What you drinking?' her colleague asked.

'Nothing for me, thanks… gotta be quick and get…'

'Hey, you promised lunch,' Kim said, trying to lighten the tension in his face.

'I'll leave you the money but I've got a meeting with the Commissioner at two o'clock.'

'Bloody hell, Tom, what's going on?'

In all the years she'd known him, through the years she'd liked him and the years she'd hated him, she'd never seen him looking like this.

Tom Travis did a lot of things well, ran a team, solved crimes, toed the line, kissed arse but he didn't do stress. Now she was intrigued.

'This case in court this week; the armed robbery.'

'What about it?' she asked coolly. This was no longer about Tom Travis. It involved Penn. One of hers.

'It's a shit storm. Whatever Penn's told you…'

'Not a lot,' she said, honestly.

He hesitated, took a breath. 'The case is falling apart to be honest. Our only witness fucked up on the stand. The wife of the accused helped nothing when she testified. Even gave the impression she only changed her statement to get him back for cheating on her.'

'Did she change her statement?'

Travis nodded. 'Retracted her alibi.'

Kim balked.

'She said he was home and then said he wasn't?'

Bryant offered a low whistle. 'Jesus. And she hinted on the witness stand that she did so out of jealousy?'

'Not in so many words but the inference was there.'

'And did she? Change her statement out of jealousy?'

'I bloody hope not or we're in even more shit than I thought.'

'There's more?'

'Oh yeah, much more. Witness for the defence, neighbour of the accused who swears he saw and heard our guy at home the night of the murder disappeared yesterday lunchtime.'

'Yeah, Penn did mention that,' she remembered.

'And turned up dead on the railway tracks this morning.'

'Suicide?'

Travis shook his head. 'Not unless he managed to tie both wrists down with garden wire.'

'Shit, Travis,' Kim said, sitting back. 'I'm assuming you need help getting out of the country.'

He smiled briefly. 'Not quite.'

'A new identity?' Bryant asked.

'Thanks, guys, I appreciate your vote of confidence.'

Kim waited, already knowing she wasn't going to like it.

'The trial has been halted and we need to go back to the beginning. We need to re-cross every T and dot every I. We've got to be sure we've got our man.'

'And are you?' Kim asked.

'Not as sure as I was yesterday,' he said, honestly.

'Jeez, Tom.'

They'd had their differences and issues in the past but regardless of any disparity in work practices, Travis was as straight as they came and wouldn't want an innocent man to go to prison.

'I need to keep Penn. At least for a couple of days until we get this thing straightened out.'

'Bloody hell, Tom, I've got a body of my own right now.'

'I know, I heard about it and I'm sorry but you can draft in help. Penn was SIO on this. No one can pick it apart like him. I swear I wouldn't ask if I wasn't desperate, but you know what could happen.'

Oh yeah, she knew what could happen and it was what the Commissioner was going to warn him of at two o'clock. If this case was going to fold, it wouldn't matter which officer had fucked up; ultimately Travis was in charge of the team and would pay the highest price.

And they both knew his personal circumstances couldn't wear that.

When they'd worked the hate crimes case she'd found out that the reason he'd acted so drastically out of character that time was because his wife had been diagnosed with early-onset dementia. The woman had been in her mid-forties and it had destroyed him. With just a few years between him and retirement he could not afford to leave the force any other way than financially secure.

'A few days, Tom, and that's it. If you're not sorted by the weekend, you'll have to learn to see in the dark, okay?'

Their eyes met and she saw the gratitude there.

'Thank you,' he said, reaching into his pocket.

'Keep it,' she insisted of the money to pay for lunch. 'Suddenly I don't have much of an appetite,' she said as her phone began to ring.

CHAPTER THIRTY-TWO

Kim entered the Timbertree housing estate and pulled up onto the kerb in front of a row of small bungalows.

Keats had disturbed them at the garden centre to tell them where but not why.

The lay-by in front of the few shops servicing the housing estate was already full of squad cars.

Vehicles were being turned and diverted and a cordon had been erected across to the other side of the road.

Most windows above the shops were wide open as the occupants shouted down to people milling outside the cordon. Everyone wanted to know what was going on. As did Kim herself.

'Oi, hope that roadblock gets shifted soon. I need to get to work,' shouted a woman from one of the windows.

If that was any time in the next few hours it was highly unlikely, Kim thought.

Keats had only told her to get to the Timbertree pub urgently. What she hadn't realised was that the Timbertree pub had gone and boarding had been erected around the site.

'Another good watering hole gone,' Bryant observed. 'Used to drink there in my twenties.'

'Been there recently?' she asked.

He shook his head.

'Well, stop moaning, then,' she snapped.

It reminded her of the outcry from the public when car makers Rover were shedding thousands of jobs, all from folks driving foreign cars. Successful companies rarely went out of business.

She approached the gap in the seven feet high white boards designed to keep vandals out. She paused for a minute and looked around.

'Get uniforms to check for CCTV, anyone looking out of the window and anyone who could have been waiting at this bus stop right here.'

'Bloody wish Penn was on our team right now,' Bryant said, heading towards a police sergeant at the edge of the hoarding.

Yes, it was exactly what he would have been tasked to do.

'Long time no see,' she called to Keats who was amongst a clutch of white techie suits.

'And I wasn't missing you a bit, Inspector,' he replied without turning. 'And thank you for your prompt attendance. I assume you were driving.' He looked around her. 'Did you kill him en route?'

'He'll live,' she said.

Keats stepped aside. 'Preliminary examination completed but we chose not to move him until you got here.'

Kim stepped around a rolled-up newspaper that had already been marked with an evidence number.

She approached the male victim lying face down on the ground, his head turned so that his right cheek lay against the gravel. A pool of blood had collected beneath him, and Kim could see the tear in the man's light sports jacket. Their victim had been stabbed from behind.

'One wound?' Kim asked, walking around the body.

Keats shook his head. 'I'm thinking two. The first one in the back to get him down and another one to the front.'

Clearly the man was local, within walking distance. A routine trip to the newsagents to collect his newspaper had ended in death. There was a sadness in the ordinariness of the circumstances. The man was fetching a bloody paper. What the hell had he done to deserve this?

She stood at the foot of his body assessing the position.

His left leg was straight but his right was bent so that his foot touched the opposite knee. His arms were to the side and not outstretched as though trying to break his fall. There was no standing position that could have led to a fall that looked like this.

'Staged?' she asked.

Keats nodded and came to stand beside her. 'Look at the edge of the blood pool. It's dry and smeared as though he was being moved around while bleeding out from the front.'

Kim took another walk around the body as the photographer took the last few shots.

She paused at his head and looked down, frowning.

'Keats, is that chalk?' she asked, looking at the faint white markings all around him.

Initially she'd thought they were faded white lines left on the tarmac from the parking area at the front of the pub.

'Not sure. We'll know more when we move him.'

She nodded; she'd seen enough.

The techies all moved forward and rolled him onto his back.

His white open-necked shirt was stained with blood proving Keats right about the second stab wound.

Kim could now see that the man was slim build, roughly her own height wearing brown trousers and blue slip-on Skechers.

His sports jacket sleeve was rolled up to reveal a standard men's sports watch and the bulge of a wallet in his front trouser pocket, ruling out a robbery gone wrong.

'Did you check for?…'

'Yes, the X has been cut into the skin on the back of the neck, post mortem.'

'Was it obvious?' Kim asked.

Keats shook his head and held up his pen. 'No, had to move the clothing aside to find it.'

'Pity you didn't bring your ruler,' she remarked.

So, the branding of the X again was not obviously on show and in the same place as Belinda Evans.

'It's like it's a message to them and not us,' Bryant observed, appearing beside her.

'Agreed,' Kim said as they both continued to stare at the area around the body, at the ground that had been uncovered because he'd been moved.

Bryant broke the silence as they both took in what was now staring them in the face.

'Guv, are those chalk marks what I think they are?'

'Yes, Bryant, I bloody well think they are.'

The body was not lying on the white lines of the pub car park at all.

He was lying on top of a hopscotch grid.

CHAPTER THIRTY-THREE

Penn placed the last of the evidence boxes on the wooden table and closed the door.

Lynne had fetched fresh coffee, and Doug was looking miffed that his easy day in court had been cut short.

Travis had secured them a small room at the station with a round table, whiteboards but no window. The DI wanted them as far away as possible from the current investigation into the murder of the defence witness, Dexter McCann. He didn't want either case tainted, and wanted the new murder to be viewed objectively by officers not directly involved.

Penn had tried to explain that the two were inextricably linked.

Travis had shaken his head, resolutely. 'Whoever killed Dexter McCann last night has no bearing on whether we got the right man last year. We have to keep the cases separate,' he'd explained, expelling them to an office in Siberia.

On the plus side they were only a short walk away from the canteen.

'Okay, guys. We gotta go through this from the beginning, just like the boss instructed,' Penn said opening the first box that contained the statements. DI Travis had made it clear that he was to lead the review, after he'd informed him that his boss had agreed to the temporary secondment.

A part of him hoped she'd fought just a little bit.

'Right, first thing I want is a timeline,' he said, taking the bandana from his suit pocket. It was afternoon and the gel used to keep his hair flat was on the losing side of the battle.

'And our man is back,' Doug said, leafing through the statements. Lynne smiled and looked away.

Penn grabbed the black marker pen. 'Okay, incident was twenty-sixth of October,' he said, noting it on the board.

'Ricky Drake identified our man on the twenty-ninth of October,' Doug called out.

'Nuryef was questioned on the thirtieth. Same day his missus said he'd been at home all night.'

Penn continued to write the timeline as his colleagues called out the facts.

'Mrs Nuryef came in to recant her statement on the thirty-first,' Doug added.

'Got warrant on the first and found bloodstained tee shirt in shed,' Lynne called out.

'Got DNA back on the third November. And charged him on the fourth.'

Penn stood back and surveyed the board.

26/10 – Incident
29/10 – Ricky Drake identified
30/10 – Nuryef questioned
31/10 – Mrs Nuryef recanted
1/11 – Found tee shirt
2/11 – Got results of DNA
4/11 – Nuryef charged with murder

'Ten days,' Penn mused, tapping the marker pen against his lip. 'We got it all wrapped up in ten days.'

'A bloody long ten days,' Doug observed.

'Yeah, twelve hours every flipping day,' Lynne agreed.

'Textbook,' Doug said.

Penn agreed. That was exactly the way cases were supposed to happen. Get a lead from an eyewitness, chase it down, question folks and find forensic evidence to support suspicion. Exactly how investigations were supposed to go. Except they very rarely did.

'When it first happened we all agreed it looked like it was gang related, yeah?'

They both nodded.

'Type of place, quiet road, no CCTV, time of night. All pointed towards—'

'Except the murder,' Lynne interrupted. 'The Reed gang don't normally kill folks. They run in, frighten the cashier with a big knife, take the money and leave.'

Penn knew that was their normal MO.

'But things go wrong sometimes. Maybe Devlin Kapoor wasn't so keen to hand over the money. Maybe he wasn't so easily frightened. He was young, fit and healthy. Probably also pissed cos his dad's business is suffering and wasn't as compliant.'

Doug raised his hand.

'What?'

'Tee shirt in the shed.'

'Put that aside for a minute,' he said.

Doug and Lynne looked at each other.

'So, why'd we stop even looking at the gang?' he asked. His gut had definitely been steering him that way.

'Ricky Drake is what happened,' Lynne said. He gave us a name and—'

'Why?' Penn asked. It was a question he'd asked at the time, but one that had been forgotten following the discovery of the tee shirt.

'Volunteered it while being questioned on another case,' Lynne answered.

Penn turned to his colleague. 'You were questioning him about the burglary, yeah?'

Lynne nodded, a wariness creeping into her features.

'How did it come about?'

She shrugged. 'Can't remember, but he definitely asked if there'd be any leniency if he were to assist us on another matter.'

'See, he knows better than that. He knows we don't do deals.'

'Which is what I told him,' she offered tightly. 'And I convinced him that he should do his civic duty and just tell us what he knew.'

'Anyone ever know him to be that helpful in the past?'

'Never,' Doug offered before getting a warning glance from Lynne. 'But if it was information he had then he had nothing to lose by trying to use it as leverage,' Doug said, backing up his colleague.

'It's not like I took his first damn word for it, Penn,' Lynne said, as the colour infused her cheeks. 'He took me through it again and again. Told me how he was walking down the street, stopped to light a smoke, which gave him time to see the killer. What did you want me to do, make him write it in fucking blood?'

'I'm not insulting you,' Penn clarified, surprised to hear her curse.

'No, you're just saying I'm shit at my job?'

'Bloody hell, Lynne. Drop the sensitivity,' he said, and then felt bad for the shadow of hurt that passed over her face. 'I know you questioned him extensively about what he did and what he saw and his story never changed, but the boss told us to go over this and look for…'

'Areas that we fucked up?' Doug asked. 'But I really don't think we did.'

'Okay, let's leave Drake for now. Our other inconsistency today came from the charming Mrs Nuryef.'

Lynne visibly relaxed as they moved on to something she'd had little to do with.

'So, after the outburst today do we question her motivation for changing her story?' He turned to Doug. 'When we questioned her on the thirtieth did you have any reason to doubt her when she swore her husband was at home?' he asked, wondering if he'd missed something in her demeanour.

'Dunno,' Doug said smirking. 'I was the one tasked with needing the bog,' he said putting invisible quote marks in the air.

Penn smiled. 'Yeah, code for a bit of a snoop around.' A ploy used on every cop drama on the telly, so he was surprised they still got away with it, but Mrs Nuryef, although pissed off and antagonistic had appeared to be honest. She had offered no detail as to why she was sure he'd been home but she'd been absolutely sure he was.

'Seemed pretty honest when she recanted the statement the next day,' Doug observed.

'And it was that recanting that secured the warrant that led to the tee shirt,' Penn observed, looking at the timeline.

'So, again I ask why she did it?'

'Moral responsibility?' Lynne asked.

'But he's her husband,' Penn pushed. 'She's got three kids, so even if it was true, why would she be so quick to blame him?' He turned to Lynne. 'If it were Simon, would you be so quick to tell the police you'd made a mistake and instantly put the man you love into the frame for murder?'

'Depends if he'd put the bog seat down that morning,' she quipped.

They all laughed.

'But it's a good question,' she said, thoughtfully. 'And I honestly don't know what I'd do or how quickly. I'm pretty sure I wouldn't believe he was capable of such an act.'

'And you're a police officer.'

Doug raised his hand again.

Penn waved it down. He already knew what his colleague was going to say.

He considered the three things that had made this case watertight.

Their eye witness – now shaky.
No alibi – questionable but still in place.
Bloodstained tee shirt – irrefutable.

On the face of it they had the right man. It was the way they'd got there that bothered him.

'So, hang on a minute,' Lynne said as lines appeared on her forehead. 'Are we reviewing this case looking for Gregor Nuryef's innocence or guilt?'

'What we're looking to find', he answered, 'is the truth.'

CHAPTER THIRTY-FOUR

'So, you reckon the hopscotch grid was there before?' Bryant asked, as they sat outside number 118 Norwood Avenue. 'And he just happened to fall on it?'

'You ever seen anyone fall over into that position?' she asked. 'And maybe we could find out a bit more if we could get in there,' she moaned.

It hadn't been difficult to locate the home of their victim whose driving licence had been in his wallet.

Uniforms had been despatched to break the news to the wife and they were waiting for the signal that she'd calmed enough to speak. Too many strangers in her house immediately would be far too overwhelming.

But they'd now been waiting for over half an hour.

'Give her chance, guv. She's just found out her husband has been murdered.'

'Yeah, and I'd like to find the bastard that did it,' she snapped.

He turned away and stared out the window.

She did the same and assessed the house. The fact it had been purchased under the right-to-buy scheme was obvious. The window frames in the houses to the left and right had seen better days but the Nixon windows were bright, shiny, new UPVC with flashings and fascias to match.

New fence panels had been fitted with gravel boards and the front garden turned into a drive.

The house looked cared for and fresh against its peers.

'What the hell does the X mean?' Kim asked.

'Not a bloody clue, guv,' Bryant answered, keeping his eyes on the door.

'There's something else bothering me, too,' Kim said, putting the time to good use.

'Of course there is.'

'Why does he put the symbol where he does? He marks them after death so they don't feel it, but it's not gratuitous, either in size or display. It doesn't make sense,' she said.

'Hmm…' Bryant said, distractedly.

'Don't throw all your theories at me in one go, will you? Pace yourself, man.'

Bryant said nothing.

'Jeez, where'd the cat take your tongue cos—'

'We're up,' he said, as a uniformed officer gave them the nod from the doorway.

'Hang on,' Kim said. 'Before we go in, tell me why you've got a face like a slapped arse.'

'We're never gonna catch him,' he answered simply.

'What are you talking about?' She could call her colleague many things but defeatist wasn't one of them.

'Clearly the two murders are linked. They've come one day after the other, so our guy is on some kind of spree. He does one at night and one in the middle of the day. He wants these folks dead, like now. He's working at speed and we're having to stick to eight-hour shifts and not more than an hour ago you gave away a quarter of our team. To be honest, our guy couldn't have timed it any better if he'd tried.'

CHAPTER THIRTY-FIVE

Stacey put the phone records of Belinda Evans to one side. Every number now had a colour except for the call made from the college.

The boss had called and asked her to look up anything to do with symbolism, particularly the letter X.

In addition, she was trying to delve deeper into the relationship between the two sisters.

Stacey wasn't given to stress normally but her workload sure was growing by the minute. And normally that would not bother her one bit. Most frustrating for her was having to try and do it all inside an eight-hour shift. Over the years she'd managed to regulate her own working practices successfully. She'd learned to prioritise the tasks, learned when to give up on a lead and change direction and most importantly she'd learned when she'd had enough and needed a rest.

More stressful for her was being forced to go home and leave tasks unfinished.

She drummed her fingers on the desk.

She'd also learned how to use the resources available to her.

She clicked on the Skype icon and pressed on the first contact in her address book.

The call was answered after two rings and a familiar face filled her screen.

'Wassup, Stace?' Alison said, smiling widely.

'Back up,' Stacey said, reminding her that she didn't have to peer so closely into the camera. It could see her fine.

Alison Lowe, profiler and behaviourist sat back in her seat.

'Better,' Stacey said. 'You busy?'

Alison blew her a raspberry.

Stacey peered closer. 'Are those pencils in your hair?'

Alison's hands rose up and felt around her head. 'Oh yeah,' she said, taking them out.

'Writing going well, then?' Stacey asked.

After the last case they'd worked together, where Alison had found herself dangling from the roof of a thirteen-storey building, she'd decided to take some time away from active investigations and write a book based on her experiences as a behaviourist and profiler. Clearly, some writing days went better than others.

Alison blew her another raspberry.

'Mature, anyway I need your help,' she said.

No one had been more surprised than her at the friendship that had developed between the two of them since working together. It had begun with an occasional early morning jog together, the novelty of which had since worn off for Stacey and now consisted of a weekly meeting for coffee or a quick lunch.

'Shoot,' Alison said, biting into an apple.

'Talk to me about branding and symbolism and—'

'Hang on, which one? They're different. Branding or stigmatising is when a symbol or pattern is burned into the skin of a living person using a hot or very cold branding iron. A bit like what's done to livestock. Do you have a victim that's been actually branded?'

'No, but I've got two victims with an X cut into the back of the neck.'

'Aaah, now that sounds more like signature which is far more interesting,' Alison said, placing the apple on the desk.

'Go on,' Stacey urged.

'The signature comes from within the psyche of the offender. It reflects a fantasy, a need that the killer has about his victims.

Fantasies develop slowly and increase over time. A signature normally involves mutilation and sometimes dismemberment of the victim's body. A killer's signature is always the same because it emerges from the fantasy and would most likely have been present before his first killing.' She picked up the apple, took another bite and put it back down.

'Any staging or posing?'

'Ugghh, Alison, chew with your mouth closed for God's sake,' Stacey said, stifling a chuckle. 'And yes, first one on a swing and the second one on a hopscotch grid.'

'Wow,' she said.

'Wow, what?'

'Wow, I wish I was working this case with you.'

'Talk to me, Alison,' Stacey said, leaning forward.

'Okay, deliberate alterations of the scene or body position can sometimes be made to confuse police, called staging. Other times they serve the fantasy and are considered part of the signature and are considered to be posing. Sometimes the posing is intended to send a message to the police or the general public. Jack the Ripper posed his victims with their legs spread apart to shock the police and onlookers in Victorian England.

'Some have positioned bodies, bitten victims, covered the face, washed the hair or tied a ligature with an unusual knot. One serial killer in India left beer cans beside his victims.'

'So, what's he trying to tell us with an X?'

Alison shrugged as she twirled one of the hair pencils between her fingers. 'Signatures can be the result of psychological deviance but some are just for effect. Some experts think that signatures are linked more closely with personality traits than what they need to do to carry out the murder. In Poland one guy was too clever for his own good. He disembowelled young blonde women and wrote cryptic letters to police in red ink revealing where bodies could be found and challenged them to catch him. They did exactly that after analysing the ink.'

'So, there's no common use of a letter X that you know of?'

Alison shook her head. 'Any symbol marked on to the victim will be completely personal to the killer. That's the whole point.'

'Got it. Thanks for—'

'Hey, I'm a recluse here. Talk to me a minute. How's Devon and?—'

'Later, I've got to go,' Stacey said, cutting the conversation short for two reasons. The first was that she didn't want to reveal what was going on in her private life and the second was the notification that had just appeared in the top right-hand corner of her screen.

'Oh nice, just cut me off, eh? Well, I'll be checking in with you later in the week, buddy.'

'Okay, chat later,' she said, ending the call and deleting Alison from her screen.

She instantly clicked on the notification she'd received from the secretary of the editor at the *Daily Telegraph*. It was a screen shot of the Skype call record between Veronica and her boss.

And there was something there that instantly commanded her attention.

CHAPTER THIRTY-SIX

Barry Nixon's wife was not what Kim had been expecting.

Beth Nixon stood at around her own height of five foot nine. She was as light in hair and features as Kim was dark.

Her snug jeans and spaghetti-strapped tee shirt showed off the slim and toned figure of a woman who was at least twenty years her husband's junior. Age-gap relationships appeared to be common this week.

The red-rimmed eyes turned on Kim hopefully.

Kim understood. She had been informed of her husband's murder by officers in uniform, but now people in suits had arrived and they were probably going to tell her it had been some kind of mistake made by the guys in uniform.

'We're deeply sorry for your loss, Mrs Nixon,' Bryant offered quickly to disabuse her of that hope.

Her long legs appeared to buckle beneath her and she half fell to the chair.

'We understand this is clearly quite a shock for you, Mrs Nixon,' Kim said. 'Is there anyone we can call?'

'She's on her way. The police officer called her,' she said, revealing a hint of a northern accent.

'Your mum?' Kim asked.

She shook her head. 'Lenora, Barry's sister, she lives just down the road. She's coming now.'

'And there's a family liaison officer on the way too,' Bryant offered.

Kim nodded for him to continue as she glanced around the room. The furnishings were matching units formed of light oak. Clutches of scented candles and small cut-glass ornaments decorated the windowsills reflecting pinpoints of light on to the walls around the room.

Kim studied every photograph seeing Barry and his daughter, Barry and Beth, one of Barry and his sister but none of Beth with anyone other than Barry. No family to call and no family on the walls.

Bryant regarded the woman apologetically. 'Mrs Nixon, we're sorry to have to ask you questions now but can you tell us if there's been anything strange in the last few?—'

'Hold your horses,' boomed a voice from the hallway.

A uniformed officer appeared behind looking apologetic. The woman who had barged in was slight but her energy was palpable.

She guessed they were now in the company of Barry Nixon's sister.

'What are you asking her and why? Obviously there's some kind of mistake,' she boomed, grabbing Beth by the hand. Beth leaned into her gratefully, clearly relieved to have someone who felt the same way.

Kim had another surprise as she realised how close the two women appeared to be. From the photographs on the wall Barry had a daughter who had graduated university and it wasn't a child he'd had with Beth. So, this was his second marriage.

Beth looked up to her sister-in law and then at the photo on the wall. 'Lenora, we have to tell…'

'We'll do nothing of the sort. We're not going to upset Katie for nothing. It's not even him. Have they shown you photos?'

New hope flickered in Beth's eyes as she shook her head and looked their way.

'We will be asking one of you to make a formal identification,' Kim advised. 'However we are sure that it is your husband, Mrs Nixon.'

She burst into tears.

Kim glanced at Bryant and raised one eyebrow.

He coughed.

'Until we have proof that it's him I'm choosing not to believe you,' said the sister-in-law, removing a thin lemon cardigan.

Bryant coughed again.

'He's far too intelligent to get himself killed. He's a very clever—'

Bryant coughed as though his lungs were full of smoke.

Mrs Nixon stopped crying and looked over as he coughed again.

'I'm sorry, officer, are you okay. Can I get you something to drink?'

'Yes, please, anything.'

She made to stand.

'I'll do it, Beth. You stay here, sweetie,' Lenora said, patting her hand.

Bryant shot her an amused look as he followed the woman out of the room. It was a tactic they used often. Divide and learn as much as you could.

But Kim had to address one point first.

'Mrs Nixon, I really must stress that however much you'd like to believe that your husband isn't dead, we are in no doubt and allowing you to think anything otherwise is just insensitive on our part. I'm sorry.'

Beth Nixon swallowed and nodded. 'My head understands but my heart is looking for any reason to disbelieve you.'

'I know, but I really need to ask you some questions so that we can find the person responsible.'

'Please, go ahead,' she said, wiping her nose.

'Was your husband having any problems with anyone that you know of?'

She shook her head. 'Barry is a wonderful man, he helps everyone.'

'Any issues at work?' Kim asked, hopefully.

'Not really. Sometimes he has to tell people things they don't want to hear but everyone is defensive when it comes to their children, aren't they?'

'Sorry, what did he do for a living?' Kim asked.

'Barry is a counsellor, for children, especially difficult cases.'

Children again. She thought about Belinda Evans.

'Please, go on,' Kim urged.

'He works with kids who have had traumatic childhoods, normally ones with violent tendencies. He practises privately and is very much in demand,' she said proudly.

Which is why he was going to the corner shop at lunchtime on a week day.

Kim couldn't help the frisson of distaste that passed through her. As a child, she'd seen plenty of Barrys, all with a different view on how to handle her but all with one thing in common: they had seen her as a personal challenge.

She had been able to smell the desperation as they'd realised just how damaged she was. Quick-fire questions, different types of questions designed to flummox and confuse her. Dolls, books, games, tricks, tests, anything to try to fool her into opening up.

Ted had been different. He had let her watch his fish swim in the small pond. He had given her lollipops and allowed her to sit in silence. She had never opened up fully to anyone, but if she'd had to choose someone it would have been him.

'So, there are parents that resent the opinion of your husband?' Kim asked. Defence of one's child had led to many a murder.

'Oh yes,' she answered, animatedly, experiencing a period of denial of current events. 'Even if they're paying for it they don't always like the truth.'

Kim was tempted to argue that it was opinion not truth, but now was not the time.

'Was there anyone in particular who had taken offence to your husband's… findings?'

Beth shook her head. 'No one recently. He'd been cutting back a bit on clients and spending a bit more time at home.'

Her ears heard the words as her brain translated it to business was drying up.

'If we could somehow get a list of your husband's recent clients.'

'Of course. I'll ask Lenora. She takes care of his appointments and his admin.'

'Mrs Nixon, does the name Belinda Evans mean anything to you?'

She considered and shook her head. 'No, should it?'

She'd hoped so based on their shared interest of broken and damaged children. Surely there had to be a link. Outside of that she could see no connection between them.

Kim felt the frustration rest heavy on her shoulders.

The clock was ticking steadily towards the end of another working day. They had clocked up another dead body but very little to help them find the person responsible.

'Okay, Mrs Nixon, thank you for your help and…'

'He really is gone, isn't he?' she whispered, staring towards the fireplace.

'I'm afraid so,' Kim said, wishing she had something to offer that would ease the pain.

'So hard to believe, and he was so looking forward to his trip tomorrow.'

CHAPTER THIRTY-SEVEN

'I'm gonna win,' Bryant said, smugly as they headed back to the car. 'Our Lenora was a mine of information.'

'Go on, let's trade.'

'Our victim is a child counsellor,' he said, getting into the car.

'Yeah, got that,' she said, closing the passenger door.

'And Lenora does his books and appointments for him.'

'Got that too,' she said.

'First wife died of cancer three years ago.'

'Didn't get that,' she admitted.

'Ah, you missed something.'

'No, just didn't think it prudent to ask the second wife too many questions about the first but you go ahead and take your glory where you can, my friend.'

'Lenora loves the bones of Beth who has made her brother very happy after the long illness of his first wife.'

'Didn't need that.'

'I'm building the tension,' he explained.

'No, you're really not and if you intend on recounting—'

'You're just no fun any more.'

'First, I was never any fun to start with and second, I found out that our guy was also going on a trip and I'm betting it was to the same place as Belinda Evans. So, come on, what you got?'

'Impressive,' he admitted. 'But did you know that Beth used to be one of her husband's patients.'

'Eww…' she said at the thought of that.

'Yeah, hooked up again on Facebook of all bloody places. Met for coffee to catch up and love blossomed, apparently.'

Yes, they were both grown adults but Kim couldn't help the acidy distaste that had landed on her tongue. Whether legal or not, there was surely an ethical or moral code against such things.

'Oh, Bryant,' she said, looking at her watch. 'We so need to be able to work longer—'

She stopped speaking as her phone began to ring.

'Sir?' she said, recognising the number of DCI Woodward, her boss.

She listened as he gave her an instruction to come to the station immediately.

'Absolutely, sir, on my way, cos I'd really like to speak to you too.'

CHAPTER THIRTY-EIGHT

Penn jumped off the bus two stops early. He knew he could have got a squad car to drop him off at the train station to pick up his car, but it felt like a piss-take to him when he had perfectly good legs and money in his pocket.

It was hard to believe he'd only parked up that morning to get the train into court. It was one of those days where three appeared to be rolling into one.

And it wasn't over yet, he thought, but didn't actually mind. Being forced to work shorter shifts for the last couple of weeks seemed to have siphoned the energy out of him. Travis wanted this thing sorted as soon as possible and hadn't read the same memo as his boss.

Luckily, they all felt the same way and neither Doug nor Lynne had wanted to clock off until they'd made some progress.

He'd tasked Doug to do some digging on Irina Nuryef to see if there was anything to the cheating rumour as a possible motivation for her changing her story. He prayed not. And Lynne had been tasked with interrogating the forensic evidence to see if anything had been missed. Again, he prayed not. And he himself had chosen to return to the petrol station to look for holes in Ricky Drake's story.

He'd stepped off the bus early to pick up the trail exactly as Drake had explained it in his statement.

The man had left the pub at ten thirty, and it was dark. Right now, it was dusky but it was close enough.

Penn stood for a minute right outside the pub and looked along the road.

On his side of the road were a few terraced houses, a closed-down wine bar, a patch of wasteland about halfway up, and the chippy Drake had been heading for was about a hundred and twenty metres ahead right before the road hit a small traffic island.

Right now, he was at the furthest point away from the chippy and could see it clearly. He wasn't sure he'd have lit a smoke only being this far away and he wasn't even close to the petrol station on the other side of the road.

He continued moving along the pavement, retracing Drake's steps as he'd explained them. Thirty metres down and Penn could see into the well-lit petrol station. He could just make out the figure of Mr Kapoor, partly because he knew the man well.

He continued to move forward. For a few seconds, his trajectory meant that a petrol pump obscured his view of the cash desk and then it came into sight again. He stood at the point Drake had claimed to be when lighting his cigarette. Right by the lamp-post in front of the wasteland.

Penn frowned. No, that couldn't be right. He looked for other lamp-posts but the space between them put any others completely out of reach.

Penn felt a seed of anxiety plant itself in his stomach as he moved back and forth in front of the petrol station, walking the whole length three more times and pausing to check with every step.

Drake had identified Nuryef clearly from this position. He had glanced and then looked closely and had recognised the accused.

From where he stood Penn could see Mr Kapoor clearly in the well-lit shop. He could see that he was conversing with someone, could even see him handing change over the counter.

But because of a chocolate display rack that stretched the length of the shop, Penn couldn't see another soul.

Ricky Drake's witness account had been a total and utter lie.

CHAPTER THIRTY-NINE

'Can't do it, sir,' Kim said, as she walked into Woody's office.

'Too damn right you can't, Stone, but I feel we may be talking about two completely different things. So, what the hell possessed you?'

'Err…' she offered, playing for time. She liked to be sure which issue they were talking about before she admitted to anything.

'You allowed Travis to keep a member of your team when you have two bodies to…'

Ah that one.

'Technically, sir, we only had one body at the time of my conversation with Travis. The second body was reported—'

'Don't play games with me. Who the hell gave you the authority to agree to an unofficial secondment? That should have been channelled to me.'

'With all due respect, Penn is a member of my team who was lost to me this week anyway sat in court twiddling his thumbs. And to be fair it looks like the case has turned into one hell of a clusterf—'

'Yes, but it's their cluster… mess and not up to us to bail them out of it.'

'It's a line on a map, sir,' she said, quoting his own words about the force boundaries. 'We're all fighting crime.'

DCI Woodward was one of the most progressive advocates of inter-force working she'd ever met. He felt the lines dividing forces were for budget and organisational purposes only as they were all trying to do the same job. Criminals crossed force borders, so procedures and working practices had to adapt too.

'You know, sir,' she continued, 'I actually thought to myself, what would the boss do in this situation? Would he dismiss the request out of hand without consideration or would he try to co-operate with his colleagues across the operational border and try to foster a more—'

'He would have consulted with his superior officer for a start, and just so as you know, that smoke you're blowing is going nowhere near my behind.'

'I could always call Travis and tell him I made a mistake and get Penn back.'

'You know damn well I'll refuse that offer. The damage is done now but I just don't understand what possessed you to act so recklessly.'

'It was his case, sir,' she said, honestly. 'Penn was the SIO and he needs to know if he f… messed up. And if he did he has to try and put it right, otherwise it'll stay with him for the rest of his career.'

'You could have just said that in the first place,' he said, wryly.

'And where's the fun in that, sir?' she asked, realising he should have known her motives were not based on inter-force co-operation. That was his job not hers and she rarely gave away or lent out anything but she knew how it felt to finish what you'd started.

'Although that does lead nicely to my reason for wanting to see you. Sir, you have to take the shackles off. Even with Penn we couldn't work this case nine to five and my team is losing the will to live. Stacey is looking for a part-time job and Bryant is on the brink of divorce. And if that wasn't bad enough, I'm actually cleaning my house.'

She saw a smile twitch at the corners of his mouth.

'Okay, Stone, some latitude but don't work them into the ground.'

'Thank you,' she said, reaching the door.

'But remember, Stone, every action has consequences and you should be ready to deal with yours.'

Kim closed the door behind her. What the hell had he meant by that?

CHAPTER FORTY

'Right, guys, it's after five o clock,' Kim said, entering the squad room.

Bryant groaned and Stacey blew a raspberry.

'But given the fact we've lost Penn and we now have two bodies, let's crack on for a bit, shall we?'

Her two colleagues high-fived each other across the room.

'Anyone need to make calls?'

'No,' Bryant said. 'My missus prefers me to ring when I'm gonna be early cos that used to be the exception.'

'No,' Stacey said, simply, but Kim caught the shadow that crossed her face. She hoped another relationship hadn't suffered as a consequence of too much time together.

'However, I am obliged to advise you both that if you start to feel tired or suffer increased levels of stress...'

'Guv, can we just get back to work?' Bryant asked.

'Fine, but just tell me, okay?'

'Okay,' Stacey agreed. 'Now, there's something I think you should know about Veronica Evans.'

'Go,' Kim said, crossing her arms.

'That Skype call she had with the editor. It was roughly the time she said but it ended at 9.52, which according to Route Planner gave her just enough time to get to Haden Hill Park and away again before her sister's body was discovered. Not sure what that means in light of the second body but...'

'Good to know, Stace, well done,' she said. Regardless of how many bodies there were Kim still wanted to know more about Belinda and her sister.

'So,' Kim said, moving towards the board. 'We have Belinda Evans on a swing and Barry Nixon on the hopscotch grid, both with the letter X cut into the back of their neck. We know that Belinda was a professor of child psychology and Barry Nixon was a counsellor, primarily for troubled kids. We also know that Barry was attending a two-day event called Brainboxes or something in Stourport-On-Severn tomorrow. I think it's safe to say that's where Belinda was going too.

'Barry Nixon's wife, who incidentally used to be one of his cases—'

'Ugghh,' Stacey said, offering Kim validation of her own feelings earlier.

'Exactly. Anyway, she insists that Barry hasn't missed one of these events in years and is paid by the organisers to attend.'

'For what?'

'Not sure but I'd like to talk to the organisers to see exactly what this event is all about. In the meantime I'd like to know more about the man himself and I'm not going to get that from either his wife or his sister who both seem to think he was some kind of god.'

Bryant cut in. 'But he didn't exactly have a boss as he worked for himself and I'm not sure he was awash with friends.'

'Hmm. You're right there, Bryant?' she said, thoughtfully. 'But I think I might know someone who can help.'

CHAPTER FORTY-ONE

Penn took a deep breath before pushing open the door and holding it open for a woman juggling her car keys and a take-out coffee.

Apart from two lads by the drinks section glancing up at the new CCTV camera, the service station was empty.

They glanced at each other and shuffled out of the shop. Teenagers – school kids – and yet either one of them could have had a knife.

Penn took the bottle to the counter.

'Mr Penn, sir. What are you doing here?'

Penn opened his mouth and closed it again as a customer ran in to pay with the money already in his hand.

Penn remembered those days. Filling up the car to the exact amount of money you had in your pocket. Careful not to go over but to get it as close as you could. A personal challenge to get it to the exact penny.

Did Mr Kapoor view every customer with caution since the death of his son? At what point did he breathe a sigh of relief that the customer was not going to produce a weapon, a knife, or worse. That they just wanted to pay for petrol and get on with their night.

He waited until the youth had left.

'Was that you over the road, pacing?' he asked, frowning.

Penn considered lying but nodded instead.

'Mr Kapoor, a lot happened in court today. Not good things from our point of view. I promised I'd keep you informed and I have to tell you that we're currently taking another look at the case.'

He frowned. 'I don't understand. Gregor Nuryef murdered my son. You told me so. You said you had your man.'

Yes, he had. Right after they'd received the results of the DNA test, he'd visited the man and his family straight after his shift and given them the news.

'The tee shirt, with Dev's blood. It was…'

'It was, Mr Kapoor. It was right there in Nuryef's shed, but there are inconsistencies that we can't ignore.'

'That man who was killed. He was going to testify that Nuryef was at home that night?'

Penn nodded. 'It's an easy mistake to make. His testimony was based on hearing his neighbour call the dog in at ten thirty every night. He was no threat to the case.'

'He was a threat to someone,' Mr Kapoor said, simply.

Penn agreed but was hoping that the team working the McCann murder case were going to turn up some indisputable reason for the defence witness's death being unrelated to the Kapoor case. Perhaps the man had defaulted on gambling debts to the wrong person or maybe he was a drug dealer murdered by a disgruntled client. His logical mind told him that the forty-six-year-old accountant was unlikely to be either, but he had to hang on to the hope.

'We're investigating every angle to ensure that—'

'Please don't do that, sir,' Mr Kapoor said, smiling sadly. 'From that first night, you've treated me with respect. We stood over Dev's body together,' he said, glancing at the spot where he'd lain. 'You explained even then that you might not find the person responsible without any CCTV, but I sensed in you the passion to do your best. You've always been fair and honest, please don't give me police-speak now.'

Penn nodded and took a deep breath. 'Mr Kapoor, we are checking to make sure we got the right man.'

'Thank you.'

'I can understand how that must make you feel. You're angry at me and us as you have every right…'

'I am angry at the person who took my son from me. I am angry at the person who robbed my wife of her first-born. I am angry at the person who has caused my young daughters to face grief, fear and mistrust earlier than they should. I was told repeatedly by the police to improve my security, and I didn't listen to you or your colleagues and I paid a high price. I have no one to blame for that but myself.'

Penn suddenly felt sick to his stomach.

'Mr Kapoor, I want you to know that we will do everything we can to get this straightened out.'

'I know you will, sir,' he said, as another customer entered the shop.

Penn nodded his goodbye and left the premises, feeling even shittier than when he'd walked in.

CHAPTER FORTY-TWO

'You sure I can come in?' Bryant asked, as he pulled the car to a stop.

'You a vampire who can't enter without an invitation?' she asked.

'You know why I'm asking.'

'Yep, but this isn't a personal visit.'

'Great, I love this guy.'

Kim rolled her eyes. She had another guy at home who got just as excited when she brought him to this address.

'Hey, Ted,' she said, as her old counsellor opened the front door.

'Hello, Kim, and I see you brought reinforcements.'

Kim smiled as she stepped into the house. 'He's got a bit of a man crush on you,' she said, walking past him.

'She's right, I do,' Bryant said, following her into the house.

'Well, thank you. And I'm guessing this must be work related,' Ted observed. 'As this is not even close to the unreasonable hour you call if it's a personal visit.'

She nodded her acknowledgment.

He tipped his head. 'So, are we just going to pretend that the last time you were here you didn't snap my head off and then storm out?'

'Absolutely,' she said. This was nothing new to them. It was how she'd grown up.

'She did?' Bryant asked, as they all stood in the small kitchen.

'Indeed, Bryant, when I told her I didn't think she should be working that copycat case.'

'Ah,' Bryant said.

'Our visit did not end well.'

'So, I'm cannon fodder?' Bryant asked.

'Oh yeah,' she said, taking a custard cream from the biscuit barrel.

'And where shall we be sitting today, my dear?' he asked with a twinkle in his eye.

During her last visit, he had explained that she chose to sit outside when she didn't want to speak. She chose to sit in the living room if she wanted his help, and she chose the kitchen if she wanted his opinion as it was the closest of the three to the door ready for when she stormed out if his opinion didn't agree with her own.

'Living room,' Kim advised. 'And I'll make the coffee while you two catch up.'

Ted nodded and guided Bryant into the lounge.

She put the kettle on and pulled down three mugs from the cupboard.

'What a lovely room,' Bryant said, as she spooned in the instant granules. 'So this is where young Kim talked to the only person she could trust?'

'Not really,' Ted said, as she poured in the milk. 'She talked very little anywhere in the house and yet still she continued to come. Every scheduled appointment she turned up and most of them for silence.'

Kim poured the water into the mugs. She remembered each and every session.

'She never let me help her and yet she still continued to come. Not sure exactly what she got—'

'Hey, Bryant, that's my seat,' Kim said, carrying the tray into the room.

Bryant moved from the single chair by the fire to the end of the sofa.

Ted looked at the drinks, shook his head and stood.

'Too strong, as usual.'

He returned from the kitchen and poured extra milk into his mug and at her colleague's agreement into his drink too.

'Wimps,' she muttered.

'So, how may I help?' Ted asked, folding his hands in his lap.

'You know anyone by the name of Barry Nixon?' she asked, figuring that the world of child counselling wasn't endless and that the two men might have encountered each other.

He thought for a second, his brows furrowed. 'The name is familiar.'

Kim got the impression he was working back through his memories. Although semi-retired now he was still called upon for the occasional tough nut to crack.

'Yes, yes, I think I recall a fellow by that name. Worked for the department about twenty years ago. Not for very long if I remember correctly.'

Kim offered Bryant a triumphant smile. This man was like an oracle.

'Hmm… case chaser he was, I remember him now. Tall, slim, fair hair, owlish features.'

Yep, that was their guy. 'Case chaser?' she asked.

'Yes, there were a few of them but he was particularly ambitious. There were certain cases that came in that caused some hands to go in the air quicker than others. He chased the juiciest, nastiest, most high-profile cases that came through the department. We're talking the most damaged, broken, angry kids the care system had to offer.'

Kids like you, she heard in the tone behind the words.

'But why particular cases?' Kim asked. 'Surely helping any child that was suffering was enough.'

'Thought he could mend anyone. But he wanted the high-profile cases for two reasons. He wanted to write papers, journals, books. He wanted to build his CV and gain a reputation as a field leader before going into private practice. There's a lot of money to be made in the private sector but a lot of competition too.'

'Go on,' Kim urged, fascinated yet horrified that treating vulnerable children had been such a calculated ambition to the man.

'A lot of counselling work involves listening, or not listening in your case,' he added, with a smirk. 'Different types of trauma require different types of approach: child abuse, neglect, PTSD, abandonment, all require a different toolkit but they all require one common denominator. Patience. You go at the speed of the child. That is—'

'She's right, Ted,' Bryant said. 'I do have a bit of a man crush on you.'

Both she and Ted laughed out loud.

'Sorry, I just couldn't keep it in any longer,' Bryant apologised.

'Thank you,' he said, continuing. 'It was a trait he didn't possess. He got into trouble a few times for rushing cases to conclusion too soon.'

'Is that why he left Children's Services?' she asked.

Ted shook his head. 'He left because he was asked to.'

'Why?' Kim asked, leaning forward.

'Tammy Hopkins.'

'Who?'

Ted took a sip of his drink. 'That's not her real name. We all called her Tammy Hopkins so we knew who we were talking about and didn't slip-up and reveal her true identity. Tammy was the eleven-year-old daughter of the singer-songwriting couple from Glasgow.'

'I remember something; about fifteen years ago?' Bryant asked.

Ted nodded.

'Murder suicide of parents. Mother stabbed father and then cut her own wrists. Tammy was ten years old and saw it all. Terrified, she hid in the outside shed for two days until a neighbour stopped by with a wrongly delivered parcel and found the whole bloody mess.'

He shuddered. 'Well, Tammy was moved down here to live with her aunt and you can guess who was first in line to take that case. Anyway, it became clear after a while that Tammy had been abused by her father making her a rape victim and...'

'Giving her lifelong anonymity.'

'Meaning he would never be able to write about or mention the case outside of the service again. He couldn't capitalise on her misery and so cut her treatment short claiming he'd helped her as much as he could.'

'And?'

'She cut her own wrists two weeks later. She died.'

Kim felt the rage build inside her for the pain of that little girl.

'How the hell was he not prosecuted?'

Ted shrugged. 'One of the most subjective areas of counselling is when to let a patient go. There's no way of knowing for sure if you've done enough. To be safe you'd have to treat them all for life,' he said, looking at her pointedly.

She laughed and felt the tension ease out of her.

'I have no idea what happened to him after that.'

'Have you heard of some kind of event called Brainboxes?'

His frown returned. 'Don't tell me he's been involved in that? If so I'm sure there are plenty of poor damaged souls there to keep him busy. Not that I know a lot about it. Some kind of mental gladiators' thing but for kids. I wouldn't like to say more as I've never been.'

She sipped the last of her drink and stood. Bryant reluctantly followed her lead.

'Can I come back without her and just listen to you?' Bryant asked, offering his hand.

'Of course,' Ted replied, smiling and patting him on the arm. 'I'm surprised you don't need extensive counselling yourself given the hours you spend with...'

'Hey, enough,' she said, turning. 'And thanks, Ted.'

'You're welcome, as ever, my dear.'

Kim followed Bryant to the car. He got in. She did not.

She went back to where Ted stood on the doorstep.

'Peace,' she said, meeting his questioning gaze. 'You told Bryant you didn't know why I came to every session to be silent. I came for peace. I came for a rest from this,' she said, tapping her temple.

'I don't understand…'

'I came because I knew that while I was here you'd never let anyone hurt me.'

She saw the emotion gather in his eyes before she turned and headed back to the car.

CHAPTER FORTY-THREE

'You know, that guy just makes me want to open up and give him all my shit. He's like Yoda.'

'I know,' Kim said, taking out her phone. Bryant started the car and waited as she pressed Stacey's number.

'Hey, boss.'

'Appears our guy was a bit of a glory hunter. Went after big cases only,' she said. 'You got anything on Brainboxes?'

'Only what the website is showing me so far. It's a two-day event for the brightest kids in the country. Been going for years. All kinds of competitions culminating in a quiz at the end of the event between the brightest boys and girls. There's prizes and everything. Lots of photos of kids enjoying themselves on the website. Current organisers are a husband and wife team who I can't get hold of at the minute as they're on their way to the venue, which happens to be The Village Hotel in Stourport.'

'Okay, Stace, call it a night,' she said, remembering Woody's warning. 'But we brief at seven,' she said ending the call.

'Guv…'

'Yep, you too, Bryant, so drop me back at the station.'

He grumbled but put the car in gear and pulled away from the kerb.

Stacey's assessment of the event seemed at odds with what they'd just learned from Ted, and yet his description had ear-wormed into her brain.

Gladiators for Kids.

CHAPTER FORTY-FOUR

'Okay, kids, how are we feeling this morning?' Kim asked.

'Like we're starting work at the right time of the day for a start,' Bryant offered brightly.

'Glad to oblige,' Kim said, feeling the exact same way. Her day had started at five with a brisk walk around the park with Barney while the coffee brewed, and no one else was around.

The dog had chowed down a bowl of dried food with added chicken pieces while she'd drunk said coffee and then they'd both stepped into the garden to watch the sky lighten as the sun came up.

Her best friend had been left munching on a carrot and his buddy, Charlie, from down the road would come pick him up later for an afternoon walk and a shift of squirrel hunting in Charlie's back garden.

Bryant referred to it as 'dog share' but it was a great arrangement that suited them all.

'So, we know our second victim was planning to attend the Brainbox thingy today. His services paid for by the organisers who we definitely want to speak with,' she said, glancing at Stacey, who nodded.

'But I would like to know why Veronica didn't share where her sister was going.'

'You think she knew?' Bryant asked.

'She knew everything else about her sister, so I'm guessing so. Carry on digging on the sisters, Stace. There's a lot there we don't know, and I want a meeting with the Brainbox folks as soon as possible. And don't forget the cross-referencing of the dates that both victims attended.'

'Will do, boss.'

Kim was aware of the workload she was throwing in Stacey's direction and glanced longingly at Penn's empty chair.

'Keats is going to let us know if there's anything more to note about Nixon once he's done the post-mortem later this—'

'Hiya,' said a bright voice from the door.

All three of them glanced towards the beaming elfin figure dressed in a constable uniform. Kim guessed her to be around five and half feet with her blonde hair pulled into a bun on the back of her head.

Kim hadn't realised it was dress your kid and bring it to work day.

'Are you lost?' Kim asked, trying to keep the edge from her voice. The door was clearly marked CID.

She shook her head, still beaming, as she stepped into the room.

'I'm Tiffany, like the singer, Tiff. I was told you were expecting me.'

'To do what?' Kim asked.

She shrugged her delicate little shoulders. 'Help out, I think.'

Kim looked to her colleagues to see if she was missing something. Their expressions said not.

'Tiffany, I'm not sure?...'

'DCI Woodward requested me,' she said, barely able to keep the joy out of her voice as though she'd been promised a trip to Disneyland. 'He said you're a team member down and I'm so excited to be asked to help.'

And still her smile hadn't wavered.

'I've heard so much about you all. You do such exciting work and I can't believe I'm here right now.'

Kim looked to Bryant who was staring with the same bewilderment as Stacey.

'I think there's been a mistake, Tiffany. If you return to your normal duties, I'll sort this with the DCI once—'

'He said you might say that,' she said, smiling even wider as though she was in on some kind of joke. 'He told me to remind you of your conversation yesterday, and oh my God, this office is fab,' she said, looking around before taking a seat.

An action that prompted Stacey's expression to change from amused curiosity to panic-stricken.

'Please use me however you want,' she offered, brightly. 'I'm just so...'

'Yeah, we get it,' Kim said, glancing at Stacey whose eyes beseeched her to remove the interloper.

I can't, her expression said back.

'I'll speak to Woo... DCI Woodward and clarify the arrangements,' she said.

Tiffany nodded enthusiastically and beamed.

'But in the meantime, I'm sure Stacey will find something you can help her with.'

'Oketty doketty,' she answered.

Kim gave Stacey an apologetic look as she grabbed her coat. She had to get out.

Suddenly their small office was way too bright for her eyes.

CHAPTER FORTY-FIVE

They had almost reached Veronica's home when Woody finally answered her call. It may have been the twenty-seven attempts in quick succession that had told him she wasn't going away.

'Good morning, Stone,' he answered.

And his cheery greeting told her he knew exactly why she was calling.

'Is she my punishment, sir?'

'I remember explaining that every action has a—'

'So, she's a consequence?' Kim corrected.

'She's a keen, gifted young police officer who is showing great—'

'How young?'

'Twenty-four.'

Kim wondered if he'd added ten years just for fun.

'Well, I suppose Santa's little helper needs something to do out of season.'

She was sure she heard a chuckle, quickly covered over with a cough.

'Don't tell me you dislike her because she's cheerful.'

'I don't know her to dislike her but you know I'm not to be trusted around people with a sunny disposition. I tend to break them without even trying. Please reconsider, sir. For her sake.'

The line grew silent.

She waited for his response, hoping he was giving her request serious consideration.

'Sir?'

'Sorry, was that a serious request? I was just taking a bite of toast and the answer is no. She's an extra pair of hands which you desperately need in Penn's absence and you've offered me no compelling reason to change my mind. And don't worry about her sensitivities as I can assure you she's much tougher than she looks. And on that note, I'm now going to finish my breakfast in peace. Have a good day.'

'Damn it,' she said as the line went dead in her hand. 'How the hell does he think having a completely new person thrown into the team is going to help in any way? I mean, how much is she going to help in between bottle feeds and potty breaks. And why pick someone so damned cheerful to put with me?'

'To be fair, guv, you really didn't give him any reason to change his mind. He can't go back on a decision because you think she's perky.'

'Bryant, I'm pretty sure I never used the word perky and I'm not sure you should either,' she said as they pulled up in front of a garage with the door open.

'Car's gone,' Bryant said, stating the obvious.

Kim could immediately see that Veronica was one of a very small minority that actually used the garage for storing her car. And only her car, Kim realised, as she saw no evidence of the normal boxes and detritus that most folks relocated out of their sight in the garage.

'Not gone far if she's left the door open.'

'Nothing in there to nick,' she answered, although she agreed with him.

'Drive around the corner,' she instructed her colleague, who reversed and turned the car.

A minute later they turned into the street where her sister had lived.

Kim narrowed her gaze, as they drew closer to Belinda's property.

'What the hell is going on here?'

CHAPTER FORTY-SIX

'You don't have to bring coffee every time we meet up, you know,' Penn said as Lynne set down the drink's holder from Costa.

'Look, I can't even think without the stuff and it'd be rude to just take care of myself,' she said, throwing a couple of sachets at Doug. 'It's only a bloody coffee.'

'I ain't complaining,' Doug said, ripping the heads off the sugar packs and emptying them into his drink. 'You wanna throw your money about I'm happy to get in the way.'

'So, how'd you get on with Mrs Nuryef?' Penn asked, cutting through the good-natured bickering.

'Ain't budging,' Doug said, shaking his head. 'Says he wasn't there and threw me out of the house.'

'Your thoughts?' Penn asked.

'I think she's telling the truth. I think her initial response of covering for him was probably denial that he could do such a thing and then panic set in. She's got kids to think of.'

'I get that,' Penn said. 'I'd expect it but then why change your mind? She's still got the kids and they're still going to need feeding with him inside. It's not even like she changed her story to "I can't remember". She went direct to "I lied and he wasn't with me".'

Doug shrugged. 'Mate, my understanding of the female species is limited at the best of times but Irina Nuryef is on another level entirely.' He leaned to his left. 'No offence, Lynne.'

'None taken but from my point of view she seemed equally as agitated and irate during both statements,' Lynne offered. 'I watched the footage back last night and I wouldn't bet this cup of coffee on which one is the truth.'

'Anything on forensics that we missed?'

'Not that I can see. We got a warrant, found the tee shirt in a carrier bag hidden behind a toolbox. Chain of evidence is all good. Forensic tests confirmed the blood to belong to Devlin Kapoor. No margin for error, no inconsistencies. Tied up nicely with a bow on. How about you?'

'Not so much,' he admitted. 'Took a trip back to the scene last night and there's a problem with Drake's witness account.'

'How so?' Doug asked.

'You can't see into the shop?'

'What?' they asked together.

'Yeah, I know,' he said. 'How did we not know this?'

The fact they'd never checked it had kept him up most of the night.

'The shop is lit up like a bloody beacon on that stretch,' Doug said.

Penn nodded. 'You can see who is behind the till but you can't see who is on the other side. Tried it from every angle and you just can't see.'

'Shit,' Lynne said, while Doug's questioning frown said he hadn't yet accepted the fact.

'Feel free to go back there tonight and prove me wrong, mate,' Penn invited. 'But how the hell he saw Gregor Nuryef there unless he was in there himself, I'll never know.'

'And could he have been?' Doug asked.

Who the hell knew?

'So, the question we were hoping not to have to ask is now front and centre,' Lynne observed. 'Who killed Dexter McCann, and why?'

'Which is going to have to wait,' said DI Travis from the doorway. 'Irina Nuryef is in reception and will only speak to you,' he said, looking right at Penn.

CHAPTER FORTY-SEVEN

'So,' Stacey said, glancing across the room. 'What's your skill set?'

Please boss make it so Woody appears in the doorway to rectify the mistake, she thought to herself. She didn't have time to play nursemaid.

'I like digging,' she said, cheerfully. 'I do it all the time out on the street. I love getting to the bottom of something.'

After looking longingly at the doorway once more, Stacey resolved that if the girl liked digging she'd give her her very own garden.

'Okay, we have two sisters involved in our current case. Belinda and Veronica Evans. Find me anything you can on either or both of them.'

'You mean like birth, marriage, kids, that kind of thing?'

'Anything at all,' Stacey answered. She'd already checked and there was nothing there but it would keep the girl busy until the boss sorted this mess out.

In the meantime, she tried the contact number again for the Brainbox organisers, Mr and Ms Welmsley. She banged the phone down in frustration. The mobile number had gone from voicemail to permanently engaged. She'd left two messages already and a third would have bordered on restraining order territory.

Okay, so the rest of her work involved the Brainbox website. She clicked the tab with the website already open and began to explore.

Everything about the site appeared friendly, accessible and inviting.

She began noting the facts.

Brainboxes had started in 1961 and was a small collection of gifted children coming together for friendly games and competition.

Popularity grew and then fizzled in the 1970s and '80s but burst back with new vigour in the mid '90s with a new two-day programme, entrance fee, prizes and a minimum IQ score to gain entry.

Hmm, Stacey wasn't sure how she felt about that last bit. She understood that the event was for child prodigies but not all kids were good at tests and, in all honesty, she hated anything for kids that excluded other kids. However, it was a private event and there was little anyone could do about it.

Looking over the years since its reinvention Stacey could see that the numbers grew steadily every year. In 1995 thirty-one children had been registered to attend but last year the number had risen to sixty-four. Clearly, gifted children were on the up.

She went to the gallery and saw that recent events had a mixture of photos and video, while the older ones had photos only.

She clicked on the images from the event the year before.

Beaming faces shone at her from the photos that had been staged in groups: all children, and then the ones taken throughout the events in different areas. Stacey saw chess, piano, a mental arithmetic competition, a spelling bee and then finally the big quiz at the end which featured the winners of all the smaller divisions.

Seemed to her like an awful lot of competition for kids in just two short days but the photos showed a lot of fun too.

Finding the attendance of Barry Nixon was easy enough. Each year had a list of event staff like a cast list and Barry was listed as event counsellor from 2003 through to last year, missing only one event a few years earlier which she suspected was when his wife died.

Stacey wrote all the years down on her notepad and then paused as an unwelcome sound punctured the silence.

'Are you whistling?' she asked Tiffany across the room.

The girl smiled. 'Yeah, show tunes. Learned when I was a kid. Fills the silence. I don't even know I'm doing it most times.'

Stacey offered her a tight smile. Just go with it, Stace, she told herself. The boss would sort it. She just had to tune herself out and she'd be fine.

Marrying up those dates with Belinda Evans was not going to be easy, and she briefly wondered if the boss had got it wrong. Belinda Evans had never been on the staff list and appeared to have attended the event in no official capacity whatsoever.

She put Belinda's full name into the website search engine and thanked God for photo tagging.

She matched up the data she could find from photos, blog posts and mentions and when she looked down at her notepad realised that the two of them had attended the event together at least ten times.

CHAPTER FORTY-EIGHT

Bryant managed to park between the skip and the cleaning company van. Kim spied Veronica's car parked on the drive of Belinda's second home next door.

'Well, she didn't waste much time,' Bryant observed.

'She didn't waste any bloody time. Property was only handed back a couple of hours ago. She must have had all these folks on standby at the top of the road.'

Mitch had texted her to say they were complete at 6 a.m. having found no evidence to link the property to the actual crime scene miles away.

Kim walked up the path sideways as two cleaning operatives passed her carrying boxes to the skip.

'No, no, clear one room at a time,' Kim heard as they entered the property.

Veronica was standing in the middle of the living room in a square of clear carpet a metre wide.

She wore light jeans and a green tee shirt. Working clothes that she didn't expect to get dirty.

She looked their way and scowled.

'Been busy here, Miss Evans,' Kim said, careful not to slip on shiny magazine covers as she moved to the middle of the room.

Kim had no clue how much she was paying these people but she could already see some wall space appearing from behind the piles.

'I really think you'd have a better chance of finding my sister's killer if you weren't so fascinated with me.'

'And perhaps if you'd been a bit more truthful…'

'What the devil?…' Veronica said, looking around them.

'Birdcage,' said the woman who had just pulled forward a pile of old bedding sheets.

'Get rid of it, but not that box to the right. Put that on the "to be checked" pile.'

Clearly Veronica wanted the focus on one room at a time so it could be closely monitored.

Perhaps Kim had got the woman wrong and she wanted to make sure that she kept hold of Belinda's personal items or keepsakes.

'A small box of jewellery over here,' said the smaller operative handing it to Veronica.

She opened it. 'Belinda's costume jewellery from the Eighties. She loved this rubbish.'

She closed the box and threw it into the nearest black bin bag.

Or maybe not, Kim thought, as her hackles began to rise.

She watched for a moment as the woman continued to direct and manage the workforce.

Despite her own shortcomings in the emotional connection department, Kim often felt a vague stirring of empathy for family members, the ones left behind, the people who now had victim-shaped holes in their lives. She felt for the people who had to rearrange their entire existence around an empty space. She empathised because she understood loss.

Yet this woman elicited no emotion from her at all. She had wondered if Veronica was burying her feelings so deeply to avoid facing them. After the involvement in each other's lives Veronica's days had to be emptier than most.

But this need to eradicate her sister's existence so soon after her death left Kim standing cold. Belinda deserved better than that. Of the hundreds of cases she'd worked she'd never seen a relative act so coldly.

'Not that one,' Veronica cried out, suddenly, causing Kim to look closely.

It was a box of old papers, textbooks and exercise books.

Veronica grabbed it and pulled it closer to her.

'Miss Evans, we know you're busy but…'

'You can talk while I watch, Inspector. I'm paying these people by the hour.'

The word unrelenting came to mind. This woman didn't give an inch to anyone on anything.

'Miss Evans, we would appreciate your full attention for just a minute or two, and if you'd prefer we could do this down the station.'

'We absolutely could,' she said without batting an eyelid. 'I'll see you some time at the end of the week. If you want my attention any sooner, I'd suggest you ask your questions, Inspector. I'm perfectly able to multitask.'

Kim glanced at Bryant to see if her inclination to put her hands around the woman's throat was an overreaction. The twitching muscle in his cheek said not.

'Miss Evans, we know where your sister was going for a couple of days and we're pretty sure you knew too.'

Veronica began to shake her head.

'Don't insult us, Miss Evans. You knew everything about your sister's movements and plans. The two of you barely made a cup of tea without consulting the other. Please explain why you chose to withhold this information from us?'

If Veronica was surprised at her change in tone she didn't show it as she continued to monitor the actions of the cleaners.

Kim continued, determined to get her point across. 'You do realise that the harder you try to hide things from us the harder I'm going to dig. So, whatever you think—'

'I told her not to go and I don't see how it is any of your business, and I will tell you nothing that will help you drag up our past.'

'As the police officers investigating this case we'll make the call on what is our business, and as Belinda's only known relative you might want to be a bit more helpful in finding her killer.'

Kim was about ten seconds away from cuffing her for obstruction.

'You should be focussing on the sicko that lured her to the park to kill her instead of trying to rake up—'

'What exactly?' Kim asked.

'Nothing, Inspector. Please continue with your questions.'

'Why was she going to the event? What's her interest?'

'The same as always: to study. There is little more fascinating than the notion of an adult brain in a child's body. She went to observe, interact, understand. That's all I know,' she said as the tension entered her jaw.

She was and would remain unapologetic for hiding this knowledge from them and any explosion from Kim was unlikely to change that.

'Miss Evans, we've investigated your Skype call with the editor of the *Telegraph* and it appears to have ended much earlier than you told us.'

Veronica shrugged, unmoved.

'I said that all books and magazines could go,' she called out over Kim's head.

One of the cleaners hesitated with a pile of books in her arms.

'But the charity shops would—'

'Skip,' Veronica instructed, clearly wanting nothing of her sister left behind.

'Miss Evans, where exactly were you on Monday night between 10.30 and 11 o'clock?'

And finally, Veronica turned towards her, face set and unyielding.

'Detective Inspector Stone, you have not cautioned me, I have not been arrested and I refuse to answer that question. I would like you to leave now and if you refuse my request I will have no alternative but to make a formal complaint.'

'Veronica, what the hell are you hiding from us?' Kim asked, unable to hold her tongue.

The woman took out her mobile phone. 'Please get out of this house and leave us in peace, immediately,' she said, resolutely.

With no choice, Kim turned on her heel and headed out wondering why Veronica had used the word 'us'.

CHAPTER FORTY-NINE

Penn kept the woman waiting for a good twenty minutes before entering the room.

Both Lynne and Doug had tried to insist on accompanying him but he'd refused. Right now, he was at boiling point with the woman but she'd requested a private meeting and that's what she'd get. As well as a piece of his mind if she carried on messing them around.

'Mrs Nuryef,' he said, coolly, as he took a seat.

He had no papers, no folders and no notepads.

She looked to the tape recorder against the wall.

He shook his head. 'No point. Whatever you've got to tell me couldn't be used in any evidential capacity. Not a jury in the land would believe a word you've got to say,' he said honestly. 'And if you want honesty, I'm not sure I would either.'

After her performance the previous day and her changing story she could admit to anything and a jury would shake their heads and dismiss her every word.

'I lied,' she whispered, laying her hands on the table.

'Well, we know that, Mrs Nuryef. We're just trying to work out which time,' he said, coldly.

She nodded her understanding.

'I know you're angry because of what I said yesterday but I can't tell these lies any more.'

Penn regarded her objectively. She looked tired; her hair was back to its straggly state. She wore no make-up at all. But her physical appearance wasn't the biggest change. It was her eyes. For the first time, he saw fear.

'Go on, Irina,' he said. 'Tell me what you've come here to say.'

She wrung her hands and swallowed deeply. 'He was with me that night. My husband was definitely at home.'

Penn tried to keep the agitation out of his voice. 'Why are you saying this?'

'Because it's true. And people are dying. My neighbour...'

'Was murdered, Irina, and we don't even know why. But how can I believe you now?' he asked, frustrated. 'And how do you explain the tee shirt in the shed, which we found after you changed your statement?'

She shrugged and then bit down on a thumb nail.

'Aside from that, why did you lie about him being gone?'

Again, she shrugged. 'I don't know, I can't explain but I'm telling you the truth now.'

'How the hell am I supposed to believe you, Irina?' he asked, as the confusion mounted in his brain.

She fixed him with a stare that although full of fear was naked and sad.

'Because I swear it on my children's lives, that on the night of the murder my husband was at home with me.'

Penn sighed heavily and looked away.

God help him, he really believed her.

CHAPTER FIFTY

Stacey sat back and stretched her neck, suddenly aware that the tune being whistled was a different one.

'Got anything?' Stacey asked, mainly to shut the girl up. Please save me soon, boss, she silently prayed.

'Not a dickie bird other than Belinda's photo and bio on the college website, which isn't really a biography at all, it's very strange. I'm looking for birth records now as a starting point.'

Yes, that's exactly what she would have done.

'I mean I wouldn't expect to see them all over social media cos they're like, too old for that, but—'

'Hey,' Stacey said. 'Our victim may have appeared too old for many things but it didn't stop her doing them. Don't underestimate folks because of their age,' she warned, wondering when being taught to respect your victims had been missed from the training curriculum.

Tiffany smiled doubtfully. 'Okay, cool. Anyway, I can't even find anything in education, so whether or not they moved around a lot or…'

'Keep going,' Stacey advised, realising she probably preferred the show tunes.

But she had to admit that the lack of information on the sisters was indeed strange. In this day and age it was growing more and more difficult to avoid a digital footprint. Especially as archives were uploaded all the time.

Stacey almost felt there was a whole section of the internet they were missing. That the two sisters were hiding out in a dark corner of cyberspace.

But right now, she had the opposite problem to Tiffany. She had too much information.

If the boss was right and the murders were linked to the Brainbox event, there were a lot of people to investigate.

So far, she'd made two lists: the children and the staff and combined there were over three hundred names.

She'd pretty much exhausted the whole website but clicked on the last tab entitled 'Hall of Fame'. The page appeared to be a still photo taken at the final event each year: the quiz. The photo showed each team behind a panel bearing their first names opposite the other team with a quizmaster in between.

Stacey smiled at the change in fashions as she scrolled through the years but the format of the photo always stayed the same. The teams of three sitting primly, hands folded behind a nameplate.

Her finger paused above the mouse button as she scrolled past the last but one photo.

Her eyes widened as she looked more closely at the screen.

'No bloody way,' she said, reaching for the phone.

CHAPTER FIFTY-ONE

'I swear to God, for being insufferable, unyielding and stubborn that woman makes it to the top of my list,' Kim said as Bryant pulled out from the kerb.

'She's second on mine,' Bryant offered, as he pointed the car towards Dudley.

It wouldn't hurt to drop in on Keats to see if he'd found anything further during the post-mortem of Barry Nixon.

'You're not even a bit funny,' Kim snapped. 'I just want to wipe that bloody look off her face. I mean how quickly does she want her sister gone?'

'To be fair, she's never pretended they were best buddies.'

'But they spoke a dozen times every day, so there was some kind of connection.'

'Or control,' he offered.

Kim hesitated and turned to her colleague. Now and again his observations were insightful and relevant.

'Go on.'

'Well, so far, Veronica has shown no emotion for the loss of her sister, but she lived close by and they spoke all the time. Normally you'd think all this was because they were close, but Veronica could have maintained this proximity to make sure she had control of her sister.'

'Bryant, I'm not sure?...'

'Okay, when I was a kid we had to take it in turns to take home the school pets over the holiday period. My mum wouldn't hear of it. She didn't want what she called rodents in the house. I was twelve at the time—'

'Bryant, your retirement is growing closer,' she moaned.

'Well, I took one home anyway. This was before all the Health and Safety and permission slips for everything. Teachers took your word for it that your parents had said yes.'

Kim banged her head against the passenger window.

'Anyway, I sneaked Rupert the guinea pig into my room, thinking it'd be easy to just leave him there and feed him when I went to bed.'

'And?' Kim asked, with no idea where this was going.

'I couldn't sit still. Every time I went downstairs I pictured someone going into my room and finding him. He was my secret, so if I wasn't in my room I was hovering around close by so that Rupert didn't get discovered.'

'You think Veronica was staying close by to guard a secret?'

'Well, it certainly wasn't for sisterly affection. She won't breathe a word about their past, so there's something she doesn't want the world to know, and we've established that Belinda was given to impulsive behaviour, so maybe Veronica stayed close by to keep her under control. There's no way she didn't know where her sister was going, but why so important to hide it from us? She's made a non-thing into a big thing.'

'Wow, Bryant,' she said.

'Yeah, I know, my observations are insightful, perceptive, valuable and—'

'You tried to hide a guinea pig from your mum?'

He huffed and she was joking because there was a chance he had a point. But what the hell was she trying to hide?

'Bryant, I only have two questions. First, do you tell me these anecdotes to calm me down?'

Because, invariably they always did.

'Let's just say I prefer you angry when it's not just the two of us in an enclosed space. So, let's call it self-preservation.'

'And finally, what happened about Rupert?'

'I kept the secret for a week. Spent the whole time in my room and not out with my mates. Come Monday morning Mum asked if I wanted a lift to school with the cage and that she hoped I'd had a nice holiday.'

Kim laughed out loud. 'Bryant, I swear...'

She stopped speaking as her phone began to ring.

'Stace, tell me you've got something good to save me from Bryant's stories from when—'

Stacey interrupted her and she let her colleague speak as her eyes grew wide.

'Bloody hell, Stace,' she said, when the constable had finished. 'Good work.'

'What?' Bryant asked as they reached the hospital island.

'Turn the car around and take me back to Belinda's house, right now.'

'Why?' Bryant asked, doing a full drive around the traffic island.

'Because Stacey made my wish come true and we are now going back to wipe that smile off Veronica's face.'

CHAPTER FIFTY-TWO

Penn wasn't surprised to see DI Travis waiting for him when he stepped out of the interview room.

'Well?'

He could see the man's anxiety, which was coupled with hope.

Penn shook his head. 'Honestly, guv, I've got no clue what's going on here. She's now reverted back to her original story. Swears he was at home with her.'

Travis leaned back against the corridor wall as two constables walked between them. He waited until they were out of earshot before speaking.

'Why has she changed her mind?'

'Scared because of her neighbour's body turning up on the train tracks.'

'Which could be completely unrelated,' Travis said.

Penn nodded even though he felt neither of them believed it.

'What's your gut say? Is she telling the truth, this time?' Travis asked.

'She's definitely scared of something. Hands trembling, voice a bit shaky and swearing on her kids' lives. Not so cocky as the two times I've met with her before.'

'It's a bloody mess, Penn. A right bloody mess.'

'Yes, guv, it is and to move this on any further there's only one person I can go and see, and you're not going to like it one little bit.'

CHAPTER FIFTY-THREE

Kim strode back into the bungalow and met Veronica head-on in the hallway.

Her set expression hardened. 'Inspector, this is becoming tiresome and I really have too much work to do.'

Kim took out her warrant card and held it aloft.

'Police,' she shouted loudly. 'Coffee break, everyone. Now.'

The two operatives close by looked around questioningly.

'Out,' Kim shouted, and the room emptied.

For the first time Kim saw uncertainty in the woman's features.

'Why didn't you tell us the truth about Belinda? That she was a child prodigy herself? That she competed in one of the first ever Brainbox competitions?'

Veronica took a step back and placed a hand on the newly cleared sideboard.

'I'm sorry but I'm not sure how that information would help you.'

'Don't act stupid, Miss Evans, when we both know you're not. You knew she was going to this event and chose not to tell us, and now we find out just how close her connection to the event is. Belinda was a child genius, wasn't she?'

Veronica nodded as though not trusting herself to utter one syllable on the subject.

'You didn't want her to go?'

She shook her head.

'For goodness' sake, speak. We know your secret but why you've guarded it so closely I'll never understand.'

'She went every year she could manage, to remind herself, to keep the memory alive of being there with our parents. She also got a kick out of studying the kids, their behaviour, attitude, even believed she could project how they were going to turn out. She would talk with them, you see, question them. Try to understand them.'

'Why?' Kim asked, simply.

'So she could understand herself.'

'I don't get it,' Bryant said, 'She was educated, had a good job, was well presented, well adjusted…'

'You call this place well adjusted?' Veronica asked, waving her arms around at the mess. 'You think this is normal? When they died Belinda kept every possession our parents owned and surrounded herself with them. Every item had a memory for her. She wanted to recapture it all.'

Kim had been watching the woman as she spoke.

'What was it like having a genius sister?'

Veronica turned hard eyes upon her. 'Totally off-limits, Inspector, and no help to you at all. But what I can tell you is that no family is ever the same again.'

'Go on,' Kim urged. 'Tell me something that will help me understand how things changed when Belinda came along.'

Veronica thought for a moment before a sad smile settled on her face. 'There was a doll. My doll. She was nothing special, made of cloth with a cotton dress sewn on, painted facial features and a few strands of yellow wool for hair. A present from my parents when I was two.'

And what a detailed description that was for a toy given to her more than sixty years ago, Kim thought.

'Belinda had colic when she was a baby and the only thing that seemed to calm her was when I waved Jemima in front of her. She would watch as I danced the doll, scrunching up its face and waving its arms. It worked for everything. She loved it and whenever she was feeling poorly or sad she'd point to Jemima and smile at me. By the time Belinda started school my doll was named "Mima" and still settled my sister when she was unhappy.'

A brief nostalgic smile fleeted across her mouth before the lips hardened.

Kim found herself fearing the eventual fate of Jemima.

'Until one day when Belinda had earache. She didn't feel well and was easily distracted from the studies our father had set her. She cried out constantly for "Mima" while rubbing at her ear. She pointed to the toybox in the hallway and wouldn't concentrate on her work. Frustrated, my father removed it from view. I found it that night, ripped up and in the bin.'

Kim now began to understand the significance of Jemima and the story that Veronica had shared.

Just like her parents, Jemima had been all hers until Belinda came along and she had shared and then lost completely.

'This is why you said if Belinda had been born first they would never have had you?'

'Who wants average after they've had perfection?' Veronica snapped.

'And was she?' Kim asked. 'Perfection, I mean.'

The woman regarded her coolly. 'It doesn't matter how many times or how many different ways you ask the question, I'm not going to tell you every detail of our past.'

'Okay, just talk to me about Belinda. Tell me the effect her past had on her present.'

Veronica hesitated as though trying to decide whether to physically throw them out or humour them.

She sighed heavily.

'You ever have your parents come to your sports day, Inspector?' she asked.

'Every year,' Bryant answered for her. 'Bean bag race champion,' he added lightly.

Veronica's expression didn't change. 'And, did you see their faces when you won?'

Bryant nodded.

'I'm sure they looked delighted, proud, as though the sun shone from your very backside.'

'Suppose so.'

'It's a heady feeling. Addictive even. We all want our parents to be proud, and when you can do it every day with very little effort, why wouldn't you?'

'But?' Kim said, hearing the word 'but' in her voice.

'How amazed would you be to see a two-year-old performing complex multiplication sums?'

'I'd certainly be impressed,' Kim agreed.

'And a teenager?'

'Still pretty special.'

'A twenty-six-year-old Oxford graduate?'

'Less so,' she said, honestly.

'There's the problem with child geniuses, officer. Eventually they grow up and the shock factor wears away. The ability is no less unique or special, as few people can do it, but the interest is. It is no longer odd or freakish or even remotely interesting.'

'Your parents bored of her?'

'As did everyone else. Child geniuses are fascinating, adult ones are not. So, of course the attention dies away. The circus eventually leaves town.'

'But the need for attention remains,' Kim realised.

'Correct.'

'And how does that tend to manifest in… gifted children?' Kim asked.

'Drugs sometimes, alcohol others, the need for sex, validation, anything that brings attention and approval.'

'All of the above?'

'Occasionally,' Veronica answered.

'I'd imagine that such individuals may need close supervision, a safety net, possibly for most, if not all of their lives.'

'Yes, Inspector, some probably do.'

Kim wondered if she was beginning to understand this woman a little better.

'And you both changed your name to Evans?'

Veronica's face hardened to granite.

'If you know that then you really don't need me at all,' she said righting herself and moving away from the sideboard.

'So, yes, Inspector, now you have access to everything.'

CHAPTER FIFTY-FOUR

HM Prison Hewell was situated in the village of Tardebigge in Worcestershire and also helped to serve West Midlands and Warwickshire.

Housing mixed-category prisons, the place had seen the Tornado squads brought in in July 2017 to deal with a prison riot following the commencement of a phased smoking ban.

Penn recalled watching footage of the elite team of prison officers bring the commotion under control and thanked the Lord for his own career choice. A couple of failed exams and that might have been him, and given the rising violence recorded in every official report he still felt the police force was a safer bet.

He drummed his fingers on the table feeling as though he was doing something wrong. He had his temporary boss's permission to be here and yet he still expected someone to tap him on the shoulder for consorting with the enemy.

Ultimately, he was the arresting police officer of a murderer visiting that murderer during the course of the trial. Oh, absolutely no codes of practice being broken there.

It didn't matter that the murderer in question looked none too pleased to see him as the guard pointed him out.

'What the fuck you want?' he asked, sitting down. His Russian accent was slightly thicker than his wife's.

Although Penn noticed that he'd aged in the time since they'd last spoken. Faint lines had appeared at the corner of his eyes.

His ruddy, healthy outdoor complexion had been replaced with pale, sallow skin.

'How's it?—'

'Fuck you,' he said, and Penn had to move back slightly to avoid a few droplets of spittle that barrelled towards him like mini torpedoes.

Penn opened his mouth to speak but lost his chance.

'What you guys gonna fuck up today, eh? You got the wrong man and built your case on my lying wife and a fucking low-level street crim.'

Penn met his gaze. There was no avoiding the red-hot rage in his eyes. And that didn't bother him. He'd put away plenty of people who now fantasised about pulling him apart limb by limb like an insect. Pissing off criminals and bad people was his job. What he didn't like seeing reflected there was accusation: the silent allegation of being told he'd got it wrong.

'You fucked up, copper,' Gregor said, bitterly.

'Did we?' Penn asked, without batting an eyelid. He would expect a man charged with murder to say exactly that. But, that's what he was here to find out. He'd spoken to just about everyone else.

'Yeah, like you're gonna fucking listen to me now. You wouldn't listen to me back then, so why you interested now? You got your guy for the crime. Well you got *a* guy for the crime, so your stats and targets are all good; so who fucking cares if I actually killed that kid, right?'

'I do,' Penn said, honestly, talking little but listening hard and watching even harder.

The man had given up. He'd shouted his innocence for months and had now accepted his fate whether he was guilty or innocent.

'Give me something, Gregor,' he said.

The man opened his hands. 'What do you want? If I'd known this was gonna happen I'd have invited the whole street round to give me an alibi. It was a normal fucking night. Two knackered parents vegging out in front of the telly, barely speaking once the kids had gone to bed. I could hardly keep my eyes open. Normal night and there's only two people who can confirm that. One is dead and the other is a lying fucking—'

'She's changed her story again, Gregor,' Penn offered.

His busy mouth fell open. 'She's what?'

'Gone back to story A. Says you were with her the whole night.'

Words appeared to fail him.

'She's offered no further explanation and she seems scared of something, but to be honest we can't trust a word she says.'

His head fell forward as though he couldn't even be bothered to summon any hope.

'There's something else,' Penn said, knowing he was divulging too much but he had to see the man's reactions.

Gregor lifted his head.

'The eye witness testimony isn't as reliable as we thought.'

'How could it be?' he asked, incredulously. 'That fucking crim couldn't have seen me cos I wasn't bloody there.'

Penn chose not to divulge that Ricky Drake couldn't actually have seen anyone. That was one fuck-up too far on their part.

'But that brings me to the tee shirt, Gregor,' Penn said, heavily. They came back to that every time.

'Never seen it before,' he said, shaking his head.

'That doesn't wash, man. The victim's blood was found on an item of clothing in your shed.'

He took a deep, defeated breath. 'Don't matter how many different ways I try to say it. I swear to you that I didn't put it there.'

Penn combed his fingers through his hair. 'You gotta give me more than that. Look, I know you've got no reason to trust

me, but work with me here. Anybody else giving you a chance
to speak lately?'

Gregor regarded him for a full minute.

'You really serious about this? You really looking at this with
your eyes open this time?'

'It's why I'm here.'

'I got nothing that's gonna help you one way or another, but I'll
tell you the whole bloody truth and you make your own mind up.'

'Go on.'

'You find the tee shirt?' he asked.

Penn nodded. 'I did the outside search.'

'Where was it?'

'Back right, furthest corner from the door.'

'What did you have to move to get in?'

Penn thought back. 'Pair of stepladders, a couple of kids'
bikes, storage boxes.'

'All at the front, right?'

Penn thought. 'Yeah, up to about halfway and then it was
clear to the back.'

'I put everything at the front, mate. Either side of the door. I
stack it up and push it around from the doorway.'

Yeah, Penn could imagine that from what he'd seen.

'Like I said before, it's nothing you can use but I can tell you
that I didn't put that tee shirt right at the back of the shed there,
cos I never even step into the thing. Never.'

Penn shook his head, not understanding

'Spiders, man. I'm not just scared of 'em. I'm absolutely terrified of the little fuckers.'

CHAPTER FIFTY-FIVE

'So, what do you think Veronica meant by access to everything?' Bryant asked as he pulled up at a zebra crossing.

Yes, Kim had been thinking about what the woman had said right before they'd walked out the door. What exactly was there to have access to? Didn't they know it all now?

'Stace and Tinkerbell are on it right now,' she replied. 'But I'm more interested in what Freddie Compton has to say.'

'You ruling Veronica out then?'

'Oh, Bryant, when do I ever rule out anyone? She's just on the back burner for now. If an obvious link to our second victim comes in I'll put her back on the boil.'

'You try cooking something last night?' he asked, giving her a sideways glance. 'Only you tend to use food analogies when you've braved the kitchen again. Unsuccessful, I'm guessing.'

'My cooker hates me.'

'You're blaming your kitchen appliances?'

'Obviously,' she said as though it was a no-brainer.

She'd tried all manner of recipes, books, internet, YouTube videos and even kiddy cooking corner and as yet there had been no success. There was only one common denominator: her cooker.

'So, no, to repeat, I'm not ruling out Veronica Evans yet. But Stacey said that this guy, Freddie Compton, organised Brainboxes for twelve years before the Welmsleys took over, so will have seen both our victims at the events. He has to have some clue as to what they've got in common, but more importantly, Bryant, where the fuck are we?' she asked looking around.

'Wondered when your anxiety levels were gonna kick in,' Bryant smirked.

Oh yeah, they were firing up. There had been a lot of green land between Kidderminster and where they were now.

'We're in a village called Cleobury Mortimer and we're taking this left turn right here,' he said, negotiating a tight bend that turned into a steep climb immediately.

'This isn't a bloody road,' she moaned as the bramble on the passenger side hit her window.

The road continued to climb and then levelled before dropping slowly beyond a grey stone farmhouse.

'Why would anyone want to live here?' she asked.

Bryant pulled on to the drive beside a Land Rover and pointed. 'For that.'

'Oh,' she said.

The house was elevated above a steep, sloping garden that ran into a valley below. The house looked out over miles of countryside.

'That's Clee Hills in the distance,' Bryant offered as they got out of the car. 'Used to take the missus up there when we were dating.'

'You cheap bas—'

'It's romantic,' he said, shaking his head.

Kim shrugged and started walking to the door on the side of the house.

'Hear that?' Bryant said, tapping her on the arm.

'Hear what?' she asked, impatiently, as he stopped walking.

'The silence.'

Oh, he was right about that. They were in the middle of nowhere. They'd turned off a decent A-road, onto a narrow bumpy B-road, before hitting a single-track lane that had led to the hilly dirt road.

She couldn't remember seeing another car for miles.

'You really don't get it, do you?'

No, she really didn't. The property was rural, isolated and to her desolate. She drew comfort from the familiarity of town noise, even the late-night noise of occasional sirens, doors slamming, tellies blaring, loud music through open windows, drunks singing on the way home from the pub, wives giving them what for once they got there.

Her only interest in the countryside was tearing through it on the Ninja to blow the cobwebs from her mind.

'Come on, country boy,' she said, knocking on the heavy wooden door. The sudden sound cut through the heavy silence.

No answer.

She knocked again.

Nothing sounded on the other side of the door.

'Bryant…'

'Yeah, I know,' he said, already looking around.

Kim headed through a waist-high side gate that led on to an area of decking supported by stilts that disappeared into the sloping ground below.

A patio window looked out on to the decking but the curtains were drawn.

Kim tried the door. It was locked.

'Damn,' she said, continuing around the property, stepping off the decking back on to hard ground.

'Kitchen window,' Kim said, holding up her hands either side of her face and peering in. Bryant did the same.

The kitchen appeared in order but empty.

'He has to be here. His car's right…'

Bryant's words trailed away as a fly hit the window.

They looked at each other.

'Time of year, guv,' Bryant said, hopefully, while taking another look.

Another two flies hit the window on the inside.

'Okay, fair enough,' he said, heading back on to the decking. He carried on towards the side door where they'd originally knocked.

She picked up a wrought-iron chair and raised it above her head.

'Guv,' Bryant shouted just in time. 'Door's open.' Well, that had just saved a chunk of their budget for new glass if their man was alive and well and just sleeping heavily.

She joined him and immediately covered her nose.

'Jesus,' she said, breathing through her fingers. There was nothing sleeping heavily in here. It was a stench they both knew well.

It was the pungent, unholy smell that could only be compared to a room full of rotting meat with the added smell of faeces. It was an odour that could live in a house for years despite deep cleaning and was unmistakeable as anything other than a dead body.

They now knew there was no need to rush as they entered the property. She turned left into the kitchen where she'd seen the flies. Bryant turned right into a small reception room.

From inside she could now see the floor of the kitchen, which was clear.

She headed into the hallway. The property appeared to be a warren of small spaces.

The room to the left of the kitchen had the door closed. A quick look at the open doors revealed a downstairs toilet and a utility room. And no shout from Bryant told her what she needed to know.

'In here, Bryant,' she called out.

Bryant joined her in the hallway and nodded that he was ready for her to open the door.

She held down the handle and pushed it open. Both the buzzing and the stench directed them before they even entered the room.

Kim filled her lungs and stepped in.

'Oh my god,' Bryant said as their eyes met the sight before them.

Freddie Compton was sitting in an easy chair, wide eyes staring towards the curtained patio window, with a kitchen knife protruding from the middle of his chest.

His white shirt, once sodden, was now stiff with the blood that had poured from the wound over his stomach, rippling along the contours and folds of his shirt, onto his legs, and staining the chair beneath him.

Flies were entering and exiting his nostrils, his slightly open mouth, hovering and buzzing around his eyes, and maggots crawled over his shirt around the wound, which would have been their first choice destination once they'd located the dead body.

She tore her eyes away from the community that had made a home within what had once been a walking, talking human being.

'Seen what's on the table, guv.'

'I have indeed,' she replied, taking out her phone.

Sitting on the table was the board game of snakes and ladders.

Bryant walked around the chair.

'Can't see it but I'm guessing the X is on his neck, and I'd say he's been dead for four to five days.'

'Yes, Bryant,' she agreed. 'I'm willing to bet this was our guy's first kill.'

CHAPTER FIFTY-SIX

'Okay, Tiff, what you got?' Stacey asked, sitting back in her chair.

Since learning the real surname of the sisters was Loftus, having later both changed to their mother's maiden name, they had researched the internet and been working their way through the hundreds of hits.

'Okay, so Veronica was four years old when Belinda came along in 1957. Born to parents Alfred and Martha Loftus. He was a professor of economics, and she raised the children. All appeared normal until Belinda was six and Veronica was ten and both kids disappeared from the school register. They hadn't moved home, so it looks like they were home schooled. Not the done thing back then and, incidentally, Mr Loftus seemed to disappear from academia at around the same time.'

'He gave up his job to school his children?' Stacey asked.

'Looks like it.'

'So, how did the family survive?'

'Ah well, it appears that Mr Loftus liked to show off his daughters, particularly Belinda who was not only a gifted mathematician but could also name every city, town and village in the UK by the time she was six years old. Mr Loftus opened his house each Friday night for people to come and play with his children.'

Stacey felt the sour taste at the back of her throat.

'Play?'

'Test, ask questions and they got to pay for the privilege.'

'So, Belinda was a freak to be exhibited and extorted. And what was Veronica's gift?'

'Spelling and a bit of piano playing. But Belinda was the star attraction.'

Stacey couldn't help wondering how much fun those nights had been for the girls.

'Well done, Tiff, that's—'

'I'm not done yet,' she said, looking back at her notes.

Over the last couple of hours Stacey had found herself hoping that Tiffany wasn't going to be whisked away quite yet. Maybe at the end of the day but not right now.

'The play nights eventually turned into radio, theatre and television appearances. The more they did the more they were in demand. Spent some time touring Europe and a trip to New York in the early Seventies. Can't find much public exposure after that, but I've got the footage of the last TV show they did.'

'Pull it up,' Stacey said, wheeling her chair across the office.

She watched as the screen sprang into life.

The set was a typical chat show arrangement, with the host named Kenny Franks sitting to the left of a glass table and the family on the right. The two girls sat side by side with their parents on higher stools sitting behind.

Stacey was first struck by the appearance of the girls. She guessed that Belinda was around ten or eleven and Veronica fourteen or so. Both were dressed in the same floral printed dress with a bow on the left of their head. Short white ankle socks and flat ballet shoes completed the look. It was an outfit suited to Belinda's age but incongruous on the older girl.

Both were sat with their legs crossed at the ankles and their hands folded neatly in their laps.

Stacey found something fairly disturbing about the whole picture.

'Turn up the volume,' Stacey said as the camera zoomed in on Kenny the host who wore a smile as wide as the lapels on his check-patterned jacket.

'…and the secret to their success is study, study, study?' Kenny asked, looking over the girls' heads to the parents.

'Absolutely,' Mr Loftus answered without humour. 'If one has a gift it must be honed and practised.'

'But with some time for fun?' he asked, smiling at the girls.

'Of course,' Mr Loftus answered but didn't elaborate.

'And you lovely young ladies are going to demonstrate the results of all that hard work for us, aren't you?'

Both girls nodded as the audience clapped expectantly.

'Is this really entertainment?' Tiff whispered, as the host took a card from the hand of an otherwise invisible producer.

'Okay, we have a few pre-prepared maths questions here. So, we'll start with Belinda.'

Stacey noted that the girl's expression didn't change at all.

'Okay, first question of three. What is three thousand, two hundred and fifty-four multiplied by seven thousand, six hundred and ninety-three?'

'That's twenty-five million, thirty-three thousand and twenty-two,' she replied after blinking twice.

'Oh my goodness,' Tiff said, leaning forward.

Kenny laughed out loud and looked around. 'I can't believe it. She's absolutely right.'

The audience cheered and clapped. Belinda smiled in response, her parents beamed with pride but Veronica remained emotionless and still. It was no surprise to her that her sister had answered the question correctly.

Kenny leaned forward towards the girl.

'Did you see my card?'

She smiled and shook her head. 'I'm not a cheat, sir.'

'Okay, let's see if we can make it a bit harder this time.'

'I don't like this,' Tiffany said.

'And yet we're still watching,' Stacey observed.

'Okay, what is seventy-three thousand and six divided by seventeen and multiplied by one hundred and forty-three?'

Three blinks. 'It's 614,109.29,' she answered.

Kenny turned to the audience in amazement. 'She's right, folks.'

The audience thundered their applause.

'You are astounding, young lady,' he said as the applause died down.

'Are you ready for your final question?'

She swallowed and nodded.

Stacey found herself leaning forward.

'Okay, here goes. What is seven hundred and sixty-seven multiplied by one hundred and ten divided by eleven and multiplied by three hundred and sixteen?'

Four blinks. 'That's two million, four hundred and twenty-three, seven hundred and twenty… one.'

Kenny's face had been forming into wonder right up until that last digit.

He frowned, as the audience waited expectantly.

'Almost,' he said, with forced cheer.

The audience waited silently.

'You were one digit off. It's seven hundred and twenty, not seven hundred and twenty-one, but that's still pretty close,' he said, as the crowd began to clap without enthusiasm.

'Blimey, that was tense,' Tiff said, as the footage continued to play. 'I mean, one mistake and the crowd are—'

'Because anyone can get the sums wrong sometimes,' Stacey observed. 'What they want to see is someone who never gets it wrong. They now know she's fallible. Forget the two impossibly difficult questions she just got right that no adult in the audience could have answered. She got it wrong and it doesn't matter by how much.'

'But she's just…'

'Tiff, do me a favour. Replay it and turn off the sound,' Stacey said. 'Just that last question.'

It was easier to spot micro expressions without the distraction of sound.

Camera on Kenny asking the question.

'I missed one,' Stacey said as she counted five blinks. More blinks than the other two questions.

'One what?'

'Micro tics: watch her eyes as she's computing the maths problem. She blinks more times on the last question.'

'It was a harder question,' Tiff answered. 'More stages for her brain to work through.'

'And I could understand if her answer was way off but it was one digit out.'

'So, what are you?…'

'It's like she was working harder to get it wrong.'

Tiffany shook her head. 'I don't think so,' she said forwarding the footage and then pressing pause.

It was a close-up of the face of Mr Loftus following the incorrect answer. He looked flushed and murderous.

Tiff turned to her. 'If that was a possible consequence, would you purposely get it wrong?'

CHAPTER FIFTY-SEVEN

Keats and Mitch arrived within a minute of each other and spent a moment chatting outside the front door.

Take your time, guys, she thought. It wasn't as though they'd been waiting for almost an hour.

Squad cars had screamed their arrival after she'd called it in, but the surrounding countryside and wildlife appeared to be less than impressed.

There were no road closures, no road diversions, just a slip of cordon tape across the front door. Not one person had turned up to see what all the fuss was about.

One of the squad cars had been tasked with questioning neighbours, once they found them, and as they'd been gone for twenty minutes she wasn't feeling hopeful. This was not door-to-door questioning as she knew it. She suspected neighbourhood watch and CCTV were going to be a bust too.

Keats bustled past the two officers in the hallway with a nod and a half-smile. One of these days she'd get one of those half-smiles. It was something she aspired to.

'Glad to see you're suitably attired,' Keats said sarcastically, glancing down at her feet.

Today was not that day.

Normally, Bryant managed to produce blue protective slippers from the boot of his car.

'Was in a bit of a rush,' she said, glancing at the victim.

'Not sure your guy was going anywhere,' he said, following her gaze.

Damn it, she had no answer to that.

'Yeah, Bryant, why didn't you remind me?' she asked, nudging him.

'Okay, my bad,' he said, holding up his hands.

'You're forgiven,' Keats said, stepping closer to the body.

A swarm of flies lifted from the body like a flock of birds. Keats didn't bat an eyelid.

'Linked to your current case?' he asked, looking at the board game.

'Oh yeah,' she answered.

'And killed before the other two,' Keats observed, catching up with her.

He walked around to the back of the chair and used his pencil to move aside the collar of the shirt.

'He has the X but of course you already know that.'

She didn't bother to argue or lie. He knew her well enough.

'Ah, just the guy,' Kim said, as Mitch entered the room. He was placing his phone back into his pocket.

'Your guy moonlighting or something?' he asked.

'Sorry?'

'Penn wants to swing by and see me later. Nothing to do with this case, I assume?'

Kim shook her head. What could Penn get from Mitch that he couldn't get from the techies over at West Mercia? She made a note to catch up with him later.

Mitch looked around, then at the body and then at her. 'You going for some kind of award this week? Let's really give the techies the worst scenes we can find?'

'No pleasing some folks,' she said, moving closer to the table. 'That board game look new to you, Mitch?'

He took a good look and shrugged.

'Not a clue. It's certainly not old and worn, why?'

'I'm just thinking that not many middle-aged widows keep brand new board games around unless they're collectors, and I'm not seeing any others around here, and look,' she said, pointing. 'Two counters placed at the start position. Why?'

'Is that rhetorical?' he asked.

'Because the game wasn't the intention,' she answered. 'Our killer didn't want to play the game, so why bother?'

Silence.

'That wasn't rhetorical, guys, so I'm open to answers.'

'First victim was on a swing,' Bryant mused. 'Second on a hopscotch and third on a board game. Not sure what he wants if it's not to actually play.'

'Me either and that's what bothers me. I don't get the point of the games judging by this. It's set up but not played, why?' she asked again.

'To prove a point?' Bryant asked.

'To who? The victim or us?'

Her colleague shrugged.

'But,' she said, thinking aloud, 'if the game is as important as the murder, it has to be done right. Our guy couldn't assume there'd be a board game here to play. He had to have brought it,' she said looking around.

'Wait just one minute,' she said, heading back to the kitchen. Bryant was close behind.

'There's the box, guv,' he said, pointing to the kitchen table.

'It's not the box I'm after,' she said, lifting the lid of the swing bin.

'Aha, there you are. Mitch,' she called over Bryant's shoulder.

He entered the room slapping on gloves.

She pointed at the cellophane wrapper. 'You can't handle that stuff without leaving your prints all over it. It's a nightmare to get off. It's like opening a packet of biscuits.'

Mitch opened an evidence bag as he reached into the bin. He extracted the cellophane and held it up to the light.

He smiled in her direction.

'Yes, Inspector, I think we might just have something.'

CHAPTER FIFTY-EIGHT

'Okay, so I can find very little in the way of public performances after that date,' Stacey said, scrolling through the google hits.

'Belinda entered Oxford aged fifteen and completed the four-year mathematics degree in half the time. Whole family moved to the city so she could come home each night. Probably wanted her back at home to be a sock drawer. Not clear where Veronica was during this time,' Tiffany said.

'Back up. What's a sock drawer?' Stacey asked, feeling her eyebrows lift.

'Her dad probably wanted her to come home each night so he could use her free time to cram in even more facts and learning. It's like my sock drawer at home. However full it is I can get one more little sucker in there.'

Stacey laughed out loud.

'Anyway, from what I can find the girls remained living with their parents until they were in their thirties, when both parents died in a car crash. The day after the funeral they both changed their names to their mother's maiden name and disappeared from view until…'

Tiffany stopped speaking as Stacey's phone rang.

She pressed a button. 'Hands free, boss,' she advised.

'Got a third victim, Stace. Our previous Brainboxes organiser. Been dead for days.'

'First victim?' she asked as Tiffany listened intently from across the room.

'Yep, I've got his phone number but Mitch has the phone, so write this down.'

Stacey wrote down the mobile number the boss recited.

'Get into it, Stace. I want to know everything about him. Especially, I want to know why he stopped arranging the Brain-boxes event and handed it over. Does it have anything to do with Belinda Evans or Barry Nixon?'

'Okay, boss, and talking of Belinda…'

'Anything that can't wait until we get back?'

'No, boss but still digging and with this—'

'Well, leave Tink to carry on…'

'It's Tiff, boss,' Stacey said, feeling the heat rush into her cheeks at the boss's mistake.

'Yeah, I know that,' was the terse response.

'Boss, you're on hands-free,' she spelled out.

'Yeah, I know that too. What's the problem?'

'Nothing, see you in a bit,' she said, ending the call.

'Tiff, I'm sorry about—'

'About what?' she asked, brightly.

'The boss forgetting your name.'

For some reason, she felt bad for the girl.

'She didn't forget it, Stacey,' she said beaming. 'The boss just gave me a nickname.'

CHAPTER FIFTY-NINE

'Glad of the break, guv, but what's up? I thought you'd want to be away from here as soon as possible.'

He was right. Kim had taken them both by surprise when she'd told him to pull over once they reached the village of Cleobury Mortimer and she saw traces of human existence once more.

A tiny café with handwritten signs and two outside tables had beckoned to her. Right now she needed fresh coffee and fresh air. The stench of Freddie Compton's rotting body was imprinted on the membranes of her nostrils. She also needed a minute to think.

'Bryant, what do all the crime scenes have in common?'

'The victims were all dead,' he offered, smartly.

'That kind of response is not gonna get you a plant,' she said, breathing deeply through her nose.

'Well, obviously the connection to playing a game of some kind and the letter X on the back of the neck.'

'Yeah, about that, about the placement. What are your thoughts?'

He shrugged. 'Easy to get to.'

'Inflicted after death, so why would that matter?' she pondered. 'He's shoved a blade inside them, pretty intimate already. He wants them dead, so why does he care?'

'Maybe the neck is important. Maybe that part of the body means something to him.'

'And the clothing?' she persisted. 'Always in place, always correct, nothing showing. It's like...'

'Respect,' Bryant said, staring over her head.

'Precisely,' Kim agreed. 'It's like he hates them but respects them too.'

'When I was a kid…'

'Oh, Lord, now is not the time for one of your—'

'When I was a kid I only ever got one smack that I remember. Nothing bad, just a slap around the back of the head. My dad hated our next-door neighbour. Constantly borrowing his tools and not bringing them back for weeks. Dad always had to go and ask for them back. I was about ten when he came to the door and asked to borrow my dad's sander. I told him he could have it when he brought the cordless drill back.'

Kim chuckled. 'You cheeky little bugger.'

'Exactly,' Bryant said. 'That's why I got the slap. You didn't cheek your elders. You showed respect, regardless.'

'We're thinking the same thing, aren't we?' Kim asked. 'That the killer is a grown-up child genius.'

CHAPTER SIXTY

'You do realise Stacey would be much quicker at this?' Bryant asked, as he scrolled through Amazon.

'You don't think she has enough to do?' Kim asked, typing keywords into Wikipedia. 'A little research won't kill us.'

'Damn it, this screen is too small,' he said, hitting the wrong key again.

'Put your glasses on and stop being so bloody vain,' she muttered as the waitress approached to take their empty cups.

They had quickly realised that they knew absolutely nothing about child geniuses and really needed advice from someone that did.

'There's got to be a book here somewhere,' Bryant said. 'Amazon has a book for everything.'

Kim worried that without his glasses he was looking straight at it.

She opened her mouth to ask when a slow smile spread across his face. 'Got something. Self-published book by Doctor Gerald Kennedy entitled, *Child Prodigies – Where are they now?*

'Sounds exactly what we need.'

'Shall I order it on Prime?'

'Forget the book, Bryant, what I really want is the author.'

CHAPTER SIXTY-ONE

For the second time in one day Penn felt as though he was doing something wrong. Only this time he was.

Earlier he'd had the permission of Travis to visit Gregor Nuryef in prison despite it being highly irregular. But this time he did not have the guv's permission or even his knowledge. It was best that none of his colleagues knew what he was doing and could not be held accountable. Any shit would be his alone.

'Hey, Mitch,' he greeted, entering the techie's half lab next to the morgue.

'Yo,' he said, chewing on a chicken salad sandwich. 'Missed lunch,' he said, putting the rest of the sandwich back into the triangular packet.

'Thanks for seeing me,' Penn said, placing an evidence bag on the counter.

'Don't thank me yet. I don't even know what you want.'

'I've been—'

'I'm off, Mitch, I'll see you... oh, what do we have here?' Keats asked, coming into the room. 'Other than the most intelligent member of Detective Inspector Stone's team.'

'Sorry?' Penn asked.

'Well, I understand you've already hotfooted it back to West Mercia, so that's a lucky escape you...'

'It's temporary,' Penn said, laughing. As the pathologist was fully aware.

'Ah, not so intelligent, then?' he said, looking at the bag on the counter. 'What's this?'

'I was just about to find out,' Mitch said, taking another bite of his sandwich.

Realising that Keats wasn't moving he opened the evidence bag and laid out the tee shirt recovered from Gregor's garden shed.

They both looked down and then up at him questioningly.

'There's a man currently on trial for murder. The case is falling apart and this is the only concrete evidence left against him.'

'Your case?' Keats asked, peering over the top of his glasses.

Penn nodded.

'And all you want is the truth regardless of the consequences?'

'Absolutely,' he said, without hesitation.

Keats began to remove his jacket and glanced sideways at Mitch.

'Well, then, I suppose we'd better get to work.'

CHAPTER SIXTY-TWO

'Do remind me why I've just driven over ninety miles to Manchester when you've been reading the book on your phone the whole time?' Bryant asked. 'Surely you know it all by now.'

Stacey had worked her magic to track down the psychology professor through his social media channels and requested an urgent meeting. He had refused until Kim had taken the number, called him and offered a little more insight. He had agreed to meet them at five o'clock at Manchester University.

She had waited until Bryant had driven fifty miles before ringing Woody and letting him know their plans. Not much point instructing her to turn around when she was already halfway there.

Kim put down her phone and began to look around.

'Do you have any idea of the research that goes into writing a book like this?' she asked.

They were entering the sprawling university campus and moseying along Oxford Road looking for Christie's Bistro, wondering why he couldn't have named any one of the Starbucks they'd already passed as a meeting place.

'Errr… no, because I'm a police officer.'

'Allegedly,' she quipped. 'What's in the book is about one tenth of his knowledge. We need to be able to ask questions, and unless technology has moved on more than I thought we can't do that with the book.'

'You know, some days seem so much longer than others,' he said, spotting the café and pulling in.

How soon her team forgot that they'd only recently been moaning about being confined to eight-hour shifts and now here the two of them were at 5 p.m. two hours away from home and with no clear end to the day in sight. There was no pleasing some folks.

She stepped into the cavernous high-ceilinged room with statues, bookshelves and sofas. Oh yeah, a chain coffee shop this was not, she admitted, savouring the aroma of freshly ground coffee beans.

She spotted Gerald Kennedy from his author photo sitting in front of a wall of leather-clad books beneath a scholarly oil portrait.

'Double espresso for me,' she said as Bryant sidled up beside her.

He headed towards the counter, and she made towards the bearded man in the corner who looked a little older than his author photo. It was the beard, she realised. Tarry black on the photos but peppered with grey in real life.

'Mr Kennedy,' she said, offering her hand. 'DI Stone and that's my colleague DS Bryant over there. Thank you for agreeing to meet with us at short notice.'

'Not at all, officer. The effort was all yours. I'm where I normally am at this time of day,' he offered with a smile as he placed his book face down on the table. 'And I must admit to being intrigued as to how you think I can help.'

He listened silently as she laid out their case in more detail, along with their suspicions.

Bryant arrived and placed their drinks on the table. The two men nodded a silent greeting to each other.

'So, you think the killer is a former child genius who has some kind of grudge against all of these people?'

'Either that or someone who really doesn't like the Brainbox event,' Bryant offered.

'Which would be understandable,' she admitted, recalling Ted's description of the event.

'I've never been,' Gerald admitted.

'You haven't?' Kim asked, surprised. 'Surely someone with your interest in gifted kids is missing out on valuable research.'

'Aah, you misunderstand my interest,' he said, sipping his drink. 'My curiosity lies in their later years. Whether they were able to lead normal, fulfilled lives once the spotlight had gone, and I focussed on five very famous historic cases. Did you know that Buster Keaton was a kid in vaudeville? He was trained to show no emotion as his father threw him around the stage. He slept in a suitcase for the first few months of his life.

'And then there was Clara Schumann, a gifted piano player who didn't talk until she was older than five. Her father made a lot of money and even wrote her diary for her. When she left him to get married she had to sue to get any of the money. My curiosity was in finding out if these poor kids can ever adapt and live a normal life.'

'And?' Kim asked.

'I finally deduced that there is no clear answer. There are parents who stop viewing their child as a life that needs protecting and see them as a tool, an asset to earn money. These kids rarely recover from the need to please and perform. On the other hand, there are some parents that handle it differently. You may have heard of *The Children on the Hill*?'

Kim shook her head.

'It's a book about a whole family of overachievers in an environment secure from outside stimulation, the absence of pressure to achieve, but full of intellectual stimulation. Encouraged to make the most of each impulse or curiosity. By all accounts all the children grew up to be valuable members of society.'

'So, you blame the parents for any eventual psychological problems?'

'I don't blame anyone. As a parent, what are you supposed to do if your child exhibits signs of gifts beyond their age? Are you supposed to ignore it, hide it, stifle it? Does that help the child or should it be encouraged to fulfil its potential? To be all that it can be?'

'At what cost?' Kim asked.

'Does it matter?' he asked, clearly playing devil's advocate. 'These are future scientists and great minds—'

'Aah, not necessarily,' Kim said. 'Your book describes a woman called Winifred Stoner who raised her child to be a genius but she did nothing after her mother died. Gifted children don't necessarily grow up to be creative adults, and creative adults were not necessarily gifted children,' she said, paraphrasing the first couple of paragraphs.

The man laughed out loud. 'Thank you for quoting my own words back to me but I am presenting both sides of the argument, Inspector. This is not an easy subject to navigate and is neither black nor white. Take your comment about this Brainbox event. You are clearly opposed to its existence?'

'Doesn't exactly sound like fun,' she admitted. 'I wonder if these kids are missing the fun of childhood, that they're growing up too quickly just to satisfy adult fascination?'

'Okay, I'm going to be as objective as I can here and ask if you think they're missing out on your idea of a fun childhood?'

'Possibly,' Kim admitted.

'What was fun for you growing up?'

'Speedway and classic bikes,' she answered.

'Okay, how many kids in your class liked doing the same thing?'

'None, that I know of,' Kim admitted.

'My idea of fun was tree numbering.'

'Huh?' Bryant asked.

'I wanted to number every tree in the world, so I'd go out and carve a number into every tree I could find.'

'Yeah, that's weird,' Kim said.

'Absolutely, but guess what, none of my peers wanted to join me.'

'Shocking.'

'So, what is normal fun? I'm not even sure there is such a thing.'

'But they're always so serious,' Bryant said, cutting in. 'And I'm not being mean but some of these kids do seem to be quite annoying.'

'As are many children that are not gifted, officer. Children of superior intelligence aren't particularly annoying, but can I ask if you've ever been in a room where you think you know more than everyone else?'

Kim nodded as Bryant coughed.

'And have you told them so?'

'Frequently,' she joked. 'Well, not really.'

'Because over time you've learned tact and diplomacy. Many of these kids know they're the most intelligent person in the room but their social skills are not as developed as their intelligence. Their problems arise from the difficulty of fitting in with an average society. They often fantasise as it's difficult to find real companions of comparable mentality and interests.'

'Imaginary friends?'

'Sometimes. They have nothing in common with peers of the same age and not a lot with fellow prodigies, only a shared higher intelligence. Still doesn't mean they like the same things. They struggle to fit in while clearly standing out. A child prodigy is defined as a person under the age of ten who produces meaningful output in some domain to the levels of an adult expert performer. So, no pressure,' he said, finishing off the last of his drink.

Kim had a sudden thought. 'You think our murderer could be doing this to get attention?'

'I wouldn't rule it out, but in all honesty, officers, I'd be more interested in knowing what's caused your killer to go on this spree right now. If indeed he or she is a former child prodigy. I've seen no evidence to suggest that any kids wake up with the sudden need to kill.'

'You think we need to find the trigger?' Bryant asked.

'Listen, my research indicated that most former child prodigies who experience difficulties later in life often turn to drugs, alcohol, sex. They may seek attention in any way they can get it. Not being in the limelight any more can devalue some kids so they don't even know who they are. It's not unusual for some to benefit from a spell in...' his words trailed away as his expression turned thoughtful. He pulled on the end of his beard as he thought, forming it into a pointy triangle of dark, course hair.

'You know, there could be another reason for the sudden rush of murders.'

'Go on,' she said.

'If the murderer is indisposed, say in some kind of institution. It's not unheard of for gifted kids to experience mental health issues later in life. I cover one of them in my book. His name was Richie Taylor from Australia in the Fifties, had an absolute meltdown when he reached his late teens. Couldn't understand why the audience that had adored his violin- playing abilities since he was six were no longer all that interested. Spent almost five years institutionalised while coming to terms with normality, but if I recall there was another case, much more recent than my studies. From your neck of the woods if I remember correctly.'

He frowned harder as he tried to recall.

'Pretty sure her name was Beth something or other.'

CHAPTER SIXTY-THREE

'Hmm…' Keats said for the seventh time.

'I was thinking that,' Mitch said, turning the tee shirt another way.

Penn stood up and stretched his legs. He'd been sitting in the corner for over an hour and these forms of half communication had been passing between the two of them at regular intervals.

Both men had suggested he leave the garment with them, but he wasn't letting it out of his sight. The chain of evidence would be preserved even if it counted for nothing any more.

'How can you know what he was thinking from half a word?' he asked, standing beside the forensic technician.

'It's the value of the word,' he explained.

Both men were wearing latex gloves and were armed with rulers, notepads, pencils and a textbook.

'Explain it again,' Keats said. 'Tell us how it happened and use Mitch,' he continued, pushing him forward. 'And here's your knife.'

Penn took the ruler from the pathologist and moved to the other side of the metal table so that he and Mitch were facing each other.

'Okay, I'm Gregor and I come in to the shop. You're Dev Kapoor on the other side of the counter. I posture and ask for money. I probably tell you I've got a knife. You don't believe me and you're angry, so you step around the side of the counter. I reach for the knife and stab you right there,' Penn said. Thrusting the ruler at the exact spot.

'And freeze,' Keats shouted.

Both men stood totally still as Keats walked around them looking through and then over his glasses.

'Hmm…' he said.

'Exactly,' Mitch agreed.

'Guys, as I didn't bring my clairvoyant head with me you're going to have to…'

'You're sure of the wound point?'

He nodded. 'Oh yeah.'

'And the trajectory?'

He took another look. 'Yes.'

'And the length of the blade given the internal wound?'

'Yes,' he said, impatiently. He'd given them every bit of information he had.

'You've got yourself a bit of a problem here, my boy,' Keats said, taking off his glasses.

'How so?' he asked, feeling the dread rise in his stomach.

He watched as Mitch went back to the tee shirt and frowned, but it was Keats who was speaking.

'That's not how it happened.'

'It has to be,' Penn said.

'You're not arguing with me, you're arguing with science and I can tell you categorically that the blood spatter marks don't match.'

'Jesus,' he said, running his hand through his curly hair. More doubt was not what he needed right now.

'Hmm…' Mitch said from beside him.

'What now?' he asked.

'I'm afraid that's not your only problem.'

CHAPTER SIXTY-FOUR

It was almost eight when Kim and Bryant found themselves knocking at the door of Beth Nixon whose social media channels were conspicuous in their absence. A woman in her late twenties with a total of eleven friends on her closed FB account and no other kind of online footprint was more unusual than unheard of.

Beth answered the door wearing a grey leisure suit that was neither day wear nor bed wear. It was just plain comfortable. Her blonde hair hung loosely around her shoulders and her face was pale and devoid of make-up. Had it only been yesterday they'd been here to tell this woman her husband was dead?

'Officers?'

'Do you mind if we come in?' Kim asked.

'Please, I'm in the kitchen,' she said, pointing the way.

Kim walked through the silent house.

'We just wanted to see if there was anything further you'd remembered,' Kim said.

'That I wouldn't have contacted you about if I had?' she asked, offering a wry smile.

Kim said nothing but sat down at the kitchen table. Bryant followed suit.

The small TV on a corner wall bracket was on but there was no sound. The whole house was steeped in an eerie silence as though it was waiting for something.

Beth followed her gaze. 'I don't watch it after the news,' she said, reaching for the remote. 'I'd rather read a book but the picture gives a bit of movement to the room.'

Kim nodded her understanding. It was a substitute for the lack of activity in the house around her.

'You don't have family that could be with you?'

'No, I have Lenora but after a while she can be… well, you met her. I think you can understand. Katie has come home but is staying with Lenora.'

'You don't get on?'

'We get on for Barry's sake but her coming here without him would be strange. Her own grief is too overwhelming for her to consider mine.'

'No family of your own?' Kim pushed. Katie was Barry's family. Lenora was Barry's family. Inherited by this woman. Not her own.

She shook her head. 'I have a brother but we haven't spoken in years. Now, how may I help you?'

'We're just re-questioning anyone close to the victims.'

'You have no idea who murdered my husband, do you?' she asked, perceptively.

'We have leads that we're following up,' Kim offered.

Despite what she'd said, this wasn't the reason for their visit.

'I don't want to be rude, but why are you here?' she asked, switching off the television completely.

'Mrs Nixon, did you and your husband originally meet at the Brainbox event, when you were a child?'

'I was fourteen,' she said, defensively, offering no reaction to the fact that Kim had mentioned the event for gifted children.

Kim held up her hands. 'There's no judgement here,' she said. Well not on your part, she thought to herself. The ethics of your husband are a different matter entirely.

'I can read that look on your face,' the woman said, folding her arms. 'And I know you don't understand.'

'So, help me,' Kim said, not bothering to lie. 'Help me understand how an intelligent, gifted teenager fell in love...'

'I didn't fall in love with him when I was fourteen, at least I wouldn't call it that. I clicked with him and if he did with me he made no sign of it. I know how he made me feel and it stuck with me.'

'And how was that?' Kim asked, wondering if they were moving into grooming territory. 'How did he make you feel?'

'He got me, totally and completely. He listened. He let me talk and he understood how I was feeling; my fears, my insecurities, my sudden bursts of anger, my hatred of—'

'Bursts of anger?' Kim asked, feeling a chill whisper up her spine.

'My childhood was not normal, Inspector. From the moment I was able to name every country on a world map an hour after looking at it. I was three years old. I was pushed, I was prodded, I was tested, I was taken out of school and isolated and I was forced to study almost every hour I was awake and guess what, sometimes it pissed me off.'

'And Barry helped you understand your feelings?' she asked.

'He did but he did more than that. He talked to me about other stuff. We talked about music, books, art. He wanted to talk to me the person and not me the genius. I always remembered it because no one else had ever made me feel that way. That I actually mattered.'

Bryant leaned forward. 'Did he contact you later?'

Beth shook her head as her arms lowered. 'No, I contacted him. It was after a particularly difficult period in my life and I reached out to him. He was grieving the loss of his wife but we met up and talked and that was when I fell in love with him. I hated the event, Inspector, but it was how I originally met the love of my life and I make no apologies for it.'

'You hated it because?'

'I was forced to do it once and there may have been kids there that enjoyed it, but not me. I'm not a natural competitor, so didn't relish being set against children who may have felt as lonely as I did.'

'But you had a brother?' Kim said, remembering her mention of him earlier.

'We were kept separate,' she admitted. 'He wasn't gifted. I envied him. He didn't have to perform and maintain expectations,' she spat.

'Is that what caused you to have some trouble a few years ago?' Kim asked.

She frowned and then realisation dawned on her. 'Oh, you mean my time away?'

Kim nodded.

'May I ask why that's relevant to the death of my husband?' she asked.

'When he's been brutally murdered everything is kind of relevant,' Kim said, not unkindly.

'It was a mixture of things, officer. Suddenly found myself in my early twenties dealing with the fact I had no friends, no hobbies and no job when a family tragedy occurred. All came at once and I needed some time out.'

'Understandable,' Kim agreed.

'I was institutionalised for seven months and it was the best decision I ever made. During that time I reinvented myself and came out as Beth the grown adult and not Beth the freak.' She tipped her head to the side. 'And now you've asked the question you came here for, may I ask a question of my own?'

'You can ask,' Kim said, standing. The woman was right. She had wanted to know what had prompted her stay at a mental health facility.

'The body of a male found in Cleobury earlier today. Is it Freddie Compton?'

'I can't answer that,' Kim said. Officers were still trying to locate next of kin.

'If it was, that would make all three victims linked to the Brainbox event in some way or another?'

'If it was, then yes, that would be a fair assessment, why?'

'It just makes me wonder what the devil are you doing here and not there?'

CHAPTER SIXTY-FIVE

'Okay, folks, where are we?' Kim asked, entering the squad room.

She'd sent Bryant on ahead to catch the team up with what they'd learned about Beth Nixon while she'd briefed Woody and given him her unconventional request. After a frown and a few questions, he'd agreed and made a phone call.

She'd share with the team later.

In her absence Bryant had brewed fresh coffee and poured her a mug.

She raised it in a salute to him and perched her bottom on Penn's empty desk.

Stacey proceeded to update her on what they'd discovered so far about the sisters. Kim drank as she listened.

'Good work, Stace,' Kim said.

'It was mainly Tiff, to be fair.'

'Well done, Tink, show me the clip.'

Tiffany loaded it, and Kim stood behind. She watched it three times with the sound on.

'Turn the sound off and go frame by frame.'

Stacey's smile told her the constable had done the exact same thing.

Kim pulled Penn's chair across the room and watched again. No one spoke.

First question. Belinda's face remained composed, relaxed but focussed. Kim could almost see the movements of her eyelids reflecting the workings of her brain.

Second question. Same response.

Third question. The blinking began before the question was even asked. Glazed eyes as her mind wrestled with the calculation.

'I think you're right. I think she answered that question wrong on purpose, and you're dead right about Dad's expression too, but there's something else,' she said, scooting closer to the computer screen.

'Watch Veronica's face this time,' Kim said, once everyone was gathered around.

'Look, see that slight lift at the corners of her mouth,' she said. 'She's pleased but also triumphant.'

Everyone nodded their agreement.

'What the hell happened to these two girls?' Kim asked, moving back to Penn's desk.

'Spent a lot of time just the four of them,' Tiffany offered. 'No friends, no boyfriends…'

'Although Belinda certainly made up in later life,' Stacey remarked, glancing at her notes. 'She's on plenty of dating sites under the name of Linda Loftus.'

'Sounds a bit porny,' Tiffany said, screwing up her nose.

'Okay, what do we know about Freddie Compton?'

Kim still wanted to know more about the sisters but it's relevance to finding the murderer was now questionable in her mind.

'He's fifty-eight years old, no kids but ran the Brainboxes event for twelve years from 2004 to 2016 when his wife was diagnosed with cancer. He was a primary school teacher who had attended the event with one of his pupils the year before he took over. Never made a lot of money out of it and took early retirement to care for his wife.'

'Enemies?' Kim asked without any real hope.

Stacey shook her head. 'Not so far.'

She growled in frustration, as she sipped the last of her drink.

'So, we're all agreed that whatever it is that links them is gonna be found at Brainboxes?'

Bryant nodded as Stacey answered an internal call, but Tiffany obviously felt too uninformed to offer her opinion.

'Okay,' Kim said, looking at her watch. 'Go home, pack an overnight bag.'

'That was Inspector Plant,' Stacey said. 'On his way with the statements from the cricket club and Belinda's neighbours.'

'It'll have to wait,' Kim said. 'We need to get to the venue and see what all this is about. Be back here in one hour,' she said, grabbing her jacket and heading out the room.

She paused and put her head back around the door in case her instruction had not been clear. 'And that includes you too, Tinkerbell.'

CHAPTER SIXTY-SIX

Penn stifled a yawn as he continued to watch the two men at work.

'Sorry if we're keeping you up while we help you out on an unrelated case from another force in our own time,' Keats said, missing nothing.

'I'm eternally grateful for your help, guys. It's just been a long day,' he said, wishing he could do more than sit and watch.

So far, he'd made coffee, phoned home to check on Jasper and his mum and paced the windowless room trying to make sense of what he'd learned.

They'd explained much about the advances made in blood spatter technology.

'Don't thank us too soon, Penn. I'm afraid we have more bad news.'

Shit, how was this day going to get any worse?

So far he'd watched as the two of them analysed the colour, shape and size of the bloodstains as well as discuss, in detail, something called fluid mechanics. They'd given attention to the angle of impact in order to determine the blood's origin and the amount of force behind it.

'Check HemoSpat again,' Keats advised as Mitch headed to the computer.

'Hemowhat?' Penn asked.

'Blood spatter analysis software. We finally agree with each other, so it's time to see if technology agrees with us.'

'It does,' Mitch said, turning around on the swivel chair.

'Oh dear,' Keats said, as Mitch came to join him at the workbench.

'Tell me,' Penn said, standing.

'The blood on this tee shirt didn't land on the fabric with any force from a violent incident, which is why we can't make any blood spatter pattern fit.'

'I don't get it,' Penn said, moving to stand beside them.

Mitch turned the garment inside out. 'The blood doesn't even go through the material. It didn't land on the tee shirt; it was smeared on there by a human hand.'

CHAPTER SIXTY-SEVEN

'You sure this is a good idea?' Bryant asked, throwing the bags into the back of the car.

Tiffany was chattering excitedly to Stacey as they got into the rear passenger seats.

Kim found it hard to believe that only a few years separated the two women; demonstrated not least by the luggage Bryant was now loading. Tiffany's backpack was covered in gaudy, bright yellow sunflowers that glowed up from the darkness of the boot.

'It'll be good to get away,' she said, slapping him on the back.

He groaned as he closed the boot and then got into the front of the car.

'Buckle up, kiddies,' he called over his shoulder.

Stacey groaned as she pulled her seat belt across her body.

Despite what she'd said to Bryant this was the last place Kim wanted to be. Right now she would have preferred to be working in her garage on the bike with Barney lying in the corner watching her.

The thought of her dog brought a pang of guilt.

She'd rushed home, put a few bits and pieces in a hold-all and then hotfooted it to Charlie's house down the road.

She'd spent half an hour walking Barney, five minutes feeding him and ten minutes silently explaining why she had to leave him at Charlie's for an overnight stay. During the last few minutes of her explanation he'd spotted the squirrel in the tree at the bottom of the garden and left her to it.

She swore that if a dog could roll its eyes Barney would be doing it twenty times a day.

Charlie had been overjoyed at keeping Barney overnight. She'd made him promise that the dog was not allowed on the bed, and she knew how long that would last.

But she also knew they needed to be at that hotel. She was sure their murderer was there and who knew who else was on his hit list.

'Feeling a bit like Hugh Hefner right now,' Bryant said, with a smirk.

'Who's that?' Tiffany asked.

The smirk disappeared. 'I don't like her any more, guv,' he said loudly.

'Don't worry about it,' Kim said to Tiff over her shoulder. 'After more than five years he still doesn't like me.'

Tiffany laughed nervously. 'I always seem to say the wrong thing. My school report always had a big tick for effort but—'

'Shush, Tink,' Kim said as something snapped in her brain.

'Sorry, I know I talk a lot.'

'That was a good shush,' Kim explained.

She turned in her seat and looked around at all three passengers.

'We've been looking at the markings on the victims' necks as an X, like the letter, wondering what it means.'

'But it is an X,' Stacey said, frowning at her.

'Yes, Stace, but it's also a cross, as opposed to a tick. He's trying to tell them, or us, that these people did something wrong.'

CHAPTER SIXTY-EIGHT

Kim opened the door to the room at two minutes past ten and nodded approvingly. The hotel was booked solid because of the event, but Woody had managed to pull some strings and the result was a two-bedroom suite with a dining area that looked out on to a small fishing lake.

'Woody did good,' Bryant observed stepping in behind her.

'Okay, just throw the stuff in for now. Restaurant closes in fifteen minutes, so get down there if you want to eat.'

'You coming?' Bryant asked.

'Yeah, be there in a bit. Get me a sandwich or something.'

He nodded and headed out with the others. She wanted to take a look around without standing out amongst a group of four adults.

The Village Hotel complex was a sprawling maze with a central driveway that cut through a car park at the front. The rooms sat to the left and the rest of the facilities were to the right with a large communal reception, bar and café separating the two halves.

She understood that the hotel had three conference rooms, a banquet hall, gym, swimming facilities and an extensive play area for kids they'd driven by on the way in.

She passed by the double doors to the restaurant and headed through the reception area which was full of parents and children sitting around the tables: just as you would expect for such an event. Books and notepads covered the tables as most appeared to be cramming in extra study in the downtime. The absence of laughter and noise amongst so many children was unsettling.

She frowned and continued her journey through to the conference facilities.

The first room she entered had three clear areas for music. A piano, a violin and a flute. A judging table sat at the top of the room with three chairs behind.

Double doors adjoined to the next room, which was set out with chessboards, again with the single table at the top of the room.

The third room, across the hall, held the same three seats and judging table with a small raised podium in front of the window. She was guessing it was for spelling or questions.

The final room was the banquet hall, which she was surprised to see wasn't empty.

Half the space was filled with seating: desks and easy chairs. The other half had already been set out for the main event the following night: the quiz that would crown one of the children Brainbox of the year.

A group of twenty parents or so were gathered, unspeaking, in a semicircle at the centre of the room.

Kim took a few steps closer and saw the reason.

A colourful clown was performing to a seated audience of about thirteen kids who all looked too old to be entertained by such an act.

She watched as the clown pulled a line of flags from his sleeve and then pretended to fall over.

'Coco the crap,' shouted one of the boys, Kim guessed to be about ten years old.

Nice, Kim thought. Not that the kid was wrong but she would have hoped for better manners.

Clearly, the organisers' attempt to inject some light-hearted humour and play into the event was not a particularly popular attraction with the kids.

With the lay of the land noted in her head she returned through the reception, which had quieted even more as families had obviously retired to their rooms. By her watch it was approaching half ten.

The restaurant was almost empty but she was pleased to see her team putting Woody's food budget to good use.

A chicken sandwich with a salad garnish had been placed before the empty seat.

She sat down and sipped the coffee that was lukewarm.

'So?' Bryant asked, spearing a forkful of tomato-covered pasta. 'Find our killer yet?'

'Eerily devoid of cheer for a kids' event,' she replied, ignoring Bryant's question. 'Makes *Mastermind* look like a blast.'

'Hey, it's a tough life for us child genius types,' Bryant offered, causing Tiffany to almost choke on her food.

'What the hell is that?' Kim asked, glancing at her plate.

'Fish-finger sandwich,' Tiff said, licking her fingers.

'Hang on, more importantly why was that so funny?' Bryant asked the constable.

She remained silent and took another bite of her sandwich.

Stacey offered no reaction as she read something on her mobile phone. Her fish and chips appeared to have been rearranged instead of eaten.

'You okay, Stace?'

'Yeah, boss,' she said, switching off her phone. She took a bite of the fish and then pushed away the plate.

Clearly, she was not, Kim noted and resolved to watch her closely.

She took a look around the almost-deserted restaurant. A dark-haired woman in her late thirties sat alone, reading a book with a half-finished dessert bowl on the table in front of her. In between turning the pages her right hand seemed to stroke her right cheek.

The only other customers in the room were a couple poring over paperwork. The woman's gaze also went occasionally to the lone female too, Kim noted.

'Stace, is that?…'

'Yep, that's the Welmsleys. Jared and Serena, the organisers.'

Kim stood at the exact second that Serena did. It was immediately clear that the woman was skeletal, but that wasn't what got her attention. It was the look in her eyes as she glanced again at the single female reading a book. Jared Welmsley placed a hand on her forearm, but she shook it off and headed across the room.

Kim sat back down and watched with interest.

The single woman did not look up until Serena Welmsley was right in front of her. No smile passed between them as Serena began to speak. The single woman's expression appeared controlled, tolerant. She tipped her head slightly as Serena appeared to get more animated, her head bobbing to and fro and her hands moving in front of her.

Kim wished she could hear the conversation as Serena placed both hands on the table and leaned towards the woman whose face had taken on a wariness at the proximity change.

Serena finished speaking and seemed to wait for a response. And the response was that the woman picked up her book and continued reading.

Kim instantly liked her style despite the tension in her jaw as the other woman walked away.

'What was all that about?' Bryant asked.

She hadn't realised he'd been watching too.

'Not sure, Bryant, but I'd sure like to find out.'

She watched as the Welmsleys drew their heads together and whispered even though there was no one anywhere near them. Even from a distance it was annoying. Furtive glances towards the bookworm told Kim they were still discussing the woman and the one-sided exchange that had just taken place.

After a minute or two they resumed their analysis of the paperwork, and Kim stood again.

Bryant looked up at her.

'Well, now seems like the perfect time to go and introduce myself.'

CHAPTER SIXTY-NINE

'Detective Inspector Stone,' Kim said, showing her badge and taking a seat.

'Pleased to meet you,' they said, together, offering her a smile that was spooky in its similarity.

Kim knew that there were some couples who had been together so long they even took on each other's characteristics.

'I assume you've heard about the murders of Belinda Evans, Barry Nixon?—'

'Terrible business,' said Serena shaking her head.

'Terrible,' Jared answered, looking down.

'And Freddie Compton, who was found—'

'Freddie's dead too?' Serena asked with wide eyes.

His name had been revealed on the nine o'clock news, but this couple had clearly been too busy with the event to notice.

'And was he?...'

Her words trailed away as she seemed unable to say the word.

Kim nodded. 'Yes, he was murdered,' she confirmed. 'Did you know any of them well?'

Both nodded but it was Serena who spoke, showing Kim that she was definitely the dominant one in this relationship.

'We knew them all. Probably Freddie the best and I can't believe he's... he's...'

'Dead,' Kim finished for her. Her limited empathy muscle was just not flexing for these two at all.

'You knew all of them but you've only been organising the event for?...'

'Oh, we've never missed a year, Inspector. Not since it started up again in 1995. We were both here that year.'

'Both?' she asked.

'Oh yes, Jared here was a chess champion and I liked to play the violin.'

'A bit modest, Serena,' Jared chastised, with a smile. 'She was world class,' he said, proudly.

There was a flash of regret in the woman's eyes as Kim joined the dots.

'You're siblings?' she asked.

'Twins,' they answered together.

And close ones at that, Kim thought, as they turned to each other and smiled.

'Quite the event you run here,' Kim said.

'It's fabulous,' Serena said, joyfully. 'A great opportunity to bring exceptional young talents together from around the country.'

'Highly competitive environment, though?' Kim asked, cutting short the sales pitch.

'No more than your usual school sports day, Inspector. Many of our attendees are not physically gifted but still welcome the opportunity to compete.'

Kim had to agree that sounded logical enough and yet there was still something that left a sour taste in her mouth.

'Okay, let me explain it another way,' Serena continued. 'The children that come here don't fit in anywhere. In a normal school environment, their intelligence is far superior to almost everyone around them, including the teachers. They become isolated by their own brilliance, usually bullied and ostracised through jealousy or just because they're different. Coming here gives them the opportunity to see that they're not alone, that there are others just like them and that their gifts are to be celebrated and not hidden.'

Again, Kim had to concede the point.

'But the intensity of the competition, the passion of the parents?' she questioned, recalling all the bent heads she'd passed in the café area during her walk around.

'Have you been to a kiddie's football game recently, officer?'

Kim shook her head.

'You should. It's brutal. Competitive parents shouting from the sidelines, insulting other children, the referee, other parents. It's no different, except for the shouting of course. We don't allow that but the children look forward to coming, to mixing amongst their peers. Just to have a couple of days not feeling like freaks or oddities.'

Kim got it but would have been happier had they been meeting up in the woods for hiking, climbing and good old-fashioned fun amongst friends, not intense competition.

'That's why we didn't cancel the event this year. The children needed to come together and—'

'You considered cancelling because of the murders?' Kim asked, which was something she could finally understand.

Serena shook her head. 'No, because of the tragic death of the Robinson boy.'

Kim frowned. 'Sorry?'

Serena appeared surprised that she didn't know.

'The Robinson family are the stars of our event.'

'And?' Kim asked, leaning in closer.

'Last week, their twelve-year-old son tragically died.'

CHAPTER SEVENTY

'Okay, folks, what we got?' Kim asked, entering the hotel room.

The team had been busy taping photographs to the wall and filling the flip charts with facts and dates while she'd been talking to Serena.

Afterwards she had taken a few minutes to wander the deserted corridors in search of the single woman she'd seen earlier who had disappeared by the time she'd finished her conversation with Jared and Serena, although Jared had barely spoken at all.

But throughout the building lights had been lowered and doors locked as everyone had turned in for the night.

The scene that had taken place between the two women was still fresh in her mind and she wanted to get to the bottom of it.

'Thanks for doing the flip charts, Tink,' Kim said, pushing her behind onto the table to look at them.

'Hey, 'Bryant protested. 'It might have been me.'

'Last I heard you didn't put little circles above your I's instead of dots,' Kim noted, looking from one board to the other. All events were recorded and the timeline was striking. Less than a week and three people were dead.

The professor's words were still circling in her mind. 'But what's the trigger?' she asked, folding her arms and staring hard. 'What the hell has caused this murder spree?'

In the silence of no responses Woody's warning sounded in her head. It was almost midnight and her team would keep going as long as she did.

'Stace, make a note of the name Stevie Robinson, a twelve-year-old boy from Evesham who died last week.'

There was a second of silence before Stacey wrote down the name and then turned to her computer. The death of a child never went unacknowledged.

'Tomorrow, Stace,' Kim said. 'It's late and I'm pretty sure Woody would have my guts for garters if he could see us right now. Time to get some rest, but seriously, great work today folks,' she acknowledged, as they began to move around the room.

'Stace, got a sec?' Kim asked as Tiff headed for one room and Bryant for the other.

'Yeah, boss.'

Kim waited for a few seconds. 'You okay?'

'Sure, boss, why?'

'Quiet, not eating. It's been a long day and you've worked…'

'I'm not stressed, boss,' Stacey said, offering her a tired smile.

'You wouldn't necessarily know, though. It can just sneak up without you knowing it.'

'Honest, boss, I'm not stressed. I'm absolutely fine, just a bit tired now but I'm good, I swear,' she said, moving towards the bedroom she was going to share with Tiff.

'If there's anything you want to talk about, you know I'm here, right?'

'Course. But I'm right as rain, I swear.'

Kim wished her good night gaining no comfort from her colleague's reassurances at all.

Stacey was clearly lying to her and she had no idea why.

CHAPTER SEVENTY-ONE

Penn crawled into bed at 2 a.m. and despite the fatigue weighing down his bones he knew he would get little sleep tonight. And he sought it desperately, not least to escape from the thoughts running around his head.

After the revelations from Keats and Mitch his brain had switched to overdrive. Long gone were his fears about having made a mistake and as the SIO he'd have to wear it. That wasn't what was keeping him awake.

Mitch had told him that he wanted to run some further tests overnight and would get back to him in the morning. He had debated for just a minute leaving the evidence in the care of the technician but he now knew the garment held nothing they could use. All he wanted now was the truth.

Exhausted, he had agreed, left the lab and come home to a quiet, empty house. He had looked in on his mother who was sleeping soundly to the soft, background noise of talk radio, her night time companion.

Jasper had been sprawled across his bed, a carefree pile of limbs and torso illuminated by his astronomy lamp that turned and reflected stars and planets on the walls and the ceiling.

Penn had watched him for a few seconds. One moment unflinching and unreactive to the occasional sudden, jerky movements from his strewn limbs.

He'd touched his brother gently on the head before quietly leaving the room.

These were his constants, his family. He was part of a team that, while welcoming and friendly, did not yet hold the long-term familiarity he'd known at West Mercia.

His old team should have felt more familiar, more like home, yet in truth he couldn't wait to get back to where he now felt he belonged.

Things had changed in his old team but he wasn't sure what. There was a guardedness from his former colleagues that had not been present before.

It was like they all knew he didn't fit any more but were doing their best to ignore it.

Despite the sadness it brought him, that wasn't the thought that was going to keep him up all night.

CHAPTER SEVENTY-TWO

'Everyone sleep well?' Kim asked, as they sat down to breakfast. It had taken almost fifteen minutes to get a table for four. Seemed everyone in the hotel had decided to eat at the exact same time. Hell, even the damn clown was chowing down on a plate of bacon and eggs.

'Like a log,' Tiff said, sipping her orange juice.

Bryant and Stacey shot daggers her way.

'What?'

'Tink, you snore,' Kim said. 'Like loud.'

'Very,' added Stacey who had shared a room with her.

Even Bryant had stepped out of his room carrying a pillow.

'A bit extreme,' she'd said at 4 a.m., from her spot on the sofa, visualising him placing it over the young constable's face.

'Damn, you've got my spot,' he'd said, hoping the extra few feet distance would lessen the sound. It didn't, Kim assured him before he turned and trundled off back to bed.

Although, it wasn't Tiffany's snoring that had kept her awake. It was her mind drawing invisible lines between everyone they'd met so far this week. Eventually she'd felt as though her head might explode.

Kim took a moment while her team ordered food to take a good look around the restaurant, full to capacity, but three sweeps of the space told her that the woman who had been dining alone the previous night was nowhere to be found. It was as though she'd simply disappeared. She'd witnessed hostility between the woman and Serena Welmsley and she wanted to know why.

'Okay, so here's the plan,' Kim said, once the waiter had left the table. 'Bryant and I will be walking around asking questions and I want you two to dig a bit deeper on Beth Nixon. I want to know if that was her only stay in an institution, and I want anything that happened for the year prior to that stay. There was some kind of family tragedy that she didn't want to talk about.'

'Okay, boss, we'll—'

'As well as that I want you to find out more about this Robinson family who recently lost their son. I don't think there's any connection but the timing stinks, so I want to rule it out.'

'No probs, I'll—'

'And once you're done on that I want you to identify the years all three of our victims attended this event and which kids came into contact with all three of them. Then look at any ex-contestants who are on the attendees' list in any capacity: parents, volunteers, judges, everyone,' Kim said, realising the volume of work she'd just thrown their way.

'You think he's here, don't you?' Tiffany asked, in a small voice, as though the idea of being in the same venue as a mass killer had only just dawned on her.

'Absolutely,' Kim said. 'Where else would he be, given our victims?' she asked.

No one argued but all three turned and looked around as though they could spot him right here in the breakfast room.

'Folks, he ain't wearing a bloody sign,' she said, with amusement.

'Could be a she,' Tiff offered.

'We never rule it out, Tink,' Kim explained. 'Trust me, we've come across our fair share of lady killers but for ease of reference we use the term "he".'

'Don't female killers tend to use poison?' she asked, finishing her second cup of tea.

'So the true crime books say, but of the female killers we've dealt with not one of them used that method,' Bryant answered.

'But keep whistling those show tunes, Tiff,' Stacey said. 'And I'll certainly consider it.'

They all chuckled as Stacey looked pointedly at Tiff's tea cup.

The smile was wiped swiftly from Kim's face as a figure she knew well appeared in the doorway.

'Okay, guys, what the hell is she doing here?'

CHAPTER SEVENTY-THREE

'You almost ready, bud?' Penn asked his brother as he took the final bite of his toast.

Always the same. Once slice, half with just butter and half with strawberry jam.

'Remind me why I pay for breakfast club?' he asked.

'Dunno,' Jasper said, rubbing his hands together furiously to despatch the crumbs from his fingers.

Jasper had been in mainstream school for five years now and loved every minute of it.

Initially Penn had been terrified of the taunts and bullying his brother would be subjected to, had wanted to protect him from the ugliness that existed in the world to people who were different.

One day Penn had asked his brother if he got bullied and called names. Jasper had nodded and told him some of the taunts.

Penn's rage had travelled around his body. He had kept his face neutral as his brother spoke but in his mind he was already heading down to that school and demanding action from the teachers or he'd pull him out of school completely. His mind had been set. His brother was not going to be forced to endure the torture of being singled out.

'Billy gets picked on cos of his limp. Sarah gets picked on cos her eyebrows are thick. Misty gets picked on cos her parents are vidorced.'

'Divorced,' Penn corrected.

''Swat I said. You know what Billy says to do with bullies?'

'What?' Penn asked.

Jasper had covered his mouth and laughed as though he was going to say something naughty.

'Go on,' Penn had urged.

'Kick 'em in the nuts.'

His brother had waited to see if he was going to be chastised, but Penn had burst out laughing, feeling all of the tension drain from his body. He'd never loved his brother, or Billy, more.

'Go on, then. Go brush your teeth,' Penn said, looking at his watch.

He heard the familiar sounds of his brother as he cleared away the breakfast dishes, placing the half slice of jam-laden toast on to a square of kitchen roll.

He heard the farewells between his brother and mother, who rarely made it down for breakfast any more.

He waited at the front door holding the backpack in one hand and the toast in the other.

As Jasper squirmed into his backpack, Penn ruffled his hair.

'Have a good day, bud.'

Jasper reached up and did the same to him. 'You too.'

Penn laughed and handed him the toast.

When his brother had first asked for the freedom of meeting his friends at the end of the road, he'd been both terrified and proud.

Unbeknown to Jasper he'd followed him for the first few mornings. He'd expected to see him munching on his jammy piece of toast as he walked, but he'd seen him meet his friends and hand the toast to his best friend, Billy.

Billy came from a family with seven brothers and sisters and very rarely got breakfast.

Most folks could learn a lot from his brother, he thought, closing the door.

With the welcome distraction of his brother gone, his thoughts turned to the day ahead, a prospect he didn't relish one little bit.

CHAPTER SEVENTY-FOUR

Kim watched the woman's every move and only when she was sitting with a coffee at a recently vacated single table did Kim stride over.

'How lovely to see you, Veronica,' Kim said, taking the empty seat. 'But what the hell are you doing here?'

'Curious,' she said, offering no emotional reaction at all to either Kim's tone or her question. 'Wanted to see what had fascinated Belinda for all these years,' she said, looking around the room. 'Wondering why she'd keep returning to this environment.'

Kim opened her mouth to speak and then paused. There was so much she wanted to know but for a split second she'd just heard a sadness in the woman's voice that she hadn't heard before. And it had found its way to somewhere inside her.

How had this woman's life turned her into the woman she was now?

'Veronica, what the hell happened to you back then?' she asked, gently.

'Nothing I care to share, Inspector,' she answered, holding tight to the barriers she'd erected around herself. Barriers that Kim herself recognised and understood, but there was something inside this woman that wanted to come out.

'Who is it going to hurt now? There's no one left. Tell me your side.'

Veronica met her gaze. 'You don't get it, do you? I don't have a side. It wasn't about me. It was all about my sister. Everything. Always.'

'Okay, tell me about Belinda. What was her childhood like? Leave yourself out.'

Although judging from the TV footage they'd seen, Veronica hadn't been left out at all.

She took a sip of her drink and Kim was surprised to see a slight tremble to her hand. All the anger and hostility towards the woman fell away. There was a human in there somewhere no matter how hard she tried to hide it. And she had suffered; somehow Kim had always sensed that.

'I was four when Belinda was born. I was pretty average and normal and definitely old enough to hear my parents tell everyone how Belinda did "everything before Veronica did". She spoke earlier; she walked earlier; she spelled her first word earlier. It was clear to everyone that she was clever. I remember her first day of school. My father collected me from class first and held my hand as we walked to Belinda's class.

'The teacher started talking to him about the extraordinary mathematical ability she'd demonstrated in just one day. She showed him the sums she'd completed, and I always remember that he dropped my hand to listen.'

The sad smile returned as she relived the memory. Kim wondered at the symbolism of that one small act for it to have remained a memory for over sixty years.

'I watched him that night when we got home. I sat on the sofa and watched him testing her and quizzing her. My mother watched too, clapping her hands in delight when my father turned the calculator to show that Belinda was getting the answers right.'

The story was about the younger girl, but Kim's attention was on the girl sitting on the sofa, watching.

'Eventually, Belinda got bored and turned back to her toys. Our parents went to the kitchen and talked privately. But that was the day everything changed. From then on, my father tested her every night.'

'Is that when Jemima was thrown out?' Kim asked.

Veronica nodded, looking surprised that she'd remembered.

'Eventually he started going to the school to see how her education was being handled. He wanted her to advance through the years more quickly, but the school couldn't oblige.'

'Why not?' Kim asked, as she realised the room was emptying around them.

'Because she lacked in other areas, Inspector. Her English was below average and her ability to retain other subjects was poor at best.'

'Really?' Kim asked, surprised. She'd assumed a child genius excelled at every subject.

'My father didn't believe them; felt they were holding her back. So, he took us out of school and gave up his job to teach us. He devised a curriculum whereby he could hone her mathematical ability and work her hard to catch up in other areas. I just learned whatever he was teaching Belinda.'

'Why did your father take you out of school?' Kim asked, not unkindly.

'Because by this time my father believed Belinda's gift was genetic and that I just wasn't trying hard enough. I was lazy. Anyway, he began reading about the father of Maria Agnesi.'

Kim shook her head.

'Maria Agnesi was born in the eighteenth century. She was a walking polyglot and spoke seven languages fluently by the time she was thirteen. She also excelled in mathematics and philosophy. Her younger sister was a musical prodigy, and her father arranged entertainment evenings.'

Jesus, Kim thought. It seemed he'd done more than study Agnesi. From what they'd learned of the sisters' childhood her father had pretty much modelled himself on the man.

'Some believe that prodigious talent arises from innate talent of the child. And some believe the environment plays the dominant role. My father decided to leave nothing to chance. At first my mother tried to object but eventually he just overruled her.'

'And how was that, the home learning?'

'My father turned the dining room into a classroom: two desks, a blackboard, shelves full of books, pictures replaced with world maps and periodic tables. All stimulus was removed and if we were caught looking out the window the blind was drawn.'

'But, how was it?' Kim asked, again. She could now picture it but she wasn't interested in the décor of the room.

'Probably took me longer to adjust. I'd been at school for a few years and had friends.'

There was no bitterness in her tone, just acceptance.

'And the one good thing about school, Inspector, is that it ends at a certain time every day.'

'He worked you hard?' Kim asked.

'Oh yes, and took away other toys as encouragement or punishment, whichever way you want to look at it.'

'That's harsh,' Kim said, remembering something from the post-mortem.

'Any physical incentives?' she asked.

'I'm guessing you already know that or you wouldn't ask,' she said.

'A ruler edge across the knuckles?'

'And the back of the head,' Veronica said, touching the nape of her neck. 'The first time he did it was because I'd made Belinda laugh with a funny face while he was out the room and she couldn't stop giggling once he returned. It was one of those fits that the more you try to stop the more you laugh. She couldn't stop, and he rapped her knuckles with the ruler in frustration and that then became the focus tool, if you like, but that's not what I remember the most about that first time.'

Kim waited.

'It was my mother standing in the doorway. I looked at her hopefully, sure she would say or do something, and for a moment I thought she was going to, but she turned and walked away.'

'He sounds like a monster to be honest,' Kim observed.

Veronica shook her head. 'He wasn't. He was never the most loving father but this gift of Belinda's compelled him to make the most of it, to explore and hone it. I'm not saying he was perfect but he wasn't a monster.'

Loyal even now, Kim observed, despite the fact that his actions had shaped the lives of both sisters.

Kim tried to imagine what it had been like for Veronica, taken form a normal school environment, away from friends, play and interaction to the cloistered, solitary existence created by her father.

'He tried so hard to mould us despite the fact that studies indicate that prodigiousness in childhood is not a strong indicator of later success. Child prodigies rarely grow into adult geniuses. There's a window of time during which it's interesting.'

'I saw the television show,' Kim said. 'Where the two—'

'Oh, I know which one, Inspector,' she said, as a multitude of emotions ran over her features. It was as though every inner feeling that had been missing all week was thrown at her face all at the same time.

'Is that why you've blocked us at every turn and kept secrets? Is that what you didn't want us to find?' Kim asked.

'It's one of the things,' she admitted. 'But mainly because it was the worst time of our lives, a time when we were treated like freaks and oddities, judged and analysed. Public scrutiny and attention are not something I want. I've built a semblance of a life and my past is a place I choose not to visit.'

Kim could easily understand that. It was how she lived her life too.

'How did your father react when Belinda got the question wrong?' Kim asked, recalling the tightness of his features in the footage.

'If you want to hear about that it's going to cost you,' Veronica said.

'What?' Kim asked, prepared to offer her house, her bike, in fact anything except her dog. She'd been wanting to hear more all week.

'At the very least, another coffee,' she said, glancing down at the empty cup.

'Is the TV show significant?' Kim asked, rising from her chair.

'Yes, Inspector, because that's when everything changed.'

CHAPTER SEVENTY-FIVE

Bryant had already decided on his target and stood when the Welmsleys finished breakfast and left the table. He tried to give the guv the nod but she seemed oblivious to anyone other than Veronica Evans, who perversely, seemed to be doing all the talking. He tried to pretend that his dislike of her was not because the woman had warmed to the guv more than to him, which almost never happened. Although he realised that the term 'warmed to' was about as loose as it could get.

But his attention was now on the woman in charge of the event. He'd found the guv's account of her conversation with the twins intriguing and wanted to hear more.

He followed the woman into the chess room, where she met up with her brother to the side of the judging table as the three judges chatted amongst themselves.

A few whispers of 'excuse me' prompted him to move along from the doorway. Although nothing was happening yet, it was as though everyone had been switched to library mode, taking heed of the 'Quiet Please' printed signs scattered around the wall.

Bryant watched as parents took seats around the edges of the room with their children. There was a stiff politeness, brief smiles or nods but then eyes would be averted. He got the feeling that real friendship amongst parents of like-minded children were not formed here.

Jared Welmsley handed a sheet of paper to the nearest judge and left the room.

Serena came to stand beside him. 'Chess fan, officer?'

They hadn't yet been introduced but he guessed she'd seen him sitting with the guv.

'Bryant,' he said, offering his hand. 'And not so much with the chess, exactly, but…'

'With the whole phenomenon of child genius?'

Although he hated to admit it, he nodded as the judge began to call out names.

'Quarter finals,' she explained as boys and girls began to take their seats.

'It'll be too quiet to talk in here, want to take a walk?'

'Of course,' he said and followed her out the door.

She turned to him as they reached the corridor. 'So what is it particularly that intrigues you, officer?' she asked, pleasantly.

'I suppose I just find this level of intelligence in children voyeuristically compelling. I don't want to use the obvious words or come off as offensive, but big brains in little bodies is unsettling for want of a better word.'

'So given your obvious interest, did you know that scientific studies have shown that the brains of child prodigies are different from ordinary brains?'

Bryant shook his head as they came to the open doorway of the music room.

'Gifted children come in all types: musicians, acrobats, artists, chess players, mathematicians, computer programmers, even magicians. We can't cater for everything here but we like to think we do okay.'

Bryant could tell she was proud of the event they'd organised. He wasn't sure if she was fishing for compliments.

'Are all the parents of gifted children pushy?' he asked. He'd half watched a programme years ago on Channel Five about pushy parents and had found himself getting annoyed at their single-minded focus on the child's gift as opposed to just the child.

She shook her head. 'Terence Tao from Australia was doing maths and reading by the age of three. By the time he was six he had taught himself BASIC and written several computer games. His parents didn't want to take credit or make money, so they managed a schedule where he could still be a little boy. He started high school at seven, and his IQ was measured at 220 against the average of 100. He scored 760 out of 800 on his SATs and passed the university entrance exam when he was eight.'

'Blimey, that's some skill.'

'It sure is but he was never pushed by his parents and is now a well-adjusted, married man with a career.'

'But is he the exception?' Bryant asked.

'But are pushy parents really so bad?' she countered.

'I suppose we all see our own childhoods as somewhat normal. My parents just wanted me to be happy. They didn't raise me to be competitive. Just to do my best.'

'I understand that and please don't take this offensively because I'm sure you do a great job as a police officer but...'

'But I'm never going to change the world,' he added for her.

'Let me put it another way. In the 1940s and '50s there were quiz kids taking part in game shows. One of them, James D. Watson, was a joint Nobel prize winner for the discovery of the structure of DNA. But to reassure you I can confirm that not every parent is a tiger,' she said, with a smile.

Bryant shook his head. He'd heard the term but wasn't entirely sure what it meant.

'It's a largely Chinese concept and depicts strict, demanding parents who push and pressure their children to be successful. Like a stage mother. They prioritise learning above all else and only allow children to participate in activities to potentially win awards. They exert a higher level of psychological control over children and tend to use emotional threats and low-impact physical punishment. They don't allow the child any decision-making freedom and ignore soft skills like socialisation, dealing with people, emotional intelligence, if you like.'

'But what happens to these kids long term?' Bryant asked. 'Surely every childhood should be balanced,' he insisted.

'Studies show they lose a sense of belonging, purpose and self-esteem. In China, there's a growing trend of children aged five to twelve seeking psychiatric help and even contemplating suicide.'

How the hell could a five-year old have such feelings? he wondered.

'They have no coping strategies. Can't manage negative feelings. Do you remember Shirley Temple?' Serena asked, moving along the corridor as a child started playing the piano.

Bryant nodded. Everyone knew of the child actress.

'Her appeal was in being a natural and that she completely enjoyed herself. No work involved and the well-constructed image that she got to enjoy a normal childhood. Except her daily regime began at seven and ended at five thirty. One critic noted something rude and rowdy about her, despite the mission of all around to keep her unspoiled.

'She had her own three-bed bungalow on the studio lot, a daily tutor, personal bodyguard, medical advisers, a system of relaxation but not movies in case they tainted her style.'

'Surely, you don't think?…'

'I'm trying to explain that pushy parents exist everywhere, officer, and always have. It's not limited to the domain of gifted children. Your average sports day will include parents pushing their kids over the line. Parents sending drunken emails to teachers and headmasters trying to control their time at school.'

'Isn't there a famous book about this tiger parenting thing?' Bryant asked, realising that's where he'd heard the term.

'Oh yes, Amy Chua's shocking account of goading her two daughters to virtuoso extremes.'

'You seem to know a great deal about this tiger parenting,' Bryant observed.

'Yes, both Jared and I were raised using the authoritarian method and look how well we turned out.'

Yes, quite, Bryant thought as he followed her along the hallway.

CHAPTER SEVENTY-SIX

'How many are you down to?' Stacey asked, across the hotel dining table. She had already identified the years that their first two victims had been present, and all ten years had fallen within the timeline that Freddie Compton had been organising it. Tiff had been trying to cross-reference kids that had come into contact with all three of them.

'There're ninety-six,' Tiff answered. 'At least.'

'Jesus,' Stacey said.

'Problem is, there's no record for the children that Belinda might have spoken to because she wasn't at the event in any professional capacity and could have had contact with the whole lot of them. Incidentally, over the ten years all three of them were present we're talking more than three hundred kids.'

'We need a team of ten to get through this lot,' Stacey noted.

'And Freddie Compton doesn't help us because as the organiser he would have come into contact with every single one of them. So, the only record we can use to narrow them down is Barry Nixon's record of children he counselled while he was here.'

'But that doesn't mean he didn't come into contact with other kids that were here,' Stacey said, seeing Tiff's logic but realistically every single kid who had attended during that ten-year period was a suspect. 'We're gonna have to try and work through them all.'

'Tell me about it,' Tiff said. 'I was hopeful about one guy who made no secret about hating this event but now works over in Akademgorodok.'

'Come again?'

'City of the gifted in Russia. It's where thousands of scientists and gifted students live and work. My guy teaches at a special boarding school for maths and physics.'

'Never heard of it,' Stacey said.

'Neither had I but the thought of the place just makes me shudder.'

'Why?' Stacey asked, smiling as the girl scrunched up her face and raised her shoulders.

'Dunno, just thinking about all these pushy parents trying to mould kids into academic superstars.'

'You don't think parents should encourage their child to fulfil their potential?'

'Wow, Stacey, that sounds awfully normal and understated and I'm not sure encourage is the correct term for some of the stories I've been reading about so far. I mean, we're talking hardcore focus to the exclusion of all else and I just think it's plain wrong.'

Oh, the black and white world of your early twenties, Stacey thought, remembering it well. The grey areas of life came a few years later.

'I understand that,' Stacey agreed, determined to make her point. 'But when you get a new smartphone what's the first thing you do?'

'Load social media and emails.'

'Next.'

'Choose a ringtone.'

'Next.'

'Check out the camera.'

'Next.'

'Fill it with apps.'

'So, you test it? See what it can do? Explore its capabilities?'

'Well, yeah but that's natural, isn't it?'

'It's absolutely natural to want to get the best out of it.'

'But where does it end?' Tiff asked. 'For people who want a gifted child and don't get one. Do they turn to eugenics?'

Stacey was well aware of the science of producing the finest offspring by selective breeding or genetic manipulation.

'You're taking the argument in a completely different direction,' Stacey said, enjoying the company of this Tiff more than the previous one. This one had an opinion and wasn't afraid to use it.

'Not really, because it's already happening. There was a Repository for Germinal Choice in California where mothers could have themselves artificially inseminated from a panel of Nobel prize winners. Already there's the expectation of greatness before the child is born and if it's not a genius there's instant disappointment. Not sure what that does to a kid.'

'But back to my phone analogy, it's advances in science that mean you can take photos play games and install a thousand apps.'

'But just because we can doesn't mean we should,' Tiff argued back.

'So, what do you want parents of gifted kids to do?' Stacey asked.

'I just want every child to have a childhood, to be a kid.'

Black and white.

'Fair enough. So, next smartphone you get, disable every function other than the ability to make calls.'

'Good point but just one problem.'

'Which is?'

'I'm not gonna irrevocably damage the psyche of my phone for the rest of its life by downloading a game of *Pet Rescue*.'

Stacey stared at her for a full twenty seconds before bursting into laughter.

'Good answer, Tiff. Good answer,' she said, turning back to her own screen. 'Now, give me just a few minutes to conclude that there's absolutely nothing interesting to find about Beth Nixon and I'll jump on to those names with you,' she said, resuming her search.

So far she'd established that Beth had been brought to the event just one time from her home in Lancashire by her maternal grandmother, who had taken on both Beth and her half-brother when their mother had died of a brain tumour. Beth had been five and her brother nineteen months. During the event the fourteen-year-old had taken two counselling sessions with Barry Nixon, her future husband, and Stacey didn't care how the woman had spun it to her boss and Bryant, that was just plain wrong in her eyes.

She had worked forward slowly through the woman's education and reached the point at which she'd voluntarily signed herself into Meadow View Psychiatric Hospital up north for a rest two months before graduating university with a physics degree. She wondered just how far she was supposed to dig to find anything more about the woman that was remotely interesting.

She sighed and glanced at her overwhelmed colleague.

'Pass me some of those names, Tiff,' she said, holding out her hand.

Beth Nixon was just going to have to wait.

CHAPTER SEVENTY-SEVEN

Penn was just a mile from the station when his phone rang.

He indicated and pulled on to an empty car park.

'Hey,' he said, answering the call.

'Hey, yourself, officer,' Mitch said in response. 'Thought you'd want to know as early as possible the results of those extra tests I ran.'

'Thanks, Mitch,' he said, not even sure what the techie had been looking for. 'So, what did you find?'

'Absolutely bugger all,' he said.

'Oh,' Penn replied, pretty sure that wasn't going to tell him much.

'Yeah, how weird is that?' Mitch asked.

'Mitch, I'm not sure…'

'I took samples from various parts of the tee shirt. As you well know we're shedding and collecting DNA all day and the majority of it lands on our clothes, but this garment is as clean as a whistle. Absolutely zilch.'

'So, what exactly are you're saying?'

'That in my opinion this tee-shirt has never been worn at all.'

CHAPTER SEVENTY-EIGHT

By the time two fresh coffees arrived the restaurant had emptied.

'So, the TV show?' Kim prompted, having paid the required toll fee for the information.

'Inspector, do you realise that you can love and hate a person at the same time?'

'Your father?' Kim asked.

'That would have been so easy, wouldn't it? But no.'

'Go on,' Kim said.

'Until I was four years old I was enough. My achievements were neither remarkable nor delayed. I was average, I was normal. I was enough. But Belinda changed all that. Belinda's brilliance changed all our lives. My father was convinced that with enough work, enough hours studying that I could be just as brilliant.

'Every day for years we were dressed the same like two little performing dolls. We woke to exist in our tiny world of just each other and study. It was an existence not a life. We were set against each other for our father's approval and even affection. Belinda craved it even more than I did. The attention was like a drug to her. She couldn't get enough. At night, we would crawl into our beds exhausted and silent, unable to bond like normal siblings as we were each other's competition.'

She shook her head as her mind travelled back to that time.

Kim remained silent.

'After the TV show my father retreated from us both completely. Belinda had proven she was human. Just one mistake and she was tarnished. Life didn't change regarding the study but my father employed a private tutor. Belinda couldn't cope with my father's withdrawal. She had monopolised his attention since she was four years old. But he wasn't interested any more. He had cancelled our trip to the Olympiad and—'

'The Olympiad?'

'The International Mathematical Olympiad, where 100 countries send 6 students. They have to solve six problems without calculators. Belinda didn't want to go anyway, but after my father withdrew his attention and affection she tried all the harder to get it back. But nothing worked. After what he saw as a very public humiliation he became indifferent. And she never stopped trying to win him back. The more she tried the more he retreated.

'When her two degrees failed to impress him she turned to more negative forms of attention.'

'Sex?' Kim asked.

'And drugs in her twenties and thirties. She needed the attention whether positive or negative; it was all she'd ever known, and she couldn't exist without it.'

'But what about you?' Kim asked. 'Was there no point at which you could break free?'

'I tried. I moved away for a few months before our parents died. With no one to give her the attention she needed she relapsed back on to the drugs. I was called to the hospital when she almost overdosed and that's when I knew I couldn't leave her again.'

'You were there to protect her from herself?'

Veronica nodded. 'I tried to.'

'And you hated her coming here, to this event?'

'In case it just brought it all back and she relapsed again.'

Kim finally began to understand better the relationship that had existed between the two of them.

Living that cloistered life had forged bonds between the sisters that only they would understand, despite being set against each other on a daily basis by their own father who had dressed them up and then paraded them and exhibited them for money and fame.

Kim could finally understand the complex web of bitterness and love that had bound the sisters for ever.

'Being a child genius is hard, Inspector, but being a sibling is no picnic either. We both lost our childhoods in one way or another.'

Kim could imagine.

'But did you have to give up your own life to protect hers?'

Veronica thought for a moment, then nodded. 'Yes, because it was all my fault.'

'The TV show?' Kim asked, remembering the expressions of the girls. 'The question that ultimately changed everything?'

Veronica nodded.

'She got it wrong on purpose?'

Veronica nodded again.

'But why?'

When the words came they were no more than a whisper.

'Because I told her to.'

CHAPTER SEVENTY-NINE

Penn was not surprised to see Travis waiting for him outside the police station.

He'd called ahead to let the boss know they needed to talk. Travis would want to hear what he had to say at the earliest opportunity.

'Your face does not look like it's about to give me good news,' Travis said, biting on his lower lip.

Penn decided there was no way to dress this one up for his ex-boss who could feel no worse about it than he did himself.

'There's no doubt in my mind, guv. Gregor Nuryef is innocent. He didn't kill anyone. We got the wrong guy.'

Travis glanced at the evidence bag and back at him without asking. Penn had swung by the morgue on his way and picked it up. The expression on Travis's face indicated that he understood that it was of little importance now. The tee shirt would be placed back in the evidence room until the internal enquiry into the case failure had been completed and a whole new chain of evidence would be initiated.

Travis motioned for him to move away from the doorway as he began to explain everything he'd found.

'We don't want this getting out before I've informed upstairs,' he said, as Penn's phone rang in his pocket.

He ignored it and continued to explain what he'd learned about the tee shirt.

His phone stopped and then instantly rang again.

Travis frowned. 'Someone wants you urgently.'

Penn nodded. 'Sir, yes, but I think there's something else you need to—'

'For God's sake, man, answer it,' he ordered.

Penn took out his phone.

Jasper's school.

'Penn,' he answered.

'Mr Penn, is everything okay?'

'Of course,' he said, frowning.

'Oh good, we just like to check seeing as we didn't receive your normal call.'

'I'm sorry, call about what?'

'Jasper not coming in today but as long as he's okay, we'll see him when he's feeling—'

'Mrs Wicks, I don't know what you're talking about. I saw Jasper off to breakfast club as normal this morning.'

An intake of breath. 'Mr Penn, Jasper is not in his classroom.'

Penn felt all kinds of sensations crawl over his body. He tried to stay calm.

'Have you checked the library?'

Jasper often lost track of time once he got in there. More than once he'd missed the start of his lesson.

'He's not there,' she said, and he knew it would have been the first place they would have checked.

'What about the toilets. The sports hall, the science lab?' he asked as his mind sprinted around the school building.

'All checked, Mr Penn,' she said, as her voice began to weaken. 'And I can tell you that your brother is nowhere in this building.'

Penn ended the call, thrust the evidence bag at Travis and ran back to his car as fast as he could.

CHAPTER EIGHTY

'What you got?' Stacey asked, when the room suddenly fell silent. A tune from *The Phantom of the Opera* had ended abruptly, which Stacey had now learned meant something had the girl's full attention.

She hoped the girl had something good so she could crack on with looking into the death of the Robinson boy; sad as it was he was no suspect in the case, whereas the people they were tracing could potentially strike again.

'Give me just one minute,' Tiff said, disappearing under the table.

The gentle whirr of the printer had been going constantly. Her temporary colleague liked paper, lots of it and had used half a ream printing out lists, timelines and attendance charts.

'Got one,' she shouted holding aloft three sheets of paper.

'Got one what?' Stacey asked. So far, they'd managed to write off approximately forty names between them through either death or emigration.

'A kid named Damien Crouch. Came here two years running when he was nine and ten years old. Chess champion both years,' she said, placing one sheet of paper on the table. 'Met with our friendly counsellor on both occasions. No criminal record, not even a speeding ticket. Happily married and now works as a microbiologist in Kent,' she said, discarding the second piece of paper.

'Okay, what makes Damien Crouch interesting?' Stacey asked. She'd shortlisted five or six similar cases herself.

Tiff held up the final piece of paper and waved it in the air.

'Because this year he's back again. With his six-and-a-half-year-old daughter.'

CHAPTER EIGHTY-ONE

Penn screeched to a halt as the school bus travelled down the single-track drive towards him.

Full of kids, it was headed to the swimming baths for second lesson. He knew because he'd packed Jasper's trunks and his brother was supposed to be on that bus.

Instead of pulling over and allowing the bus to pass he parked right in front of it and got out of the car.

The driver was making angry signals as he pounded on the door to be let on.

'I know these kids,' he shouted, pointing to the door, understanding the man's reluctance to allow him on board.

A teacher he knew tapped the driver on the shoulder and the doors opened.

'Has he turned up yet?' he asked, breathlessly.

She shook her head. 'Have you tried his?…'

'Straight to voicemail every time,' he answered, heading past her. He'd given Jasper a mobile phone for emergencies a few years ago and he always answered when Penn called.

'Billy,' he shouted out, and the boy's dark head popped up at the back of the coach.

'Hey mate,' he said, trying to keep his voice calm. 'What happened to Jasper this morning?'

He shrugged as fear filled his eyes. Penn realised he was towering over the kid and his manner was frantic.

He sat down on the seat opposite and smiled, trying to force a calming smile on to his face. 'It's okay, Billy. You've not done anything wrong. I just need to find him. Did he meet you at the end of the road?'

Billy nodded, and Penn felt a huge surge of relief. He'd made it to the meeting point, so Billy had to know where he'd gone.

'He give you your toast?'

A slight smile and a nod.

'So, where'd he go, mate? Why didn't he come into school with you?'

'I was only looking on Lucy's phone for a minute. She'd got a video of a dog water skiing. It was funny and—'

'Where was Jasper, Billy?' Penn pushed, trying to keep the urgency out of his voice.

'Dunno. There was a car and…'

'Jasper got into a car?' Penn asked, hearing how his voice had risen.

'Y… yeah,' he answered, as his eyes widened and his lower lip started to quiver.

'It's okay, mate. You've not done anything wrong,' he said, heading to the front of the bus.

Penn tried to think. His confusion was clouding his brain but he knew Jasper was a sensible kid.

Jasper understood that he mustn't go anywhere with strangers, which caused Penn's heart to beat loudly in his chest because it could only mean one thing.

His brother had got into a car with someone he already knew.

CHAPTER EIGHTY-TWO

'Damien Crouch,' Kim said to Bryant, ending the call that had come from Stacey while she'd been briefing her colleague on her conversation with Veronica. 'He's twenty-seven years of age, ex-chess champion here with his young daughter. Stace is looking for an up-to-date photo now.' She looked around. 'And then we gotta go looking for him,' she said, striding over to the reception desk.

This was a good, solid lead that Tink and Stacey had uncovered and was exactly the type of person she was looking for. History with the event and right here, right now.

She held up her ID to the male receptionist, glancing at his name badge.

'Raymond, we need to speak to one of your guests immediately. His name is Damien Crouch and his car has just been hit out there on the car park.'

Concern immediately registered on his features.

'It's okay, no one was hurt but my colleague witnessed the whole thing,' she said, as he began to tap away on the computer.

'Does your impatience have no limits?' Bryant asked, turning his back on Raymond.

'That's clearly rhetorical,' she answered, following suit as Raymond picked up the phone.

From the activity around them it appeared that sessions were ending for break time. There was a sudden rush of voices and movement like a train emptying on to a quiet platform. With

this level of movement, even with a photo they could be chasing around the venue after him all day.

She watched as a dark-haired man wearing an expression of concern cut around the meandering crowds and headed straight towards the desk. He wore black jeans, trainers and a casual sweatshirt.

'Here he comes,' Kim said, stepping forward into his path.

She held up her ID. 'Mr Crouch?'

He looked beyond her to the reception to confirm this was who he'd been called to see.

Raymond nodded.

'You want to speak to me about my car?' he asked, looking towards the hotel entrance and the car park beyond.

'Your car is fine, Mr Crouch,' she said. 'We need to speak to you on another matter.'

'But…' he said, glancing around.

'Oh, never mind Raymond. He got it wrong. He's very busy. We don't want to talk about your car. We'd much prefer to talk to you about murder.'

CHAPTER EIGHTY-THREE

Penn watched the school bus drive away, everyone on it going about their normal business while his own world was crumbling around him. He wasn't sure what he expected them to do. Right now he knew he was on his own.

When the call had first come through from the school he'd decided to delay letting his mother know. Her ailing health could do without the stress. Especially when he'd been convinced that he could locate Jasper in a few short minutes, but the hours were growing since his brother had last been seen. His fear for his brother's safety was now very real, and the call to his mother was inevitable.

'He'll be fine, he'll be fine, he's a sensible kid, he'll be fine,' he chanted to himself as he took out his phone. He had to convince his mother that everything would be fine and that he would find Jasper. But first he had to convince himself.

He hesitated before making the call, feeling as though he had failed her somehow. That he had been responsible for his brother's disappearance. He wished that Jasper had simply wandered off on foot. Limiting the distance he could travel. In a car, he could be anywhere by now.

'Where are you, buddy, and who are you with?' he whispered.

The events of the week began to circle in his brain. The coincidence of his brother going missing during the week he was reviewing an old case. Everything he'd uncovered had confirmed that Gregor Nuryef was not responsible for the murder of Devlin

Kapoor. He'd been about to tell Travis that he thought the murder was related to the Reed gang and that was a whole new set of problems for them all.

His mind started to unravel the ball of string that had just started to come loose in his brain. Had the Reed gang got wind of the internal investigation and worked out that he was going to point the finger at them? Did they know they were his first suspicion before the evidence against Nuryef began piling up?

The panic notched up a gear. If he was right, he knew these people would think nothing of disposing of Jasper, to teach him a lesson; but then he'd have nothing left to lose.

No, if they had him it was to bargain, to force his hand, to back off and leave the investigation alone.

But where was the call? Where was the contact from the Reed gang to tell him what they wanted, to threaten him into keeping quiet? He checked his phone again. There was nothing new. His last text message was from Mitch. Just confirming all of his findings on the tee shirt. He hadn't read it because he'd already been told.

But there was something different about seeing the results listed in bullet form. There was something clearer about the information once removed from the doubt about Gregor's innocence or guilt.

It brought a clarity he'd not had before and the events of the week suddenly fell into place.

He knew where his brother was.

And more importantly, who he was with.

CHAPTER EIGHTY-FOUR

The two of them followed Damien back to the great hall, where his daughter was sitting at one of the tables beside the woman she'd seen reading a book in the restaurant the night before.

Damien sat where his jacket and bag had been left beside a laptop open on the next chair. He closed the lid as he sat.

She took a seat on the row of chairs in front, and Bryant stood, glancing around the room.

'Your daughter?' Kim asked as the little girl turned and gave him a wave.

He winked and waved back.

'Yes, Matilda is having a private lesson.'

'The woman is a tutor?' Kim asked.

He nodded. 'And a very good one.'

Again, Kim couldn't help wondering what was at the root of the animosity she'd witnessed between this private tutor and the event organiser.

She turned her attention back to Damien Crouch. 'You have quite a history with this event?'

'By quite a history I assume you mean my two visits to the event when I was a child?'

She nodded and waited for him to speak. He met her gaze with confidence.

'Please ask me anything. I have nothing to hide.'

'You knew all three victims?' she asked.

'Absolutely. Everyone knew Freddie Compton. He made a point of having a quick chat with all the kids to tell them to have fun. Serena and Jared don't seem to do that but hey ho. I had one counselling session with Barry Nixon after losing my first chess game, and Belinda Evans asked me a few questions when I won the entire tournament for the second time.'

'And you only came twice?' she asked.

He nodded.

'Why?'

'Truthfully, Inspector. I got bored. Chess was my life from the moment I pulled myself to a standing position using my parents' marble chess table. I played every minute of the day and when I wasn't playing it I was thinking about it or reading about it or watching famous games on the internet. At night I lay in bed replaying in my head the games I'd watched, analysing any games I'd lost. I played and I practised and I played and I practised and loved every minute of it. I was shit in other areas, don't get me wrong. Couldn't spell for toffee and my maths was limited but I didn't care. It was all about the game.'

Kim leaned forward, intrigued by this man's refreshing honesty. Even Bryant had taken a seat and was listening intently.

'Until?' she asked.

'Until I discovered something that puzzled me way more than the game, officer.'

'Which was?'

'Girls.'

'I hear ya,' Bryant muttered beside her.

Kim couldn't help the smile that teased at her lips.

'Puberty,' he continued. 'Hit me like a torpedo. Suddenly the opposite sex was not the disgusting enemy I'd always assumed them to be. So, lost interest in chess, discovered girls and told my parents I didn't want to play any more.'

'And?'

'And what?' he asked, looking puzzled.

'How did they take the news?'

His frown deepened. 'Not sure what you mean. They seemed a bit relieved to be honest, but you seem surprised.'

'Just what I've learned about pushy parents over the last few days.'

'Not all parents are pushy and not all gifted kids have a shit childhood if that's what you think. My parents were and still are supportive of my choices and my childhood was great. Sure, some kids could be mean because I was a chess geek and I kept myself to myself, but kids pick on anyone who is different. It didn't bother me.'

'And yet, here you are again?' Kim asked, not totally convinced.

'She likes spelling. What can I tell you? She's a performer and likes to show off,' he said, smiling fondly at the back of her dark, curly hair.

'She's got another round in about half an hour and she'll be wiped out by the older kids,' he said, shrugging. 'But she'll still want to stay and watch the quiz cos a little piano playing girl is already through and they're best buddies,' he said, raising an eyebrow. He tipped his head. 'Oh, hang on, you think I'm one of those pushy parents myself forcing my daughter to attend this event?'

Kim shrugged. 'She's taking private lessons in between events,' she challenged.

He tapped the laptop beside him. 'And Dad needs just an hour or two to catch up on work,' he said, good-naturedly. 'But go on, I'll play along. Mattie,' he called out.

She turned, her face full of colour and joy.

'Show me,' he said.

Matilda held up a canvas, daubed with bright colours. Orange, smeared into yellow, a flash of pink, a stroke of green.

Damien gave her the thumbs up. 'Great picture, sweetie.'

She chuckled and turned back to her work.

'What was it?' Kim asked, seeing absolutely no artistic talent there at all.

'Who cares?' he answered. 'Her favourite thing to do in the whole wide world is paint and if she's happy, I'm happy.'

'I don't get it,' Kim said, honestly. 'You bring her here to compete but your whole ethos seems at odds with the spirit of the event.'

'Officers,' he said, looking from her to Bryant and back again. 'You're not the only ones confused right now. I'm trying to understand why you think that every kid who came here had a miserable time. I loved coming here. I hated sports, couldn't kick a football if my life depended on it and couldn't hit a cricket ball if I'd had three bats glued together. I had no enjoyment in physical activity. When I was here I didn't feel like I was a freak. Yeah, some parents were overbearing but mine weren't. They got to know a few of the parents and I made a couple of good friends. I came here and enjoyed myself. And when I didn't want to come any more I just stopped. It really is that simple.'

There was a part of Kim that wanted to believe him and accept this event had been and still was a positive experience for some. And yet another part of her wondered if he protested too much.

He shook his head and continued. 'I don't even mind that you've chosen to talk to me. The fact that you have indicates that you think the killer could be a child who attended Brainboxes at some point in the past. From what I've heard about these murders, Inspector, you've got one pissed off person on your hands.'

He paused and opened his hands. 'And I'm sorry to have to tell you that I'm not the tree you should be barking up cos I'm not angry at all.'

CHAPTER EIGHTY-FIVE

'Do you think he protests too much?' Bryant asked as Matilda's lesson came to an end.

She watched as the man exchanged pleasantries with the tutor before taking his daughter's hand. Matilda skipped away with her prized painting clutched in her palm.

'Dunno,' she answered. The man had seemed well balanced, astute, intelligent and on the face of it a loving and supportive father.

Kim continued to watch the tutor pack away her belongings into a pull-along case.

'I don't see what she's got to offer us,' Bryant said, following her gaze.

'She teaches these kids. She may have some insight for us,' Kim argued.

'We're wasting our time, guv,' he said, moving away.

She stayed still. 'Feel free to wander around the hotel asking folks if they've been on a murder spree recently, but I'm gonna find out what's between this woman and our effervescent organiser.'

Bryant shrugged and followed Damien Crouch and his daughter towards the exit.

Kim approached her from the left.

The women's eyes filled with wariness before she nodded, looking around at the empty tables. She frowned and turned her head, revealing a thin white scar that travelled from her cheekbone to the corner of her mouth.

The woman's expression dared her to ignore its presence.

'DI Kim Stone,' she said, offering her hand. The woman lowered the pile of papers back down to the table and shook her hand. No wedding rings, just a simple signet ring on her right hand.

'Ellie Lewis,' she said, offering no more. 'How can I help you?' No small talk. Kim liked that.

'You're here with the event, obviously?' Kim clarified.

The woman shook her head. 'I'm not connected with the event. I'm here under instruction from the parents. I'm a private tutor, paid for my services to ensure that their children's continued education doesn't suffer during the event.'

'It's two days' long,' Kim said, wondering how much learning they could lose in such a short space of time. 'And isn't this event kind of studying?' she asked.

'No, officer. Many gifted children are taught to see learning as fun.'

Yeah. Kim wasn't too sure about that.

'So, you and Serena get along?'

'As well as we need to,' she answered.

Bloody hell this woman was making her look like a chatterbox. 'Feel free to…'

'I don't care much for skirting, officer,' she said with a half-smile. 'If there's a question in your mouth then ask it.'

'Okay, you two appeared to be having words in the restaurant last night.'

'I think you'll find Serena did most of the talking.'

'If you could just…'

'But you're right. She was unhappy with me. I was tutoring an eleven-year-old girl named Carrie Bruce whose mother wanted a ninety-eight per cent pass rate on the history test I'd set her. The child had to re-sit the test and was late to a chess game. Serena tried to insist that I work with her to ensure the children get to their events on time.'

'And?'

'She doesn't pay me. Carrie's mother does.'

Kim liked the way the woman had stayed calm in the face of the woman's anger. She suspected that Serena was used to being in charge. She could barely remember what her brother, Jared, had sounded like at all.

'Do you know about the murder of the victims connected to the event?'

'No, Inspector, because I've been under a rock for the last few days,' she snapped, and then offered an apologetic smile. 'I'm sorry, tiredness seems to be linked directly to my enjoyment of sarcasm.'

'I don't generally need an excuse for mine to put in an appearance,' Kim admitted. There was something about this woman she liked. Probably her direct approach.

'Did you know any of them?'

'All of them, in passing, if you know what I mean.'

'You mean you just met them a couple of times?'

'No, I met them many times. I've been doing this event for fourteen years but I prefer to know people only in passing.'

Kim almost offered the woman a high-five. She resisted and frowned.

'Forgive me but you look a little young to have attended so many times.'

'I was twenty-four when I first attended and I'll accept the compliment. Thank you.'

'And how did you get into?…'

'Do you have any further questions for me, officer?'

Wow, when this woman didn't want to talk she shut you down pretty quick.

Kim made a mental note for later. There was a story here, she could feel it, but pressing her further would result in total shut down.

'So, you probably know some of the kids and the parents?' Kim asked.

'The ones that pay for my time, yes.'

'Like Damien Crouch?' she asked, not yet ready to let go of a perfect fit for her suspect profile.

'Damien pays me to play with his daughter for a couple of hours so he can keep up with work. No learning, just playing,' she said, almost smiling. 'She's a pretty special kid but he won't push her.'

'How do these parents even know their child is a genius?' Kim asked.

'They don't. They normally look to Mensa for clarification, and they have seventeen signs or behaviours that gifted children may display.'

Kim's eyes widened.

'Including unusual memory, hobbies, intolerance of other children, passing intellectual milestones early, setting themselves high standards, liking to be in control... to name a few but genius is rarely maintained into adulthood.'

'But how can that be?' Kim asked.

'Kids can eventually fall behind due to lack of effort, such as when success comes at an early age with little to no effort. Some kids then believe they can succeed without effort in the future.

'It's understood that genius kids have five special needs. Firstly, they struggle to pay attention in class – many have originally been diagnosed with ADD or ADHD. They lack the motivation to complete certain tasks. Often, they become perfectionists and struggle to achieve their own expectations and finally they can struggle with speaking; may hesitate or stutter as they try to translate complex ideas from their heads into language that a similar age can understand.'

'Surely the parenting can affect how they'll develop in later life?'

'Now you're getting into child psychology territory that is way beyond my knowledge base but I can speak from what I've seen. The authoritative approach is child centred. Kids are taught to

regulate their feelings. It's warm and nurturing. Positive encouragement but with punishments that are measured and consistent.
Normally produces independent, self-reliant kids.'

'Sounds ideal,' Kim said, wondering if that method of parenting had made it to the Hollytree Estate.

'Then you have authoritarian which would cover most tiger
parents. Children are given instruction without explanation. It's
punishment-heavy with spanking and shouting. The goal is to
teach the child to behave, survive and thrive in a harsh world.
These kids often experience abuse.'

Kim instantly thought of Belinda.

'And finally, indulgent style which is pretty much do what
you like when you like without fear of consequence. Of course
the danger here is that the child never learns to avoid behaviours
which will annoy other people and will expect to always get its
own way.'

Her mind turned to Veronica. 'How does this whole thing
affect other kids in the family?' Kim asked.

'Again, that's not my area of expertise.'

'Yeah but you've spent more time around kids than I have.'

'Okay, in my experience, other kids in the family don't do so
well at all.'

CHAPTER EIGHTY-SIX

Penn felt himself bounce up and down as he tried to speed over the potholes gouged into the dirt track that was no longer used.

He reached the gate that screamed 'No Entry' and got out of the car. The chain tying the two sides of the gate together had been cut.

He pushed the left side of the gate open and walked through. Whatever was happening here would not be helped by him running in all guns blazing even though that was exactly what he wanted to do.

In front of him was the main building of the abandoned go-kart facility. It had closed three years ago following the death of a child who had fallen into the ravine, a seventy-foot drop on to a bed of rocks.

The main building held a couple of back offices, a reception area, toilets and a small café. Beyond that, out of sight, was the go-karting track and a shack for hiring out the safety helmets.

He moved closer to the main building and edged along it, ducking and moving below the windows.

He listened keenly for any sound from his brother. He heard nothing but the distant rumble of traffic on the road he'd just left.

He took two more steps towards the edge of the building. Once he reached the corner and turned he would be in full view of the track and the smaller building.

He tried to take deep breaths to still the trembling that was vibrating around his body, terrified at what he was going to find.

He swallowed deeply as he reached the edge of the wall; the end of his cover.

One more intake of breath and then he turned.

That last breath got trapped somewhere inside his chest as he saw his brother standing blindfolded at the edge of the ravine.

CHAPTER EIGHTY-SEVEN

'How many you got left?' Stacey asked, leaning back in her chair. The wooden bars across the back creaked as she tried to get some lumbar support digging, into her flesh. Boy, she was missing the ergonomically designed chair the boss had procured back at the office.

'Just ruled out another sixteen which leaves me…' she checked down her list. 'Nineteen kids left to check.'

'I have seventeen and am rapidly losing the will to live,' she answered, getting up from her seat. She stretched and groaned at the same time.

'I'm gonna join you,' Tiff said, pushing her chair back.

They paced the hotel room on opposite sides. 'Still having fun, Tiff?' Stacey asked as the woman did a couple of star jumps in the middle of the room.

'Would you think any less of me if I said yes?' she asked, heading towards the tea and coffee tray.

Stacey shook her head. 'Nah, I get it.'

She continued to pace as Tiff made herself an instant black coffee and reached for one of Stacey's diet Cokes from the fridge.

'You know, I don't…'

'I'm not sure we're…'

They both chuckled at starting their sentences at the exact same time and appearing to be having the same thought.

'It's not working, is it?' Stacey asked the question in its entirety.

'I see the boss's logic but we could have another couple of murders on our hands by the time we've finished checking and verifying the whereabouts of all these kids.'

Stacey couldn't have put it any better herself.

She popped the ring on her can of Coke and took a swig, looking at the flip charts for inspiration.

'You know, the boss said that professor guy in Manchester talked a lot about the trigger. He suggested we identify what's set off this killing spree.'

'So, something must have happened recently to set our guy off,' Tiff answered, retaking her seat.

Stacey's eyes went to one particular event in the chronology of what they'd learned since Tuesday.

She rushed back to retake her chair opposite Tiffany.

'I think I know just where to start.'

CHAPTER EIGHTY-EIGHT

Bryant grabbed a coffee and looked around the crowded social area for a seat. Right now he was feeling a bit twilight zone about the hotel and wondered if he was ever going to escape.

'This seat taken, buddy?' he asked a boy sitting alone with a book.

'Taken where?' he asked, peering over his reading glasses. 'Do you mean occupied?'

Bryant looked around again but there were no other seats available.

'I'm gonna take that as a no,' he said, pulling the chair towards him.

The boy regarded him seriously, and Bryant guessed him to be ten or eleven years old with fair hair and clear hazel eyes, enlarged by the thick spectacles.

'Is it appropriate for a middle-aged man to seek the company of an unattended child?' the boy asked, seriously.

'Blimey, bud, I only wanted to take the weight off for a minute,' he said, trying not to laugh at the kid's earnest expression, which was clearly still waiting for a response.

Bryant took out his ID. 'I'm a police officer.'

'So?' he asked, pushing his glasses further up his nose.

'So I protect people not hurt them,' he explained.

'I'm not sure the two are mutually exclusive. You could still be a bad man.'

Bryant shook his head as he put his ID back in his pocket. 'Where are your parents?'

'Speaking to the head judge of the general knowledge competition.'

'Why?' he asked, taking a sip of his drink as Serena and Jared came from opposite directions and met in front of the café counter.

'They're appealing the decision to remove a point from my score for a wrong answer which led to my loss of the competition.'

'And was the answer wrong?'

He shrugged. 'Yes and no.'

'How can it be both?' Bryant asked, watching as the siblings to his left appeared to engage in animated conversation.

'I was asked who invented the loudspeaker. Their answer was Edward W. Kellogg and Chester W. Rice, but they are wrong,' he said, imperiously.

'How so?'

'Johann Philipp Reis installed a loudspeaker in his telephone in 1861, some sixty-four years before Kellogg and Rice invented the dynamic speaker in 1925.'

'And your parents are arguing this on your behalf?' Bryant asked. He would have been mortified if his parents were arguing with judges on his behalf.

'Yes, because they are wrong,' he offered definitely. 'At the very least they should accept that they made an error in the clarity of the question.'

Bryant really would have felt the need to laugh out loud had he not noticed Serena's hand on Jared's arm.

To the untrained onlooker it may have appeared that Serena was engaging in casual physical contact with her brother, but the trained eye could tell that her fingers were clenched, tense, her nails digging in.

'So, what's your view on what I've just told you?' the boy asked.

'Kid, I reckon you're way too serious for your own good,' he answered as Jared leaned in closely to his sister, said something into her ear before snatching his arm from her grip and storming away.

He watched the dismay form on the woman's features as his phone began to ring.

The kid regarded him with irritation.

Bryant was sorely tempted to bob out his tongue before he answered the call but refrained. He really had just wanted to take the weight off.

'Hey, Stace,' he said.

'Can't get the boss,' she explained. 'But there's something you need to know.'

He sat forward as the boss came through the doors from the great hall.

'It's that Robinson kid,' she explained. 'The one who died recently.'

'What about him?' Bryant asked as the guv spotted him.

'I've been through all the media reports and there's not a great deal of detail, but he didn't just die, Bryant. This twelve-year-old kid took his own life.'

CHAPTER EIGHTY-NINE

Penn resisted the urge to call out to his trembling brother for fear it could startle him into falling over the edge.

He could hear a faint whimpering coming from behind the woollen hat that had been pulled down over his head.

He ached to run to Jasper across the forty feet of tarmac racetrack that led to the grassy verge at the edge of the site. But he knew that his brother was not here alone.

'Aah, so you've finally worked it out,' Doug said, appearing from behind the building.

'Yeah, I followed your trail of breadcrumbs, you bastard, now get my brother away from that edge.'

'Jasper's okay, aren't you mate? I explained to him that we're gonna play a little game and that you were coming to play too.'

Penn was watching Jasper's body twitch and try to turn away from the ravine because he'd heard his voice. He was looking at the back of his brother's head. One false move and he knew his brother would step forward and fall to his death.

'Jasper knows to stay perfectly still until I tell him to move,' Doug said, standing approximately ten feet away from his brother. All that separated them was a cut-out in the ground. At any second Doug could leap the two-foot gap and push Jasper down into the ravine, but if Jasper tried to move towards Doug's voice he would fall through the cut in the ground.

'Stay still, buddy,' Penn called. 'Everything is gonna be okay. I promise. Just don't move.'

'O… Okay, Ozzy,' his brother said, and Penn could have cried.

His brother had never been able to say Austen, so he'd been Aussie and then become Ozzy over time.

'Doug and I are just going to have a chat and I need you to stay still for me. Okay?'

He nodded.

Penn turned his attention to his former colleague.

'How could you do it, you bastard?'

'What exactly did I do?' he asked, popping a piece of gum into his mouth.

'Was it the money? Was that it? They pay you well?'

'Still don't know what you're saying, mate,' he said, smartly.

'You must have been laughing your fucking head off while I've been chasing my own tail all week. But I've got it all now.

'I wondered why Mr Kapoor kept saying he'd been told numerous times about his security. I knew of only once but you went back, didn't you? To find out if he'd made any improvements, and when he hadn't you informed the Reed gang that the place was good for it. Told them the dummy camera wasn't real so they could hit it. How many others have you done it with, Doug? How long you been telling them who to hit?'

'I knew you'd work it out eventually but no one's gonna believe you. Cos let's be honest, that's pretty fucking thin.'

'I noticed that you kept pointing towards Lynne having new things. Her car, flashing her cash about buying drinks. Always trying to cover yourself, Doug, but you won't get out of this.'

Doug smiled. 'Oh, I think I will, but tell me more.'

'You found Ricky Drake and sent him into Lynne to interview. No link back to you, but you overplayed your hand with Irina. You told her she'd best keep her mouth shut when I sent you to check on her story. She panicked and realised she was in too deep after the neighbour was killed. She came and told the truth.

'It was you that planted the blood-soaked tee shirt in Nuryef's shed and then directed me to find it. You bought a brand new tee shirt and smeared it with blood from the clothes or shoes of the real killer.'

'And of course you can prove all of this, eh, mate? Ah, actually it's getting thinner every time you open your mouth. Even if it was all true, you can't prove a fucking thing.'

Penn stole a glance at his brother who was trying his hardest to stand still, but his muscles were fidgeting of their own accord.

'Actually I can, Doug. You made absolutely sure that I'd find the tee shirt. You sent me out there. Again, no line back to you. Except that's the mistake that will convict you.'

Penn saw indecision pass over his face trying to work out where he'd gone wrong.

'If you'd gone and searched the shed for the tee shirt you'd have covered your own tracks. But now you're gonna have absolutely no excuse for the fingerprints that will be found on the dozen or so items you had to move to get to the back of the shed.'

Doug started to clap. 'Bloody hell, mate, you always were too clever for your own good but this time it's not going to work. No one's gonna know how clever you are cos they'll be too busy mourning the tragic accident that happened here today.'

'Doug, what the?...'

'This isn't what you think, buddy. I've not brought Jasper here to bargain with you. There's no point anyway. You'd never go for it. Nope, sorry mate but this is the endgame.'

Penn could barely believe this was his old friend speaking.

'When did you turn from being a bent copper to a kidnapper and a killer, Doug?'

'I ain't going down, Penn. Not for you. Not for anyone. Twenty fucking years I've given to the force and it's given me nothing back except an ulcer and two failed marriages. Yeah, I could have kept watching folks around me go for promotion and earn bigger bucks, leaving me behind, but that's just a piss-take too far. I wanted a few more quid in my pocket.'

'This is about money, you bastard?' Penn said.

'Yep, mate, it really is that simple. When the Reed boys offered me an opportunity to earn a few hundred extra a month for passing on information, I couldn't see the harm in it and I still can't, so things will just carry on as they were before once you're out of the picture.'

'A man lost his life, Doug. That mean nothing to you?'

He shrugged and finally Penn saw the coldness behind the mask.

'He was nothing to me. Didn't know the guy, so I won't miss him.'

A deathly chill passed through Penn's body as he realised that this man he'd known for years really was capable of hurting both him and Jasper without a second thought.

'If I let you live, I lose everything, buddy. My job, my house, my pension and the nice little earner I've got going with the Reed boys, but I'll do you one favour,' he said, glancing at Jasper. 'For him I'll make it quick.'

'You hurt one hair on his head and I swear to God I'll fucking—'

'Hey, Jasper, I was only kidding about hurting you. The game's over now, so walk towards me and I'll—'

'Jasper, no,' Penn screamed. If he took two steps towards Doug's voice he would walk straight into the fall away that separated them. 'Buddy, don't listen to him. Only listen to me. Just hear my voice.'

'It's okay, buddy,' Doug said. 'The game's over. Your brother didn't find it funny, so we're gonna stop now.'

'Jasper, don't move,' Penn screamed but he could see his brother's feet move as he stepped from one foot to the other.

'Ozzy,' he called out as a dark stain began to colour the crotch of his trousers. 'Ozzy, I don't know what?...'

'Don't move, bud. I promise it'll be okay, just stay still and listen to only me.'

'Oh, for fuck's sake,' Doug said, striding across the cut and landing a foot away from Jasper.

Penn knew there was no way he could reach him in time.

Doug grabbed Jasper and turned him around, to face him, sideways on to Penn.

'I swear to God if you want something doing…'

'Ozzy… Ozzy… what?…'

'Jasper… what would Billy do?' Penn shouted at the top of his lungs.

Doug turned towards him, confused, which gave Jasper just enough time to process his words.

Jasper's knee rose up sharply and caught Doug squarely in the genitals.

Pain and surprise doubled him over as Penn sprinted towards them. He grabbed a disoriented Jasper and pushed him away from the edge.

'Sit down on the ground,' he said, forcefully, so he couldn't wander back towards danger.

Doug was clutching his genitals and had rolled closer to the edge.

'Oh no you fucking don't,' Penn said, rolling him back.

Doug made one attempt to get to his feet, but a meaningful right hook knocked him clean out.

Penn ran back to his brother and ripped the woollen hat from his face. Jasper's eyes were watery and wide with fear.

'I weed myself, Ozzy,' he whispered.

Penn pulled him close, as he took out his phone. 'It's okay, buddy,' he said, kissing the side of his head. 'No one is going to hurt you again.'

CHAPTER NINETY

The market town of Evesham was located twenty-six miles south-east of Stourport, and also lay on the banks of the River Severn, on a horseshoe-shaped peninsula almost completely surrounded by water.

Due to its exceptionally fertile soil the area was renowned for its market gardening trade around the Vale of Evesham.

Not that you would have known it here, Kim thought, as Bryant pulled up outside a terraced house with no front garden in a row of twenty. The windows on either side were covered in metal grating.

Kim stepped between two wheelie bins and over a bunch of flowers lying on the doorstep to ring the bell.

A man in his late thirties opened the door. The jogging bottoms and sweatshirt did nothing to hide the fact that there was barely any flesh on those bones.

'Mr Robinson?' Bryant asked.

He nodded and waited.

Bryant introduced them both. 'May we come in for a minute?'

'Social Services send you?' he asked, frowning. 'Said I was all clear for…'

'Nothing to do with Social Services,' Kim reassured him. 'And if you allow us to come inside, we'd like to explain.'

He stepped aside for them to enter a small reception room. They passed the stairs and entered a second reception room that had been crudely knocked into the kitchen, exposing bare wall that formed a double archway.

The kitchen table was a varnished picnic bench. He sat and pointed for them to do the same.

'Mr Robinson, we're sorry for your loss and for intruding at this time but a great deal of death has surrounded the Brainbox event this year and we'd just like to—'

'I'd blow every one of 'em up if I could,' he said, reaching for his cigarettes. He lit one and inhaled deeply. 'Fucking hate it but the missus wouldn't give over. Sold the bloody car to get him entered into the competition last year. He didn't want to do it. I didn't want him to do it, but she wouldn't leave it alone.'

Bitterness and anger dripped from his words.

'The kid was throwing daily tantrums to get his point across.'

Had the kid been unable to tell his parents he didn't want to do it? Had that failure this year led to his suicide? 'Couldn't he just say he didn't?…'

'No, officer, he couldn't.' He paused and turned tired eyes on her. 'You know what savant syndrome is?'

Kim shook her head.

'You seen *Rain Man*?'

She nodded.

'Dustin Hoffman has savant syndrome, same as Stevie. It's where someone with significant mental disabilities demonstrates certain abilities far in excess of average. Often rapid calculation, like in *Rain Man* or a musical ability but just the one skill.'

'Is it common?' Kim asked. She'd seen the film but had had no clue of what the condition was called or the level or types of genius that came with it.

He shook his head. 'It's rare, just one in a million which is why it wasn't picked up even though he was a slow developer. He didn't walk until he was eighteen months or utter a word until after his second birthday. Basic physical tests were normal, so doc told us to take him to playgroups to interact with other kids to catch him up. I took him. Crawled straight over to some other kid's keyboard and started playing it until people stopped and listened. He didn't like that.

'Missus was straight out to get him one. Pawned her jewellery at Cash Converters and put it in his room. He played and played and played as long as no one was watching. Then the missus had the brainwave of taking him to that Brainbox thing and the kid went ape. Missus insisted he'd be fine once he was there. I tried to talk her out of it, but she's a bloody stubborn cow when she wants to be. She wanted to turn him into some kind of star, and I just wanted to play footie with a normal kid.'

'So, Stevie went to Brainboxes last year?' Kim asked, feeling the man's palpable rage. Had the child met with all three of their victims and this man somehow wanted vengeance for his son's suicide?

'Yeah, we went. Bloody competition. Stevie didn't speak for the whole time. Missus tried to get him to mix, and I tried to explain that he just wasn't built that way. He sat at the piano and froze, wouldn't play a note and then started keening. Worst sound I ever heard in my life. It was bloody miserable. We all hated every minute of it, except for the missus who only went and signed him up for it again this year.'

'And where's the missus now?' Kim asked.

'Fucked if I know. We had a bust-up. Legged it when I told her our son's death was all her fault.'

Kim wondered at the harshness of such a statement made to someone who must already have been feeling responsible.

'I don't care what you think,' he said, shrugging. 'It was her fault. You should arrest the bitch for murder.' He swallowed down his anger as a tear rolled over his cheek. He wiped it away roughly. 'Every bit of her attention on Stevie all the time. Poor kid couldn't cope. She killed our son and I'll never forgive her. May she rot in hell.'

Kim was about to stand when Bryant beat her to it. This man's anger was borne of grief and despite his comments to the contrary she couldn't see him being responsible for anyone's murder. He possessed all of the anger but none of the control.

Bryant offered the man his hand. 'We're sorry for intruding on…' his words trailed away as piano music suddenly sounded from above.

The man didn't bat an eyelid.

'Mr Robinson, who is?…'

'I already told you, didn't I? Stevie loves to play the piano.'

She locked gazes with Bryant to see she hadn't missed anything. His expression said not.

'But Stevie is dead… he killed himself?'

'Who told you that? It's his brother, Ryan, the normal kid that did himself in,' he said, looking upwards. 'And as you can hear, our genius kid is still very much alive.'

CHAPTER NINETY-ONE

Kim let out a breath as she and Bryant got back into the car.

'How the hell did we not know which kid had died?' Bryant asked.

Yes, it was annoying that they'd been ill-prepared but it was no one's fault. 'Serena never mentioned the first name of the boy that died, and Stacey wasn't to know by the vague police statements. The news articles, as always, read between the lines.'

Kim knew that the press would not report fully on the full names and details until after the inquest and then would be guided by the Samaritans' guidelines.

'You think this is linked to our investigation?' Bryant asked.

'I don't think the family is linked, but I can't help feeling that the boy's suicide was the catalyst. Hang on, so what day did he die?' she asked, looking at her colleague.

'Thursday afternoon.'

She counted backwards. 'Around the time our first victim, Freddie Compton, met his end over a board game.'

Kim didn't wait for a reply.

'Bryant, I think we just found our trigger.'

'Slow down, guv, that's a bit of a...'

'Bryant, it's too coincidental that Ryan Robinson took his own life around the time of our first murder. I'm sure it's the trigger but I just don't know what it was that was triggered,' she said, tapping her phone absently. 'Unless... oh shit...'

'Oh no, where's that mind of yours going now?' he asked with dread in his voice.

Kim thought back over what she'd learned so far that day, initially from Veronica, from Ellie and indirectly from the dead boy.

'Bryant, if you don't like bad language, I'd cover your ears now.'

'Why, who is gonna get it?'

'It's not going to be me that's doing the swearing,' she answered, scrolling down her contacts list.

'Hey Stace,' she said, grimacing. Bryant turned to listen with interest.

'How's it going with narrowing down the kids that came into contact with all of our victims?'

'What do you need, boss?' Stacey asked, perceptively. 'Cos you only check on my progress with a task if you're about to say something to throw a spanner in my works.'

Kim allowed the smile on to her face. 'Yeah, well about that. I'm gonna need another list.'

'Other than any kids that could have known all victims?'

Kim prepared to hold the phone away as Bryant looked on with amusement.

'Yeah, I want to know which ones had brothers and sisters.'

CHAPTER NINETY-TWO

'Go on up,' Kim said as they entered the hotel foyer.

'Cannon fodder?' Bryant asked. 'You know Stacey's gonna be raging.'

'Tink will protect you,' she said, heading for the café bar.

In truth she wanted just a few minutes to herself. She felt as though she hadn't been in her own company for days.

She also knew that Bryant couldn't understand her niggling feeling about the tutor she'd spoken to earlier. The scar, her guardedness, her deflection of any questions that even remotely bordered on personal.

Snippets of their earlier conversation kept flashing through her mind. But nothing more so than the woman herself. There was an aloofness there that hid a warmth that she didn't want shown. She possessed the gift of sarcasm, which Kim appreciated, but there was a sense of caution draped around her that belied the person inside. And why the hell had she been private tutoring at such a young age?

She took a seat at the edge of the café area, fired up Google and entered the name 'Ellie Lewis'. She scrolled down through nothing of interest.

'Ah, hang on,' she said out loud.

Three heads at the next table turned towards her.

She ignored them and retyped the name. Ellie was normally short for Eleanor. She tried the search again and Google offered her more than ten thousand results.

Her mouth dropped further open the more she read.

Eleanor Lewis had graduated from teaching college when she was twenty-four years old. A year later she'd found herself teaching English Language to teenagers in a particularly run-down area of Staffordshire. One evening when she was leaving she was jumped by three students who raped her, cut her face and left her for dead.

The horror in Kim's stomach grew as she read each article. The assault, the recovery, the court case. It was all covered in minute, sordid detail.

It was no surprise that she'd been unable to return to the education system and now used her skills to tutor privately. One-on-one. Safe.

And the bastards, all of them fifteen to sixteen years of age, hadn't served ten years between them.

That she had survived such an ordeal just made Kim want to go find her again and shake her hand.

The external scars were completely obvious to anyone with a pair of eyes but Kim couldn't help but wonder about the ones inside.

CHAPTER NINETY-THREE

It was almost six when Kim entered the hotel room and she could swear that every time she left and returned someone had shrunk it.

With four people in the small sitting area, surrounded by wipe boards and laptops, the space was beginning to feel like a broom cupboard.

'What you got, Stace?' she asked, switching on the kettle.

'The urge to find another job,' she grumbled, as the portable printer kicked into life behind her.

'What can I?…'

'Nothing right now, boss, we got a system going and another pair of hands is just gonna confuse me,' Stacey said, handing a printed sheet to Tiff. 'Cross-reference that with what Bryant's got.'

Bryant glanced at her in an 'I'm in with the cool kids' kind of way, and she burst out laughing. Everyone knew that Bryant and data mining were not great bedfellows.

She threw herself into the vacant chair fighting her frustration. She knew without a shadow of a doubt that their killer was here somewhere. After all the miles, all the probing, the interviews and following leads, she suspected the answer lay in the work being done by the rest of her team, and much as she wanted a name and description right now they couldn't magic it out of thin air.

As she listened she realised the process was like panning gold. Each swill of the water washed away some dirt bringing them closer to the nuggets at the bottom. Every cross-reference they made weeded out unlikely suspects.

She trusted Stacey's methods more than she resented being left out of the process.

She checked her emails, registering the only new message from Keats containing the toxicology reports from all three crime scenes. She opened the first one and began to scroll right through it. There was nothing unexpected except a note advising possible cross-contamination from a police officer's boots which had recorded a high level of NaCl at the first crime scene at Haden Hill Park. A strange result, but nothing that could help her now. She'd ask Keats to check his results later. She closed it and scrolled to the second report.

'Okay, I'm ready,' Stacey said, sitting back in her chair.

'Go,' Kim said, closing her emails and turning to face her colleague.

'Okay, I've got a total of seventeen kids who had contact with all three of our victims; Belinda Evans, Barry Nixon and Freddie Compton.'

'Okay, let's look at—'

'Hang on, boss. Of these seventeen kids eight of them had siblings.'

'Okay, great, let's—'

'Of these eight…'

'Stace, at this rate will there be any kids left to investigate?' Kim asked, folding her arms.

'Of these eight,' Stacey continued. 'There are three that are of particular interest and we should look at first.'

Kim was tempted to disagree but she had learned to trust her colleague.

'So, first we have a young girl named Carly Benz. Her brother Laurence was a star chess player who had contact with all the victims. She was four years younger than him and he died of a brain tumour when he was eighteen years old.'

'Why relevant?' Kim asked, wondering why this particular story had made Stacey's top three.

'Sister went off the rails after his death. Got in all kinds of trouble: stealing, violence, antisocial behaviour. But nothing since. I can find no trace of her since a court case when she was sixteen years old. No social media channels, nothing. It's like she simply disappeared. She'd be mid-twenties now and could be punishing our victims for some perceived misdeed against her brother.'

'Interesting, Stace,' Kim acknowledged as Tiff noted the bullet points on the flip chart.

'Oh, it gets better. Our runner-up is Mrs Beth Nixon herself, brought to the event by her grandmother. There's not much about her visits to the event except a blog post about her younger brother heckling her performance in the final event. No name but he managed to disrupt the quiz.'

'Bloody hell,' Kim said, realising that just about everyone they'd spoken to was tied to this event in one way or another.

'Not sure how you're gonna top that one, Stace,' Kim admitted.

'Ah well, I like to save the best for last,' she said, raising her eyebrows.

'The final sibling connection I can find where there was contact with all three of our victims and have been right under our nose the whole time, are our very own Serena and Jared Welmsley, the organisers of the whole event.'

CHAPTER NINETY-FOUR

Kim stood aside for a family barrelling down the corridor towards them, chatting and laughing as a little boy beamed holding a sizeable glass trophy.

'He's a happy chappie,' Bryant remarked, with a smile.

'Course he is, he won,' she replied, as she headed into the reception area. Squeals of delight reached her as parents and children pored over certificates, cups, badges and trophies. She spotted Damien Crouch watching proudly as his daughter Matilda showed off a pink ribboned rosette pinned to her cardigan.

'Looks like we're at the tail end of it,' Bryant observed. 'Just the last main quiz to go and no incidents…'

'Don't even jinx us, Bryant. Our killer is here somewhere and we've got to make sure we catch him before the event ends completely. If there's anyone else on his kill list, they're gonna be right—'

'Inspector, still here I see?' Serena said from behind them.

The woman was carrying a clutch of rosettes, a clipboard and a single child's trainer.

She followed Kim's gaze. 'Don't ask.'

'Almost done?' Bryant asked.

She beamed happily, glancing around at the children and parents finally making some noise.

'The event has been a huge success,' she said, and then seemed to remember herself. 'Apart from the recent tragedies of course,' she acknowledged. 'But just the quiz to go now and then we're done for another year.'

'Splendid,' Kim said. 'Serena, did Barry Nixon ever bring his wife with him to this event?'

'Just last year, she came along with him. It was lovely to see her again after all these—'

'And was a ticket put aside for her this year?'

'Of course. I understood that they were attending together.'

'And has her ticket been claimed?' Kim asked, as her stomach flipped.

'I'm sorry, officer, I have no idea,' she said, edging away. 'Jared takes care of the attendance records.'

'And would you mind telling me where I can find your brother?'

Serena looked genuinely taken aback by the question.

'My brother, Inspector? I'm sorry but I haven't seen Jared for hours.'

CHAPTER NINETY-FIVE

'You reckon Jared could be our guy?' Bryant asked as they headed for the main hall. After there'd been no reply from his mobile phone it had been Serena's best guess before hurrying off to lost property.

'I'll let you know after he explains where he's been during all of our murders, but I still have a feeling there's much more to learn about Beth Nixon. We still don't know what prompted her stay in a mental health facility, and she was due to come here with her husband.'

'You think she could have killed her own husband though, guv?' Bryant asked, doubtfully. 'She seems to have loved him very much.'

'Yeah that's the impression I get too but it wouldn't be the first time we've questioned a serial killer and not known it. We're dealing with some pretty clever folks here.'

'Yeah, and how do you catch a killer who is more intelligent than you?'

Kim thought for a minute. 'You hope that they're far too clever for their own good.'

'Great words, oh wise one,' he said, as they reached the hall.

The majority of the space had been prepared ready for the final event. Two long tables faced each other with three seats behind each. Nameplates were in position for the finalists and a judging table was located in between.

Two tripods ready for camera equipment had been positioned to catch all the action and a hundred or so spectator seats had been placed to witness the battle of the brainboxes.

A few seats on the front row had been taken already by the early birds. One woman was busy combing her child's hair and adding a spotted bow to the top of her head.

The child ripped it out and threw it on the floor.

'Charming,' Bryant observed.

'Unsurprising,' Kim noted, looking around the room. 'Act like a mini adult but look like a kid. No wonder the child is confused.'

'Good point,' he answered as her gaze searched a group of kids sitting in a huddle, waiting, over in the far corner.

'He's not here, guv.'

'I can see that, Bryant,' she said as a tingle shivered down her spine. 'And as this competition comes to a close and he's one of the organisers where the hell else would he be?'

CHAPTER NINETY-SIX

'It's a bit like one long shift, isn't it?' Tiff asked, stifling a yawn.

Stacey smiled. 'Yeah, that's why we like it.'

'Don't your partners and families mind?'

'For the most part they get it,' Stacey offered, tightly. In her case Devon understood most things, but what Devon was failing to understand was her inability to answer the question that had been put to her at the beginning of the week, that she'd successfully avoided through work.

'Oh, there's no better feeling than when your other half just gets you. When you finish each other's—'

'Tiff, I've really got to crack on with digging on Beth...'

'But the boss says she's looking for siblings now, so why are you still working on the wife of one of the victims?'

'It's a suspicion, Tiff. Just cos the boss has had another idea we don't leave leads dangling in mid-air. It's about finishing what you started.'

'I get it,' she said, stretching her arms above her head. 'But I need to get out, just for a short while. Need anything?'

'Diet Coke,' Stacey answered as she drained the bottom of her can, pleased to finally get a few minutes to herself.

Despite being exhausted Stacey hated that she'd been pulled off researching Beth Nixon to look at siblings of child geniuses. Secretly she thought it was a bit of a long shot but the boss was convinced it was a possibility.

But, her time with Beth was not yet over because she didn't have all the answers.

'Right, Beth Nixon,' she said to the empty room. 'What exactly have you been trying to hide?'

CHAPTER NINETY-SEVEN

Ten minutes later they were back outside the main hall which was beginning to fill up. The smaller rooms had all been cleared and handed back to the hotel, and Jared was still nowhere to be found.

'Okay, Bryant. I don't like the fact that Jared Welmsley is missing cos you know who else we haven't seen?'

He shook his head.

'Ellie Lewis, the tutor.'

'Probably already left,' he said, logically. 'Not sure why she'd be interested in the quiz.'

'Hmm…' she said, heading back to reception. She jumped ahead in front of a few families waiting to check out. Somehow she felt the woman wouldn't leave before seeing if any of her potential students had made the quiz. But her colleague might be right. It had been known to happen.

Bryant followed, making her apologies.

'Excuse me,' she said, showing her badge. 'Has Eleanor Lewis checked out yet?'

The woman hesitated, as though toying with telling her to join the queue. She thrust her badge forward. Where was Raymond when you needed him?

'Please,' Bryant added. 'It may be important.'

She relented, tapped a few keys and shook her head.

'Not yet.'

'Ring her room,' she instructed

She did so and listened as the phone rang out.

She shook her head.

'Can I get her contact number?' Kim asked taking out her phone.

The receptionist shook her head. 'I'm sorry but I can't—'

'Bryant, ask her nicely,' she said, turning to her colleague.

The family behind huffed. She turned and offered them a withering glance. They turned away.

'Lisa,' he said, reading her name badge. 'We believe Ms Lewis may be in danger. If we can just call her to...'

'Here,' said the receptionist, handing him a pink Post-it note.

Kim shook her head as she took out her phone.

'You could thank me,' Bryant moaned.

'I'd rather thank your mum and dad for giving you manners,' she said, keying in the number.

'Fair point,' he admitted.

The call went straight to voicemail.

'Damn,' she said, trying again.

Same response.

She dialled another number.

'Stace, take this number down.'

Stacey listened as she read it out. 'Belongs to Ellie Lewis, the private tutor. Keep trying it. We can't find her.'

'Hang on, didn't you say she was late thirties?'

'She's thirty-eight.'

'That wouldn't make sense. She couldn't possibly have been here teaching when Jared was a child so—'

'Right now, both of them are missing, Stace. Everyone else is accounted for, so there's something,' Kim said. 'Just keep trying her and let me know.'

'Will do, boss,' Stacey said, ending the call.

'She's just raised a fair point, though, about—'

'Sorry to interrupt but I couldn't help overhearing,' said the woman who had huffed at her in the queue.

Kim frowned at the intrusion but nodded for her to go on.

'Well, Ellie tutors our son, Marcus, in Geography. He had a session with her earlier today. Just after lunch.'

Kim tried to hide her irritation. The woman was trying to be helpful but Ellie's movements of five or six hours ago were of little use to her now.

'Thank you for—'

'No, you don't understand. The session was rescheduled. Originally planned for tea time but she said she was going to meet an old friend.'

CHAPTER NINETY-EIGHT

'Dead spots?' Kim asked, pushing herself back to the top of the queue, waving her mobile phone at Lisa. 'Where are they?'

It took every ounce of customer service training she'd had to bury her irritation.

'We don't have any…'

'Of course, you do,' Kim said. 'Every venue has them.'

Kim knew that despite the best efforts of phone networks dead spots still existed caused usually by hilly terrain, dense foliage or physical distance. In an urban area other factors contributed to patchy signals.

'Lisa, where are your thickest walls or metal constructions?' she asked. Even the dense rebar in concrete could cause a problem.

'Please, just tell her and she'll be gone quicker,' Bryant advised.

'He's right,' she offered.

Lisa lowered her head. 'Store rooms at the end of the kitchen leading out into the service yard and the locker rooms between the gym and the pool.'

'Thank you,' Kim said, taking out her phone. She tried the number again.

Nothing.

'Guv, those places couldn't be further apart.'

'I know, Bryant. We're gonna have to split up. You take the pool and I'll take the kitchen.'

He nodded his understanding as they turned and went their separate ways.

CHAPTER NINETY-NINE

Ellie stifled a yawn and sat back against the bench as she felt in her pocket for reassurance. The personal attack alarm was nestled right against the seam.

She'd been surprised at the text message she'd received earlier. Any message that came from an unknown number sent shivers down her spine. And the mystery of the first message had done nothing to allay her fears as she'd read the words:

'Care to meet later for a catch up?'

Her immediate thoughts had gone to her attackers. It was where her thoughts always went, she realised, as her hand automatically went to her face. It wasn't as though she could ever forget it. The proof and memory of it stared back at her with every task that required her to look at her reflection: brushing her teeth, combing her hair, applying make-up.

And if she fell unaware of it for even a few moments she saw it reflected in other people's eyes. It wasn't a scar that was satisfied with a fleeting, passing glance. People didn't look away once seen. They stared and watched it move as she spoke as though it was a living thing. She understood completely the irritation of glamour models when people talked only to their breasts. If she'd been better endowed in that area, she might have tried using them for distraction now and again.

She closed her eyes for a moment, relieved that the event was finally over. It had been tough, emotionally exhausting being around so many people.

In normal life she avoided crowded areas, stayed away from curious eyes and intrusive stares. Easy to do in this day and age. She left her home, drove to the homes of her clients, tutored their children, got back in her car and went home. And there was little she couldn't buy online.

Except it was getting harder to come here to this event, harder to put herself on open display, but it was something she had to do to satisfy her clients.

And that was what had prompted her to come to this meeting.

Her first response had been to wonder about her attackers but she knew where they were. She always knew where they were. Almost sixteen years on and she still feared that they would come back to finish her off.

But that had been reduced from three fears to two since the oldest had been killed in a gang-related stabbing five years ago. That night she had celebrated not so much out of revenge but that it was one less she had to worry about. One less to search for on the internet. One less to monitor.

The youngest of the three was back behind bars after a string of brutal attacks on young women. Safe for now. And the other was now married with two young children working as a roofer in Stoke.

The first text message had been followed a few minutes later and her fears had been calmed when she'd read:

'Sorry, forgot you didn't have my work number. Matilda has a little present she'd like to give you. Damien.'

The message had ended with a smiley face and an eye roll that had instantly made her smile.

Normally she would have refused but once the initial anxiety had passed she'd remembered the conversation with the police inspector. She'd enjoyed talking. She'd actually appreciated the art of conversing with an adult. Sharing her knowledge, her experience and she had been sad to see the woman walk away. Using her training and education to teach young minds one-on-one satisfied part of her needs but she was coming to realise that maybe not all her needs were being met. Adult conversation was one of them, and besides, Matilda was an absolute sweetheart and her father was a kind and caring man.

The sound of a twig cracking snapped her eyelids open.

It took a few seconds for her eyes to adjust in the falling dusk but when she did, her mouth fell open at the figure coming towards her.

CHAPTER ONE HUNDRED

Kim hurried along the corridors of hotel rooms towards the industrial kitchen at the far end of the hotel. The facility had two kitchens: a smaller one to service the café and restaurant that was on the leisure side of the facility and an industrial space for catering to room service and events.

She held her phone in front of her as she walked, watching the signal bars bounce up and down. The second she lost signal she'd start searching.

The smell and the clatter told her she was drawing near to the dead spot, but her focus was being disturbed by something she'd seen earlier that hadn't yet registered in her brain.

'Jesus,' she cried, as a white clad kitchen worker almost knocked her over while carrying a side of beef.

His look of apology turned to concern. 'Are you lost?'

She flashed her ID. 'No, now tell me where this dead spot starts?'

He frowned.

'Phones,' she said, holding hers aloft.

He looked down the corridor towards the fire exit door.

'Starts just past that extinguisher on the wall and carries on out the door and to the edge of the scented garden.'

'Got it,' Kim said, hurrying away.

Sure enough the bars stopped dancing completely as she passed the fire extinguisher.

With no further rooms beyond this point she pushed open the fire exit door and headed outside.

Her nostrils were assaulted by a combination of summer blooms. A single ornamental lamp post cast light on to the bench beneath. A quick look around the area told Kim there was no one here.

But had she been? Kim wondered, standing beside the bench.

The end of the scented garden, the kitchen guy had said and the bench was just inside it.

She hurried to the end of the space along the path that led around to the front of the hotel. She checked her phone. Still no signal. She couldn't even call Bryant to see if he was having any better luck than she was.

Damn, damn, damn, which way to go? she wondered turning to face each direction.

And then she remembered what she'd seen that hadn't yet made it to her brain.

Searching all of the rooms for Jared.

Children sitting in a group.

All facing the same direction, waiting.

She'd lied when she'd told Stacey that everyone was accounted for.

Where the hell was the fucking clown?

CHAPTER ONE HUNDRED ONE

'Anybody in here?' Bryant shouted, knocking on doors in the male locker room.

So far, he'd ruled out the gym, the badminton court, the Pilates and Zumba room and all areas of the swimming pool. Only the sauna and the ladies rooms were left.

The last door swung open to reveal a pile of neatly folded clothes. He banged on the sauna door as it began to open out towards him.

'What the?…'

'Mr Welmsley, where the hell have you been?' Bryant asked, averting his eyes from the nether regions of the naked male covered only by a very small towel.

'Umm… in there,' he said, nodding towards the steam wafting over his head.

Ask a stupid question, Bryant thought.

'But the event, the quiz, your sister…'

'Is perfectly capable of keeping things running until I get there, but what the hell do you want anyway?' he asked, stepping into the cubicle and closing the door.

'Have you seen Eleanor Lewis?' he asked, as the man ducked down behind the door.

The crisp white towel appeared and Bryant didn't want to picture what was behind.

'Ellie, the tutor?'

'Yes, have you?…'

'You're banging on doors like a madman to ask me if I've seen someone I've barely ever spoken to in my life?'

Bryant didn't like the way this man was able to make everything he said sound ridiculous. He worked all day with someone like that.

'Well, have you?' he pushed.

Jared's head appeared and shook as Bryant heard the buckle of his belt snap shut.

He began to walk away when a sudden thought occurred to him. 'Everything okay with you and your sister?'

'Excuse me?' he said, pulling on his shirt.

'I saw you earlier, having an argument, in the reception.'

Jared frowned and then relaxed when he seemed to recall the episode. 'Oh that. It was nothing. If you've spoken to her you'll know she's a bit of a control freak. Sometimes gets a bit much. But that wasn't even a disagreement,' he said, disappearing from view once again. 'You should see us…'

Bryant walked away, realising he was gaining nothing from this conversation.

His first instinct was to head away from the complex and go find the boss, but he hadn't checked the whole area yet.

If he left prematurely and his instinct about this guy was wrong he might be leaving Ellie Lewis bleeding to death against a wall somewhere.

He thanked Jared for his help and headed towards the female changing rooms.

For now, the boss was on her own.

CHAPTER ONE HUNDRED TWO

Think, think, think, she told herself as she left the scented garden.

What did she know so far? Board games, hopscotch and the swings at the park. The killer had to keep the pattern. They were in a hotel. Where the hell could he?...

Play area, she suddenly realised. He had to have taken her to the play area.

Every death had been symbolic of playing some kind of game. He made them play and then killed them, normally with a stab wound.

A knife.

Ellie and her previous attack.

Kim caught her breath. The woman would be terrified.

She sprinted around the building and headed along the gravel drive towards the play area she'd seen on their way in.

She swallowed her indecision. If she was wrong about the location there was a good chance Ellie was going to die. The killer would only play with them for so long.

A single light illuminated the area in the distance but she was approximately one hundred metres away and could see nothing beyond the framework of the wooden castle.

She continued heading towards it replaying everything that had happened during the week, searching for something that would give her a clue as to who and what she was dealing with. Any small point that had gone unnoticed.

She tried to calm her breathing as she approached the entrance to the park. She covered her mouth with her hand and listened keenly.

In the distance, she could hear a rhythmic sound.

Squeak

Four seconds.

Squeak

Four seconds.

And then a laugh of pure delight that chilled the blood in her veins.

She knew she had to get closer but she had to do it quietly. Who knew what was going on.

A pair of bolt cutters had been placed against the gate to close it. The heavy chain lay on the ground.

She reached over the waist-high fencing and picked them up as quietly as she could. She laid them down on the grass and pushed open the gate, her whole body tense as though that would prevent any rattle or sound alerting her arrival.

Squeak

Four seconds.

Squeak

Kim was relieved to hear the sound. The play came before death. If he was still playing there was hope for Ellie Lewis.

But who the hell was she dealing with?

She moved slowly, stepping around a spillage of crisps that had not yet been cleared.

The movement jolted a memory into her brain. It travelled along the events of the week and finally hooked up to a random finding like a magnet.

The trace of NaCl.

Sodium Chloride.

And finally, she knew who it was.

CHAPTER ONE HUNDRED THREE

Bryant headed out of the leisure complex and took out his phone.

He'd been careful to check every inch of the place to make sure Jared Welmsley hadn't done the deed and then jumped into the steam room to clean himself off.

'Hey, Stace, I've—'

'Bryant, where the hell have you been? I've been trying to reach you.'

'I'm in the leisure complex. No signal. Area checked and it ain't Welmsley.'

'I told you that makes no sense but can you pass me to the boss?'

'Not with her, Stace. She's at the other dead spot.'

Silence for a second.

'So, you both go to communication dead spots, alone, without telling me?'

Bryant could hear the scold in her voice.

'Stace, what have you got?'

'The traumatic event, Bryant. The one that drove Beth Nixon into the mental health facility. It was her grandmother, her legal guardian. She was murdered eight years ago.'

'Jeez, Stace, that's bad but what does that have to do with us?'

'It's the way she was killed: on a roundabout at a park up in Burnley, a spider's web. Tied to it with barbed wire, turned and turned until her brain smashed all over the ground.'

Bryant didn't even speak as he ended the call and started moving quickly.

He had to find the boss and he had to do it quick.

CHAPTER ONE HUNDRED FOUR

Kim took a deep breath and stepped out from behind the castle.

'Hello, Eric, nice to see you again,' she said to the man she'd interviewed at the very first crime scene. The man who had thrown up and whose vomit had contained high traces of sodium chloride – salt – found on the boots of one of the attending police officers. Because he'd made himself sick from the bottled water for effect.

'Inspector, lovely to see you, too,' he said, calmly, as he glanced towards his companion.

Kim tried to appraise the scene before her without allowing the horror to show on her face.

Eric sat astride one side of the see-saw still wearing the clown costume he'd used to infiltrate the event. The yellow half and the red half were separated by two blue pompoms on his stomach and chest. The multicoloured wig had been removed, but the white face and grotesquely painted red lips remained.

At the other end of the see-saw was Ellie. Her hands were tied around the handle and a scarf gagged her mouth. Terror shone from her eyes.

Kim briefly wondered how he'd managed to get her so trussed up, but given Ellie's earlier encounter with a knife, she would have been petrified and would have done whatever she was told.

Ellie made a sound as her half of the see-saw came down, and Kim suddenly saw why.

The knife had been rigged to stand in an upright position so that every time her side of the see-saw came down the knife sliced into the flesh on the back of her leg between her ankle and her calf. If she didn't push back up, the point of the blade would bury itself firmly in her flesh. Her feet were bound, so Ellie couldn't control the angle at which her legs were going to fall.

Eric was forcing Ellie to play with him, and the pool of glistening blood beneath her seat told Kim they'd been playing now for quite a while. Eric was having the time of his life while Ellie was getting weaker.

Kim knew she had only one option and that was to get him off the see-saw.

She took a second to do the maths. Ellie had been tutoring privately for fourteen years. Fourteen years ago Beth Nixon had attended the Brainbox event. Ellie must have ignored this kid too.

Kim moved forward.

'Take one more step and I do this,' he said, speeding up the see-saw.

He pushed harder and quicker so that Ellie had no choice but to match his pace to avoid the blade burying into her flesh but that meant even more slices to the back of her leg. This was lose or lose more.

The woman cried into the gag as blood began to drip from the extra wounds.

Kim stopped moving.

'You didn't seem surprised to see me, Inspector?' he said, disappointed. 'What gave me away?'

Kim was tempted to tell him he'd been too clever for his own good, but she had to try and think how best to get him off that see-saw.

'Salt, Eric,' she said, calmly. 'You overcooked your reaction to finding the body of Belinda Evans. Your vomit contained high levels of sodium chloride that was in your water bottle to make you throw up once you'd killed her. You refused to take a drink of it when I told you to.

'You wanted people to see how clever you are. You got no gratification from your first kill. No one found Freddie Compton for days, so when you killed Belinda you wanted to see what you'd caused while sitting there with your head bowed, feigning shock.'

He smiled appreciatively, and the see-saw had slowed while she had his attention.

He clearly enjoyed having his actions replayed to him. She would try and take advantage of that fact.

'You went into the college on open day and called Belinda from that cleaner's room. You arranged a meeting at the...'

'Yeah, she was a dirty old bitch all right.'

Kim ignored the insult, knowing the woman had been so much more than that.

'Your last victim wasn't hard to find, was he, being your brother-in-law?' Kim said, remembering the last three cases Stacey had highlighted.

The brother heckling Beth's performance when they were kids. Trying to take the attention away from her.

'And that poor boy's suicide pushed you over the edge, didn't it? The brother of a genius who felt the only way out was death.'

Kim knew she had to keep him focussed, keep his attention on her until she could work out how to get him off the see-saw.

'You were always second fiddle to your sister. Weren't you?' she asked gently.

She had no weapon and no help but the one thing she did have was knowledge, her mouth and the seedling of a plan to divert his attention and anger away from Ellie.

'I get it, Eric,' she said. 'I understand how awful it must have been as a child when Beth was getting all the attention. All these people played with your sister, lavished attention on her while completely ignoring you. None of these people saw how special you are. None of them took the time to play with you.'

His eyes were on her and he opened his mouth but she didn't want him to speak. She wanted him to listen. She needed her words to enter his brain and register. For her plan to work she needed to pick at the scab of rejection in his mind.

'I bet she even got special treatment, didn't she? More presents, more treats, more toys. Everyone thought she was cleverer, funnier, cuter. Your parents showed her off at parties, telling everyone what she could do, bragging about her achievements. You were totally forgotten, constantly in her shadow, trying to get some attention for yourself. Trying to stand out, be noticed. I can't even imagine what that could do to a child. All that rejection so young.'

She knew she had him. The see-saw had slowed and Ellie had had the sense to match his speed so that her leg was getting less nicks and the blood loss had slowed.

And now for the gamble that fresh hurt cut deeper than old wounds.

'So difficult for a child to take that level of rejection, except it doesn't end there, does it, Eric?' she asked as her voice hardened.

'Especially when it follows you into adulthood, cos I've met both you and your sister and I have to say I liked her much better than I liked you.'

Her eyes challenged him.

'So, why don't you come play with me?'

CHAPTER ONE HUNDRED FIVE

'Jesus, will you get out of the way, man?' Bryant growled when he got to the fire exit door that led out on to the scented garden.

'Just a sec, mate, gotta make sure the magnets are holding and the activation is received back at the control room.'

The security guy was holding his radio up to his ear awaiting a response.

Bryant tried to control his breathing after his sprint through the building. His only alternative had been a two-mile run from one end of the complex to the other.

And now he was just a couple of minutes away from the play area where he was guessing his boss was facing down psycho Beth or her half-brother alone.

'Too many activations from these doors, mate. Gotta make sure they're all in order.'

Bryant nudged him out of the way and pushed hard.

The doors opened.

'They're working,' he called back as he ran as fast as he could across the plants.

CHAPTER ONE HUNDRED SIX

Kim saw the expression in his eyes turn murderous as he dismounted the see-saw. The second he was off Kim sprinted to Ellie's side of the see-saw as her legs headed towards the knives.

Kim managed one swift kick at the blades before Eric grabbed hold of her hair and pulled her down to the ground.

The sting went from her scalp to her eyes. She prepared her body for an onslaught as he dragged her across the tarmac.

'You've spoiled it all, you fucking…'

His words trailed away as the grip loosened on her hair. She lifted her head to see him looking beyond her.

A figure was rushing towards them.

Eric pushed her to the ground and ran.

'Get Ellie,' she shouted to her colleague. 'And stay with her,' she instructed, getting to her feet.

The woman would be absolutely terrified by her ordeal.

She set off in the direction she thought he'd gone. He could easily climb the fence around the play area and get lost in the Worcestershire countryside.

She ran around the castle and spied him launching himself at the metal fencing. His left foot had managed to get hold and he was scaling it like Spiderman.

She heard him curse as one of his clown suit bobbles got caught on a join in the wire. He shouted out with frustration as he was frozen halfway up the fencing, unable to move up or down.

She reached him as he gave one almighty roar. She heard the fabric of his suit rip as his left leg came free. Too late she realised that his left foot was aiming straight for her as he kicked down.

She managed to turn her head so the heel missed the middle of her face but caught her on the left temple. The force of it knocked her to the ground. The nausea threatened to engulf her but she pushed herself back to her feet and began climbing the fence as he dropped down the other side.

She fought the dizziness as she pulled herself up feeling the burn right through her muscles but she knew she had to catch him.

The grounds of the hotel led on to open countryside but a few lights littering the driveway to the main building told her he had a good thirty to forty metres head start.

Gotta go quicker, she silently told her muscles as she tried to increase her speed.

The lights she'd thought were fixed appeared to be moving towards her. Maybe people with torches coming to help.

Damn it, her one hope had been that Eric might get disoriented in the semi-darkness and lose his bearings, taking him away from the exit and potential freedom and giving her time to catch him before he got away.

She shook her head to clear them from her vision but still the lights to her right came towards her, moving much quicker than she had thought. But they were still helping to drive Eric towards the exit.

She focussed her gaze on Eric and wasn't sure if she'd managed to close the gap by a few metres. She realised he was losing ground by keeping on looking behind to see where she was.

If she could just find another gear she could get to him before he left the grounds.

She followed his trajectory trying to ignore the two lights in her peripheral vision.

Her muscles burned as though they were detaching from her bone; her breathing was laboured as she tried to force more air down into her lungs. The process brought back the nausea from the kick to the head.

But she knew she was gaining on him as he turned again because now she could see the expression on his face.

Come on, she told herself as the lights to her right burned brighter.

They weren't torches, she realised.

They were the headlights of a car, travelling along the gravel path towards the exit.

She looked again towards Eric, running at speed, looking behind him, checking where she was.

The car continued to travel.

Eric continued to run.

One last look.

And then the sound of metal hitting flesh.

Kim's legs faltered but she pushed them on, staring at the inert figure on the ground.

Oh, no, she thought. It doesn't end like this. Three people dead. Countless lives ruined. The bastard had to stand trial.

As she neared, the car door opened and Veronica Evans stepped out. Her face ashen.

'Oh no, oh my god, oh no.'

Kim took a few deep breaths as the figure on the ground groaned.

'I can't… oh no…. I didn't see… I'm so sorry…'

'He's not dead,' Kim offered breathlessly.

'Oh my goodness… I hit a… children's clown,' she said as the horror on her face grew.

Kim looked down into the pain-contorted features of Eric Hanson, all the more grotesque with the smeared clown make-up and felt nothing but disgust for him, for the lives he'd taken in what was little more than a fourteen-year long tantrum.

'Don't be too sorry, Veronica,' Kim said, taking out her phone. 'This is the bastard that killed your sister.'

CHAPTER ONE HUNDRED SEVEN

Stacey let herself into the flat at almost one in the morning.

The scent of jasmine welcomed her even though she'd been avoiding it all week. Along with the familiar aroma she detected a sweet, sickly, cloying smell in the air. Some kind of fruit pie, she guessed. Devon baked when she was stressed.

She removed her coat and laid it over the back of the sofa. She didn't turn on the lights. She didn't need to. She knew Devon's flat almost as well as she knew her own.

As she walked through the lounge she took care to avoid the brightly coloured craft bag containing Devon's numerous failed attempts at knitting. The oversize needles had been used more for sword fights between the two of them than for actual garment making.

Against the wall between the bathroom and the bedroom was a two-foot high stuffed dog with a misshapen face, so ugly that he'd been in their favourite vintage store for months. Eventually they'd felt so sorry for him and given him a home.

Feeling sorry for a stuffed toy, she thought, shaking her head.

She slipped soundlessly into the bathroom and quickly brushed her teeth while waiting for the anxiety to pass. This was a conversation she'd avoided all week, and she was being unfair to them both. And perhaps she had left it too late.

She opened the bedroom door into total darkness. Blackout blinds covered both windows. Night raids as an immigration officer often meant Devon had to try to catch sleep in the day.

Stacey undressed silently and crawled into bed.

Devon's deep rhythmic breathing drained the tension from her body.

'You know that I know you're here, right?' Devon asked, clearly.

'Of course,' Stacey said, moving a little closer.

Devon moved away without turning. 'Why are you?'

Oh, she wasn't going to make this easy and nor should she.

Stacey had been tempted to talk to her boss, seek an opinion from a completely objective person, but earlier tonight she'd realised that she didn't need to.

All week she had been thinking of what she could possibly lose but tonight she had been surrounded by pain. To her left had been Ellie Lewis, already damaged and barely holding on to her sanity. A man being rushed to hospital after murdering three innocent people, and a woman who had lost everything sobbing beside her car.

And all she could think of was what she had to gain.

Yes, she'd panicked. Yes, she'd been frightened and yes, she'd acted like a stupid child.

'Ask me again, Dee,' she said, tracing a finger gently down her lover's spine.

No response.

'Please,' she whispered.

Devon turned in the bed and faced her. No light shone upon them but Stacey knew every feature by heart.

Devon cleared her throat and reached for Stacey's hand.

Her voice was quiet and nervous when she spoke.

'Stacey Wood, will you do me the honour of becoming my wife?'

Stacey beamed in the darkness.

'Yes, my sweetheart. I will.'

CHAPTER ONE HUNDRED EIGHT

Kim sat outside the property for just a few minutes before getting out of the car.

She had just finished questioning Eric Hanson following the events of two nights ago. Luckily, Veronica's twenty miles an hour speed had caused nothing more than a fractured rib, a dislocated shoulder and mild concussion.

Despite the lack of forensic evidence against him, bar the fingerprint on the board game wrapper, Eric had confessed to all the murders offering a blow-by-blow account of each one. He had recounted the murder of his brother-in-law with no more emotion than the others, referring to him as a dirty old bastard.

Eric had gone on to describe a childhood so warped and twisted that she had struggled to remember she was speaking to a fully grown man and not an injured young boy.

He had openly explained how his one single possession left behind by his father had been sold to buy books for his sister. He told of his grandmother removing Beth from school, and the beatings he'd received if he even spoke during lesson time. He explained that he'd also been taken out of school because his nan hadn't been prepared to traipse down to the school for just one.

But most of all he spoke of being ignored, of being made to feel invisible, worthless. When he'd read of the suicide of Stevie's brother, Ryan, it had brought back every inadequate feeling he'd ever had, which he'd buried after killing the person who had caused it.

Throughout the four hours it had taken for his statement Kim had forced herself to remember that she was questioning a man that had killed four people including the brutal murder of his grandmother on the spider's web. Four families changed for ever because of one damaged, broken soul.

Ellie Lewis had been released from hospital the following day with her physical injuries treated.

Kim had no clue about the long-term psychological scars of her ordeal. Her phone was switched off, her rented address empty and her private clients cancelled.

Right now, Ellie Lewis did not want to be found by anyone, and Kim could respect that.

Beth Nixon was preparing to bury the husband who had been murdered by her own brother. The grief and the love had been real and she was unlikely to speak to her brother again.

Jared and Serena were making the most of the publicity surrounding the Brainbox event to try to defend the whole process, although public opinion was not on their side.

She'd caught up with Penn, who had recounted the events of the service station murders and his colleague's involvement. She knew he'd played down what had happened with his brother at the old go-karting track, but Travis had filled her in fully. She'd met people like Doug before; officers who wanted promotion without the work, officers who felt they were entitled to more without the hard graft. It seemed that over the years Doug had grown steadily more bitter and resentful of the people around him as they progressed. Travis admitted that he'd advised Doug against taking the sergeant's exam a third time, pretty much sealing his fate. Kim wondered if that had been the straw that had broken that particular camel's back.

She knew that Penn would beat himself up for a long time for not spotting his colleague's true nature earlier, but he'd stuck with his instinct that there was something amiss in the case against

Gregor Nuryef, who was back home with his wife and children. She was proud of her colleague's unwillingness to let it go and to fight hard for the truth.

And whatever had been wrong with Stacey was all good now. She'd turned up for work the day after they'd caught Hanson with a spring in her step and a smile that blinded them all. First into the office at 7 a.m. she had shared her news with Kim before the others had arrived. Kim was truly happy for the constable and thought the two of them made a pretty good match.

And Bryant, as ever, was Bryant.

Despite the slow start due to Woody's restrictions, the case had been exhausting, taking them away from their loved ones as they tried to unravel sibling rivalry, neglect, cruelty and lies.

And once the statements had been signed just one person had remained on her mind, she thought, as she knocked the door to the three-storey town house.

Veronica answered with a quizzical expression.

'May I come in?'

Veronica frowned. 'I gave my statement. Is there…'

'Veronica, will you please just let me in?'

'Of course,' she said, stepping aside.

Kim headed up the stairs to the library on the first floor.

She was not surprised to see the box of exercise books from their childhood nestled in the corner. However painful the past, it was still her history.

'Is there… did I forget…'

'Veronica, everything is fine. You're not being charged with anything. It was an accident; I am your witness and the man is very much alive.'

'Oh, okay,' she said, relaxing visibly. 'So, why are you…'

'I just wanted to talk,' Kim said, reading her surprise. 'Is it really so difficult to believe that someone might want to come round for a chat with you?'

'You? Yes, definitely,' she said, with a glint of amusement. 'You seem even less socially adjusted than I am.'

Kim smiled in response. She was not offended as the assessment wasn't wrong. But throughout the case this woman had blocked them, antagonised them, held out on them, frustrated them and yet not once had Kim found herself unable to dislike her.

There was something in Veronica that she recognised, understood. A deep, dark hurt that had damaged something unreachable inside her. Had stopped her from granting herself a normal life.

'You have to let it go, Veronica,' she said, once she'd sat down.

Veronica followed and folded her long legs beneath her.

'If you say he's not seriously hurt then I'll…'

'Not that,' Kim said, tipping her head. 'Your guilt. It wasn't your fault. You were not responsible for everything that happened after the TV show. It wasn't your fault and yet you've spent your whole life making up for it.'

'But if I hadn't advised her, things would have stayed the same and our father wouldn't have rejected her.'

'But, it would always have changed some time. Don't you understand that your father's disappointment was only ever one wrong answer away? He'd put your sister on such a pedestal that it was inevitable that Belinda wouldn't live up to his expectations. Yes, you advised her but she made the decision to do it.'

Veronica stood and walked the room. 'But I destroyed any chance of us being sisters, normal sisters.'

'In my experience, there is no such thing,' Kim said, honestly. 'And if there is it's your father who spoiled that for you.'

'But we could have loved each other,' she said with a break in her voice.

'You did,' Kim offered. 'You never left her side. You never let her down. She was never alone and she knew she could count on you. You stayed close and gave up your own life to take care of her. You protected her as best you could but she was an adult.

She always knew she had you. You loved her very much when she gave you little in return.'

A tear slid over Veronica's cheek. She wiped it away.

'It's not her fault. She couldn't love me. Not after what I'd done, what I'd caused. She blamed me. She hated me.'

'No, she didn't,' Kim said. 'Because she never told you to go away. She loved you just as much as you loved her. In fact, she always had.'

Veronica frowned. 'You can't possibly know that.'

Kim was surprised at how the simplest of facts were overlooked by the people that needed them the most and yet obvious to someone outside the situation.

'I do know it and it's because of one single fact. Everything changed for her after the TV show. She lost your father's love, his attention, his respect. And she could have got it all back by doing one simple thing.'

Veronica's gaze narrowed. 'How?'

'She could have told the truth.'

Kim watched as the realisation dawned on her that her sister had never admitted that Veronica had told her to get that question wrong. Had she done so she would have been forgiven everything and her life would have returned to normal, but she had protected her older sister instead.

'She loved you too much to turn your father's displeasure your way.'

'How could I… I mean… I never thought… she…'

Kim stood and offered her hand to the stern, formidable woman who had intrigued her from the moment they'd met.

'Thank you, Inspector, I really don't know what to say.'

'You're welcome,' she said, heading out and down the stairs.

She took a deep, contented breath and reached for her helmet as her phone began to ring.

A LETTER FROM ANGELA

First of all, I want to say a huge thank you for choosing to read *Child's Play*, the eleventh instalment of the Kim Stone series and to many of you for sticking with Kim Stone and her team since the very beginning. If you'd like to keep up to date with all my latest releases, just sign up at the website link below.

www.bookouture.com/angela-marsons

For as long as I can remember I have been intrigued by Child Prodigies. I have wanted to explore their home lives, parenting styles and the effects of such pressure and attention later in life. As ever, the story took a turn I wasn't expecting as the characters and personalities began to come to life in my mind.

Adapting the things that interest me into a crime procedural can sometimes pose a challenge but this was a book I enjoyed writing from the moment I began to research subjects such as Tiger Parenting until the minute I finished the book. I hope you enjoy reading the end result.

If you did enjoy it, I would be forever grateful if you'd write a review. I'd love to hear what you think, and it can also help other readers discover one of my books for the first time. Or maybe you can recommend it to your friends and family...

I'd love to hear from you – so please get in touch on my Facebook or Goodreads page, twitter or through my website.

If you haven't read any of the previous books in the DI Kim Stone series, you can find them here:

Silent Scream
Evil Games
Lost Girls
Play Dead
Blood Lines
Dead Souls
Broken Bones
Dying Truth
Fatal Promise
Dead Memories

Thank you so much for your support, it is hugely appreciated.

Angela Marsons

 www.angelamarsons-books.com

angelamarsonsauthor

@WriteAngie

ACKNOWLEDGEMENTS

As always I must first acknowledge the contribution to these books from my partner, Julie. She is involved in every part of the process and never lets me forget how lucky I am to be able to do what I love and call it work. The books would not exist without her and I am truly grateful to her every single day.

Thank you to my Mum and Dad who continue to spread the word proudly to anyone who will listen. And to my sister Lyn, her husband Clive and my nephews Matthew and Christopher for their support too.

Thank you to Amanda and Steve Nicol who support us in so many ways and to Kyle Nicol for book-spotting my books everywhere he goes.

A special acknowledgement goes to an exceptional man named Jez Edwards who so kindly offered me assistance in all things related to police procedure and who sadly passed away following a short illness. You will be missed.

I would like to thank the team at Bookouture for their continued enthusiasm for Kim Stone and her stories and especially to Oliver Rhodes who gave Kim Stone an opportunity to exist.

Special thanks to my editor, Claire Bord, whose patience and understanding is truly appreciated. She greets every book with enthusiasm and sound advice and again, I look forward to working on the next.

To Kim Nash (Mama Bear) who works tirelessly to promote our books and protect us from the world. To Noelle Holten who has limitless enthusiasm and passion for our work.

Thank you to the fantastic Kim Slater who has been an incredible support and friend to me for many years now and to the fabulous Caroline Mitchell, Renita D'Silva and Sue Watson without whom this journey would be impossible. Huge thanks to the growing family of Bookouture authors who continue to amuse, encourage and inspire me on a daily basis.

My eternal gratitude goes to all the wonderful bloggers and reviewers who have taken the time to get to know Kim Stone and follow her story. These wonderful people shout loudly and share generously not because it is their job but because it is their passion. I will never tire of thanking this community for their support of both myself and my books. Thank you all so much.

Massive thanks to all my fabulous readers, especially the ones that have taken time out of their busy day to visit me on my website, Facebook page, Goodreads or Twitter.